Arthur:

The Struggle Continues
Arthur Series, Book2

Walter Stoffel

Copyright/Disclaimer

walterstoffelauthor.com

Walter Stoffel (2021-4-15).
Arthur: The Struggle Continues, Arthur Series Book 2
ISBN-13: 9798737804930

❧
Dedication

Arthur: The Struggle Continues is dedicated to those in our society that are fated to live a challenged life from the day they are born. Abuse and neglect can take many forms and be inflicted in varying degrees but the end result is the same—a damaged soul. You may know someone like Arthur. Perhaps that someone is the person you see in the mirror.

In a truly humane society children would not be forced to continue suffering at the hands of their caretakers while the rest of society wrings its hands and then sits on them.

My hope is that Arthur's story sheds light on child abuse—a perpetual pandemic for which there is no current vaccination. May heightened awareness of this scourge lead to meaningful change for the better.

Arthur:

The Struggle Continues

Arthur Berndt is an eleven-year-old boy growing up on 1950s Long Island. His life revolves around one, overriding task: surviving under the same roof with his abusive father August.

In response to the world he is trapped in at home, outside his house he lives a life that consists of equal parts delinquency and isolation. Only in school has Arthur found a measure of normalcy. There, he is succeeding academically and has found a measure of predictability and stability that exists nowhere else for the youngster.

Over the years of his short life, Arthur has gradually gained a sense that he isn't growing up like other children. This awareness has only increased his self-consciousness—and anger. The self-consciousness has led to keeping secrets, both about himself and his family. Arthur is driven to hide who he is and where he is from. He spends much of his time in the nearby woods, finding there a measure of safety and anonymity that he desperately craves. As for his anger, he acts out on the streets, fearing the rest of the world less than he does his father.

Arthur has been headed down the wrong road since he could walk. It remains to be seen if someone will come to Arthur's rescue and point him in the right direction.

Chapter 1

Due to his well-earned reputation as a troublemaker, Arthur became a persona non grata in his neighborhood. As a result, he often faced the task of entertaining himself when not in school.

Five houses sat on Lowell Place, including the Berndt residence. The road was subject to virtually no through traffic. One weekday afternoon in late June, 1955, Arthur was outside sitting in the middle of the road in front of his house, sorting baseball cards. Arthur called to his German shepherd Rex, who was lying comfortably on the front lawn and reluctant to respond. Not taking his dog's rebuff personally, Arthur continued arranging his cards into two piles—those he'd keep in his room and those that would be relegated to serving as noisemakers on his bicycle. Like other children his age, Arthur loved to attach baseball cards to his bike, utilizing clothespins, so that they flapped against the tire's spokes when pedaling the bike. Arthur was the judge and jury charged with selecting the cards that would be doomed to die a slow death on his bicycle, while sparing others such a dark fate. Brooklyn Dodger players were protected merchandise. Lesser known players on other teams and, of course, any hated Yankees were to be ridden to death. Arthur was so engrossed in his work, he was taken by surprise when a speeding car approached and came to a screeching halt just a few feet behind him. Arthur turned around and saw the front end of a huge Cadillac staring him in the face.

The driver stuck his head out of the window and threatened, "Get the hell out of the road, German boy!" Arthur remained seated, not certain what was happening or what to do. Mr.

Baldwin, a resident of Suassa Park that Arthur recognized but didn't know by name, revved his car's engine. "I told you—get the hell out of the road!"

Arthur, leaving his baseball cards behind, walked to the side of the road, turned around and stood looking at the car's driver. Mr. Baldwin slammed his car in reverse, turned the steering wheel counter-clockwise and gunned his car forward, again heading directly towards Arthur. At the last minute, he yanked the wheel clockwise and stopped his car alongside the youngster.

Mr. Baldwin draped his arm on the outside of the driver's door, leaned his head out the car window, and said, "Listen, you piece-of-shit Kraut. I killed a few of your kind in the war. One more wouldn't matter, especially a troublemaker like you."

Arthur grabbed the first rock he found and hurled it at the car. "Go away!"

The rock hit Mr. Baldwin on his elbow. "Why, you little punk!"

Rex was now taking an interest in the activities and trotted over to his young master. Before things could escalate further, the unfriendly neighbor drove away, purposely running over the youngster's baseball cards.

Marguerite, Arthur's mother, came to the front screen door and yelled, "What's going on, Art?"

"Some bad man said bad stuff."

"Do you know who it was?"

"No."

"Why would he pick on you?" Spotting the baseball cards scattered on the road, Marguerite continued. "I've told you not to play in the road. How many times is it now?" Without waiting for her son to respond she added, "Pick all those cards up and come inside."

Under the watchful eye of his mother, Arthur dutifully did as he was told. Some of the cards had been scuffed and bent by Mr. Baldwin's car.

"Ma, look at what he did to my cards!"

"I'm sure he didn't run over them on purpose. That's what happens when you have your valuables on the street like that. Finish up out there. I want you to wash the dishes. I have a surprise for you. I'm making a pineapple upside down cake. Your favorite!"

"Oh boy!"

Picturing a huge slice of his favorite cake, the youngster quickly shoved aside any thoughts of his recent near-death experience...at least for the time being.

Chapter 2

"Get out of the road German boy!"

So had begun Arthur's summer vacation from school. A few days after his encounter with Mr. Baldwin, Arthur was at home watching television. His thoughts, however, were not on the *Popeye* cartoon being broadcast. All his life Arthur had been hoping to go to the movies. Up until now, that hadn't happened. All he knew about the movies was second-hand knowledge gained from listening to other kids' accounts of films they had seen. He knew that children's fare was usually shown on Saturday afternoons, but he couldn't count on his parents to take him. On weekends, his mother was usually too busy with household chores and his father often put in extra hours as a freelance gardener. There had been that one time August had promised to take him to see a Roy Rogers film, but after the youngster wet his bed the previous night, he lost his chance to see his favorite cowboy on the big screen. At the time, Arthur was both disappointed and relieved—relieved because, as badly as he wanted to visit a movie house, he would have felt uncomfortable sitting in the dark for several hours next to the man he feared the most. Both his parents had expressly forbidden the youngster from going to the movies alone.

With Popeye mumbling in the background, Arthur hatched a plan. He was allowed to go bicycle riding by himself as long as he stayed within the environs of Suassa Park. Why not leave the house on that pretext, but then head for the movie house in downtown Port Jefferson? Arthur convinced himself there was no reason to delay putting his plan into action. He had the money—his allowance. Target date: the upcoming weekend.

***

July 2. A scorcher.

Arthur left his house to set out on his supposed bike ride. Not wanting his bycycle to be spotted downtown, he ditched it in the woods not far from his house. Then, in the boiling heat, he set out for downtown, a little under a mile away. Since he was on a forbidden journey, every once in a while the youngster ducked into the woods to avoid being seen by a passing motorist who might recognize him and inform his parents.

Reaching downtown, Arthur walked along Main Street until he reached the Port Jefferson Theater. The young boy didn't bother to check what was playing: seeing so many other excited youngsters headed inside convinced him to follow their lead.

This was the first time he'd ever entered a movie house—and he was doing it by himself! After paying the admission fee to the man sitting inside the ticket booth, he took his stub and walked over to the vending machines in the lobby. This was another first for Arthur. All the candy he had ever gotten in the past he'd stolen or purchased directly from people. The young boy stood in front of one of the metallic contraptions, not exactly sure how to proceed.

"Hurry it up, kid," an impatient teenager barked from behind him.

"Well, how do you get stuff?" Arthur asked.

Pointing at the machine, the older boy replied, "You put your money in that slot, dummy!"

"Oh."

Arthur did as directed. He purchased ten cents worth of candy. Then, after an usher tore off half his ticket and gave Arthur the remainder of it, the young boy walked up a flight of stairs that led to a huge, dimly lit room filled with rows of seats facing a huge curtain. The rest of the children in the theater were either accompanied by an adult or, if not, were older than Arthur. The young boy felt out of place, not an unaccustomed experience for him.

Arthur walked down one of the two flat, slanted aisles, stopped and entered a row of seats, stumbled past a mother with her two daughters, and found himself a seat. Then, like everyone else in the theater, Arthur sat waiting for something to happen.

Unlike everyone else, Arthur wasn't exactly sure what that "something" was going to be. To kill time, he opened his package of Chuckles and went right for the red one. Just as he was going to work on his box of Good & Plenty, the already-weak lights were completely extinguished and the curtain began to draw open. For the next two hours, the only world Arthur knew was on the screen in front of him. The first images presented on the huge screen were the coming attractions for the upcoming weeks. Next Saturday's full-length feature was *Creature from the Black Lagoon*. That further cemented a decision Arthur had already made—he'd be back the following Saturday and all the Saturdays for the rest of the summer, if he had his way.

Next came a cartoon featuring Porky Pig, one of Arthur's favorite characters. At home his father discouraged his son from watching "such childishness". Here in the movie house, the youngster, at least temporarily, could relish being a child. By the time the cartoon ended, Arthur had finished his box of Good & Plenty and, since he was out of money, braced himself for sugar withdrawal.

Then, something else came onto the screen—the third episode of *Radar Men from the Moon*, featuring Commando Cody. Arthur hadn't seen the first two episodes but that didn't dampen his fascination. A hero that flew with a tank on his back, aliens that lived on the moon, rocket ships—television's *Captain Video* suddenly paled by comparison. True to form, the episode ended with the good guys apparently being drowned in molten lava produced by a ray gun shooting at them from the moonmen's tank. Had Commando Cody and his assistant met their fate? Arthur would have to come back the following Saturday to find out. He'd already decided to be there.

After a brief pause it was time for the feature—Gene Autry. He was no Roy Rogers in Arthur's book, but well worth the twenty-cent price of admission. Arthur's self-consciousness at being the only person sitting alone in the theater evaporated as he became transfixed by what he was watching on the screen. This was way neater than television! As he watched Gene and his sidekick Smiley Burnette bring the bad guys to justice, Arthur took comfort in knowing this was how he would spend every Saturday that summer. Most every child likes to escape into fantasy; Arthur *needed* to escape his reality. The movie house was just the place to do that.

7

After more than two hours of cinematic entertainment, the screen went dark, the curtain began to close and the dimmed lights came back on. Everybody left their seat and headed for the exits. When Arthur walked back out onto the Main Street sidewalk, it was like coming out of another world. The bright sunlight, passing cars and pedestrians brought the young boy back to reality. The trek back home felt a bit more strenuous than the walk to the movie house had been. Perhaps that was because the trip to the movie house had been made with pleasant anticipation.

During the return trip, Arthur thought of only one downside to his movie house visit: he'd run out of candy way too early in the program. The young boy had been suppressing the temptation to steal money from his mother. Now, he felt the need to reconsider that policy. Sitting more than two hours at the movies demanded a significant increase in his supply of snacks.

Arthur retrieved his bike from the woods and pedaled one block to Lowell Place and home. He was relieved when his mother greeted him with nothing more than, "Art, you must be exhausted. That's a lot of bike riding." Acknowledging her son's history of antisocial behavior in the neighborhood, Marguerite added with uncharacteristic sarcasm, "And there were no phone calls from any of the neighbors, either." Arthur knew why there weren't, but kept that knowledge to himself.

A weekly visit to the movie house soon became something more than just a source of entertainment for Arthur—going to the movies helped take the edge off his life.

***

Three Saturdays later, Arthur was scanning the comic books available on a large magazine rack in Cooper's Stationery store. He had his favorites—*Superman, Little Lulu, Archie, Donald Duck, Captain Marvel, Popeye. Classics Illustrated* didn't do it for him. Too boring.

He'd just come from the movie house, where he had been able to curb his candy cravings and thus hold on to a dime. With only ten cents to spend, he'd have to limit his purchase to a single comic book. The problem was he couldn't decide between the latest *Superman* and *Donald Duck* issues. He wanted both. Usually, he would have been able to purchase the two of them and more with money he stole from his mother, but he hadn't

8

been able to gain access to his mom's pocketbook earlier in the day.

The magazine rack was situated next to the store entrance. Mr. Cooper was standing at the counter forty feet away, ringing up a customer. Arthur grabbed the two comic books he craved and, standing behind a six-foot high rack featuring postcards for sale, shoved them under his shirt. He tucked his shirt back underneath the waist of his shorts and left the store. His body now drenched with excitement-produced adrenalin, Arthur immediately sprinted into a nearby alley and came out behind the Bohack grocery store. He kept running until he got to Barnum Avenue. There, he slowed down and took out the products of his thievery.

This was the day Arthur began his career as a solo shoplifter. He no longer needed Ronnie Simpson, his one-time shoplifting partner in crime with whom he'd had a falling out. From now on, everything Arthur stole was his and his alone. Later on, he'd decide which of the "hot" comics to read first. Since there was so much he was unjustly punished for, any time Arthur got away with doing something that merited punishment, it was posted on his mental scoreboard as a home run that evened the score.

As he continued his walk home, Arthur calculated the benefits of his criminal career move. Stealing from stores would be easier than stealing money from his mother. At home, he was forced to live at the scene of his crime and, more importantly, he always had his father to worry about. He had gotten caught that one time when his mom found his stash and he'd suffered the consequences. Since then, he was never certain if he was getting away with robbery due to his expertise or because his mother was looking the other way to spare him from his father. If the latter were true, how long would his mother keep giving him a pass? He'd have no need to worry about that when stealing from local businesses.

Every store in Port Jefferson was now fair game except Brown's Pharmacy, where his reputation preceded him. What if he got caught? He had little to fear—all the shopkeepers were men not named August Berndt. No other adult male had ever hit Arthur. Even the police never beat him up. Besides, he was sure he'd never get caught.

While making the steep ascent up Brook Road, Arthur mentally cased the stores in Port Jefferson. There was Smitty's (the ice cream freezer), Terry's Sporting-Goods (toys), Anderson's Market (candy and more ice cream), Woolworths (all kinds of stuff), and, of course, Cooper's. Arthur would return to the scene of today's crime again and again. The Crystal Fountain was not included on his hit list, thanks to that darn glass case that stood between him and his sugary treasures.

Arthur second-guessed himself. Maybe he wouldn't completely keep his hands off his mother's pocketbook, after all. It would remain as a secondary option. Any good crook has to have a backup plan. Arthur had always been a thief. From this day on, he took his five-finger discounting to a higher level.

By the time he reached the driveway at Twenty-one Lowell Place, Arthur decided he'd hide his two comic books in the deepest recesses of a desk drawer in his bedroom. *Superman* would be his first read.

Chapter 3

Mid-July on a Sunday afternoon.

The day before Arthur had enjoyed a double feature at the movies—*Rocket Man* and *The Atomic Kid*. Next Saturday he'd have to settle for a single feature, but it was *Them!* Any movie featuring huge, mutated, killer ants had to be worth the price of admission.

At the moment, he was watching baseball on the TV set with his mother. The Dodgers were in the process of losing to Cincinnati. Arthur was glad his father was outside in the backyard widening a drainage ditch. August Berndt got especially surly when watching the Dodgers perform poorly.

The game was in the bottom of the seventh inning. Down 6-3, the Dodgers had loaded the bases with nobody out and Roy Campanella was striding up to the plate. The crowd was making lots of noise, encouraging one of its favorite hometown heroes.

Over the fans' clamoring that was coming out of the television, Arthur heard yelling much closer to home. He immediately made out his father's voice. Arthur rushed to the window from which he spotted his father engaging in a shouting match with Evelyn Sinclair, a next-door neighbor. She was accusing August of having encroached on her property with his digging, and damaging some of her flowers in the process. Marguerite Berndt went outside in what would prove to be an unsuccessful attempt at peacemaking. Arthur stayed inside and turned down the volume on the television set in order to better hear an argument between two adults that showed no signs of abating. The youngster did this out of a need to be self-

11

protective. Whatever and whoever may have initially provoked his father's ire, the elder Berndt often would customarily inflict any lingering foul mood on family members, particularly his son. Today, as he did on so many other days, young Arthur was gauging the potential side effects of his father's bad mood.

"You know damn well you did this on purpose!"

"What the hell are you talking about?"

"I know you don't like me. That's why you did it. Look at my poor flowers!"

"You did that yourself. It helps to water plants, you know."

"Don't be a smart aleck. I've been watching you from my window."

"Yeah, well watch this!" Arthur Berndt purposely scooped up a large shovelful of soil, dumping it on Mrs. Sinclair's property.

"That's it! I'm getting a surveyor—and a lawyer!"

"Get all the lawyers you want, ya old crow!"

By now several neighbors had come out onto their properties, eyeballing the spectacle. Inside his house, Arthur sensed an opportunity. For a long time there had been something in the Berndt household in the kitchen that he had wanted to get his hands on. He sprinted into the kitchen, climbed up on a stool, opened a cabinet door and reached in to get his prize—a box of safety matches. He placed the box on the kitchen counter and climbed off the stool, moving it to another part of the kitchen, away from the crime scene in order not to arouse suspicion. He tried jamming the box of safety matches into his pocket but it didn't fit so he stuffed it down his shirt and left the house via the front door.

As he headed for the woods, Arthur heard the continuing adult spat slowly fade away behind him. He walked onto the dirt path he so often tread when seeking a timeout from the battle he was constantly fighting with his father at home. The young boy proceeded thirty yards and then veered into the woods. Once he felt safely hidden by the thick foliage, he pulled out the box of matches from under his shirt. After sitting down on a tree stump, he took a match out of the box and proceeded to slowly rub it along the black surface on the side of the box. Nothing happened. He tried another match, which again did not produce the results the young boy was looking for. Why was nothing happening? He'd seen his father use the matches to start a fire in the fireplace and his mother occasionally used them to light the gas stove. Arthur took out another match. He struck it with increased force. Whoosh! Arthur heard the gentle sound of the match catching fire. The young boy stared at it with fascination. He watched as the matchstick briefly burned and then went out. Wasting no time, he immediately took out another match, struck it with equal force, resulting in another lit match in his hand. This one he held against some dead leaves resting on the ground. All the youngster got for his efforts was the briefest of flames on one of the leaves and then a short-lived wisp of smoke.

Arthur was nothing if not determined. He'd always been fascinated by watching the blazing spectacle his father produced in the fireplace at home. He gathered some dried leaves and twigs, stuck a few matches among them, lit another match and started his first "successful" fire. Occasionally, one of the matches lying among the leaves and twigs would catch fire, briefly intensifying the burning process. After a few minutes, all that was left was a small patch of gray and black ashes. This was not enough for Arthur. He collected an even greater amount of leaves and sticks. Before attempting to start another fire, Arthur realized something was missing. He remembered that his father often used newspapers to get a fire going at home. He also remembered how fiercely the newspapers would burn. The youngster knew what he had to do. He placed the box of matches on the ground, walked through the woods out onto the dirt path, and proceeded back towards Old Post Road.

After leaving the house earlier, Arthur had passed the Sinclair house and seen that the Sunday newspaper had been delivered and was sitting on the Sinclair's front stoop. With that in mind, Arthur crossed Old Post Road and entered the wooded lot that abutted the south side of the Sinclair property. In the distance, he heard the two adults still going verbally toe-to-toe. For a split second, the youngster wondered if the two grownups would hit each other. He knew his father had fought with men before. Would the fact Mrs. Sinclair was a woman make a difference? The youngster often heard his father threaten his mother verbally but wasn't sure he'd ever hit her—the fleeting thoughts of an eleven-year-old.

Arthur reached the southern edge of the Sinclair property. The Sinclair house sat between Arthur and the two arguing adults, giving the youngster cover. All the spectators, including his mother, had gone back inside. That made his task even easier.

As soon as he set foot on the lawn, the young boy made a mad dash for the stoop, grabbed the newspaper and headed back into the woods. Mission accomplished! The rest was relatively easy. He hurried through the wooded lot in a southerly direction, came back out onto Old Post Road, crossed it and again walked onto the dirt path. He proceeded back into the woods up to the spot where he'd left his matches and two small piles of ashes. Then, the youngster got down to business. He took a section of the newspaper, spread its pages on the ground and lit them. Lesson learned: paper catches fire more easily than leaves. When he sensed the fire was abating, Arthur grabbed more newspaper to keep the flame going.

There hadn't been rain for weeks and everything lying on the ground was extremely dry, so it wasn't long before leaves, twigs and other foliage caught fire. Arthur watched with rapt attention.

At some point, his enjoyment morphed into concern. This fire was not lessening as the others had. In fact, it was spreading. Everything Arthur's fire was reaching eagerly joined the conflagration. Now, not only leaves and twigs, but even bushes were aflame. This wasn't a fire Arthur dared try to stomp out. He grabbed at some dirt and threw it in an attempt to put out his creation but his efforts proved futile. Arthur was no longer in control—the fire was. Panic set in. Flames covered thirty, then forty, then fifty yards in circumference with no sign of slowing down. The fire had now reached several medium-sized trees, lapping at their trunks. Arthur had to back off, a helpless but still willing onlooker, mesmerized by his fiery creation.

Since there was nothing he could do to put the fire out, it was time to leave the scene of his first act of arson. He hustled through the woods and out onto the dirt road. Looking back, the foliage was too thick for him to see the flames, but he heard the fire's crackling sound and could see smoke wafting above the treetops.

Arthur headed towards Old Post Road. Suddenly, he heard a siren. He knew this wasn't the twelve o'clock whistle. It wasn't noon, and besides, the whistle didn't sound on Sundays. This was the fire department's alarm! Arthur knew fire trucks would soon be arriving on the scene. Instead of walking out onto Old Post Road and risking apprehension, he entered the woods on the other side of the dirt path and ran as fast as he could.

As he continued his escape, he heard a fire truck, siren

14

blaring, barrel off Old Post Road and onto the dirt road. Arthur kept running until he reached a spot where he felt safe enough to peek out onto the road. Seeing no vehicles coming from either direction, he ran across the road onto Whittier Place. Then, he cut across the lawn of the house sitting behind his and came out on the backyard at Twenty-one Lowell Place.

The un-neighborly confrontation between his father and Mrs. Sinclair had ended and all was quiet, save for the activities of the firemen in the not-so-far distance as they worked to put out Arthur's fiery handiwork.

Walking up the back steps Arthur entered the kitchen. There, he found his father putting the finishing touches on a can of Rheingold beer while sitting on the same stool the youngster had used an hour earlier to steal the box of matches. Another empty can sat next to him on the kitchen counter. By this time Arthur had witnessed his father's drinking habits enough to recognize a pattern. While ingesting the first and second cans of beer his father entered a sweet (and ever-so-short) spot. He looked and acted as if he was at peace with the world. If he continued on to a third beer and beyond, which he usually did, all bets were off. Things could, and often did, get ugly. Without a word between them, Arthur continued into the living room where he found his mother and his sister Ruth watching television.

"Art, where did you go?"

"I went outside and walked around to see if there were any kids doing anything."

"You missed a great game. The Dodgers pulled it out in the ninth-inning. You know, you should've taken Rex with you. He's overdue for a walk. Were you over near where the fire trucks were?"

"No, I went the other way."

Ruth chimed in. "Yeah, you probably started the fire. "

Arthur filled with panic. How could his sister know? The youngster responded defensively. "I did not."

Ruth shot back snidely, "I'm so sorry. You probably aren't smart enough to start a fire."

His sister's sarcasm tempted Arthur to respond with *I am too!* but he realized that might be giving himself away. Besides, it was clear his sister had no evidence to convict him.

"Ma, I guess I'll walk Rex now."

"Atta boy! Just don't go near where firemen are."

15

Boy and dog left the house. The youngster started to walk his dog towards Hawthorne Street when behind him he heard the sound of a large vehicle. He turned around to see a fire truck fly past the other end of Lowell Place, heading in the direction of the firehouse from where it came. Seconds later, a second truck followed. Arthur did a U-turn. The boy now had a destination in mind. If it's true that the criminal always returns to the scene of the crime, Arthur Berndt was no exception. He was overcome with curiosity—the need to see what he had wrought.

Arthur and Rex scooted up Lowell Place, across Old Post Road, and onto the dirt path. The youngster was running now, eager to see his handiwork. He entered the woods at the same spot he had entered it just a few hours earlier. At first it was as if nothing in the woods had changed at all. Then, he walked out on a huge swath of water-soaked, fire-damaged foliage. The ground had been scorched, but the firemen had seen to it that nothing was left smoldering. Countless trees had caught on fire, leaving flame-scarred tree trunks and limbs as silent victims. Yet, observing the damage he had done, the only word that came to the young boy's mind was *Neat!* His only regret? In his haste, he'd left the unused matches behind and they had been consumed by the fire.

Experts have written that three major childhood precursors of adult sociopathy are bedwetting, fire starting, and cruelty to animals. Arthur loved his dog Rex.

Chapter 4

"Arthur, we're going to visit your cousins today."

Those words from his mother's lips were a godsend to the young boy. It had been several weeks since Arthur's self-initiation as an arsonist. Since then he'd spent most of his waking hours outside the house with Rex, save for his Saturday visits to the movies. Of course, since today was a Saturday, he'd have to miss the movies but, in his eyes, spending a day with his cousins was worth it.

Arthur relished these day trips to faraway Brentwood. All three of August Berndt's brothers lived there with their families. Visiting them was time well spent in Arthur's world. While his father was preoccupied in conversation with his own adult siblings, Arthur got to play with his cousins, relatively free from his father's fear-provoking scrutiny. Traveling to Brentwood to visit his cousins was a timeout, a rest between rounds in his ongoing fight to survive a fearsome opponent—his father.

August, Marguerite, and their three children—Liz, Ruth, and Arthur—climbed into the family's 1940 Dodge and headed southwest towards Brentwood, which sat seventeen miles away in the center of Suffolk County. In the early 1950s, Brentwood was sparsely populated, featuring large tracts of vacant land, sandy soil and scrub pines. In comparison, August and Marguerite Berndt, though of somewhat limited means, lived in the more upscale Suassa Park.

The first stop was at Karl Berndt's place, where he and his wife Bernice lived unhappily with their five children. Liz had once told Arthur that Karl was even more of a tyrant than their own father was. Arthur didn't see it that way. The youngster paid little attention to how Karl treated his own children. Uncle Karl left Arthur alone and that's all that mattered to the youngster.

The adults, including Liz who was now twenty-two years old, spent a few hours watching television. Or, rather, they talked about this, that, and everything else while the TV droned on in the background. In the kitchen, Ruth joined her cousins Joyce and Carol in listening to a collection of 78 and 45 RPM records on an RCA portable record player. Arthur chose to play catch-a-fly-you're-up outside with his cousins Peter and Paul. One batter would hit a softball, hopefully in the air. If either of the two fielders caught it on the fly, he became the new batter. Unlike his cousins, Arthur had to play without a glove. This didn't prevent him from making numerous catches and thereby earning multiple turns at bat.

Around noon, a lunch was served consisting of bologna, head cheese and salami sandwiches, pickles and homemade beet salad. Lunch over, it was time for Arthur's family to head for their next stop. Marguerite and Bernice hugged, August and Karl shook hands, and the cousins simply said goodbye to each other.

August and Marguerite wouldn't be visiting Joe Berndt today. His wife Olga had just come home from Pilgrim State Hospital following another nervous breakdown. Joe and Olga were not currently up to receiving guests.

After a short drive of a few blocks, the family vehicle pulled up in front of 38 Washington Avenue, where John and Ella Berndt lived with their three boys John Jr., Henry, and Skipper. This was Arthur's favorite stop in Brentwood. The youngster savored the comparatively upbeat atmosphere he found in no other Berndt household. Another positive was the fact that Aunt Ella worked in a bakery and always had great pastries on hand.

As his father pulled the car into the driveway, Arthur saw his three cousins on the front lawn. He jumped out of the car and rushed over to where they were playing croquet, hoping to insert himself into the game.

"Can I play?"

"Yeah, as soon as I'm done winning this game," Johnny said. Arthur sat down on the lawn and began impatiently waiting.

The rest of Arthur's family went inside. Soon, Ella, Ruth, and Liz began taking turns demonstrating their skills on the piano, while August listened critically and John listened disinterestedly.

"Can't someone play something by Beethoven?" August asked. Ella took that as a cue and proceeded to butcher the first movement of the Moonlight Sonata. Never the diplomat, August mumbled only slightly under his breath, "I'm sorry I asked."

Ella turned around on the piano chair, shot him a cold look and then—out of spite—segued to a piece by Frédéric Chopin. She knew August loathed Chopin.

The phone rang and John answered it. While he conversed, his wife kept playing the piano. Just as Ella finished the Etude Number One, John hung up the phone. "Bernice called. They're all coming over. And Joe is bringing his two kids with him too. Just not Olga."

This was the first time in years so many Berndts would be under the same roof. With all four brothers in attendance, the occasion called for beer, lots of beer. With that in mind, John and August drove to a nearby delicatessen to answer the challenge.

Outside, the game of croquet continued. Not surprisingly, Johnny, age seventeen, had the upper hand against his brothers Henry and Skipper, age fourteen and ten respectively. It was Johnny's turn. His ball was resting against Henry's. Johnny, foot firmly planted on his ball, gave it a hard whack, sending Henry's ball out into the road. That did it for Henry. "I quit!"

Skipper, trailing badly in the contest, signaled he was also through by picking up his ball and walking over to hand it to his oldest brother.

Johnny turned to Arthur and said, "See? I told you this game was gonna end real quick."

Arthur leapt to his feet, ready to join the fray. He had only played croquet a handful of times. His sisters didn't like playing with him because of his bad sportsmanship. Furthermore, his father discouraged playing the game at home, claiming it was injurious to his lawn. Undaunted by his lack of experience and the age gap between him and two of his potential opponents, Arthur brazenly grabbed a mallet. Game on! The youngster was short on skill and knowledge of croquet but long on enthusiasm for competing—and winning, by any means possible.

At that moment Karl's son Paul pedaled his bicycle up to where the boys were playing. He'd decided not to wait to come over in the family car. "Can I be on one of the teams?" Arthur was quick to respond. "No you can't! I had to wait my turn."

19

Though he'd never seen Arthur play croquet, Paul was sure he lacked talent. "You stink."

Arthur responded. "So what, you smell."

"Do not."

Johnny stepped in as the arbiter. "Arthur goes first. This game will be over in no time and then you can go."

Glumly, Paul took a seat on the grass approximately where Arthur had been sitting.

Fresh from retrieving his ball from the road, Henry had a suggestion for his older brother. "Hey, there's four of us. Now we can have teams like it's supposed to be. You and me against Skipper and Arthur."

"Are you kidding? That'd be a slaughter. Let's make it me and Skipper against you and Art." Skeptical of his would-be partner's talents, Henry turned to Arthur and asked, "Do you even know how to play?" Defensively Arthur answered, "Yup, and I'm good too."

"Yeah, sure," Henry answered, unconvinced.

To decide which team would go first, the two oldest boys played odds/evens with their fingers. Johnny won, meaning his team got the blue and black balls. Henry's team got the red and yellow ones. Johnny went first and after his turn, his ball sat just short of the third wicket. Henry followed. He inadvertently knocked Johnny's ball through the third wicket while leaving his own ball short of that same wicket. Skipper followed, but failed to clear the second wicket. It was Arthur's turn. He held his mallet clumsily and took some practice swings. Johnny sarcastically said, "Look out! We've got a real expert here." Johnny walked over to the youngster and adjusted his grip for him. "There, that's how you hold the damn thing, chump...I mean champ!"

The older boy stepped back and Arthur swung his mallet. The ball went through the first wicket and though it grazed the second one, cleared that also. That entitled him to another turn. He slammed the ball with all his might. As a result his ball went past wicket #3 all the way to the edge of the front lawn. Johnny laughed. "Hey, Babe Ruth. This is croquet, not baseball. I wonder how many turns it'll take you to get through the third wicket." Johnny laughed. Arthur was not amused. It was Johnny's turn, but Arthur didn't care. He hit his ball, ran to it and then hit it again until it landed near the third wicket.

20

Johnny protested. "Hey, you can't do that, cheater!"

Henry added, "Hey, Arthur, don't be stupid. You're screwing up our chances to win."

Johnny warned his brother, "You better keep your teammate under control."

Things briefly calmed down. By the time Johnny finished his turn, his ball was sitting just short of the fifth wicket." Hey, this is so easy. I've got four more (wickets) to go. Don't mess up, Skipper. We got this game in the bag." Henry then advanced his ball until it sat alongside wicket #4. Skipper cleared the first two wickets. "Hey, Arthur's ball is in the way. He shouldn't be there anyway."

Johnny agreed. "Yeah, Arthur's a crumby player and a cheat."

"Am not."

Johnny picked Arthur's ball up and walked across the playing field.

"Hey, you can't do that! " Arthur complained.

"I just did, didn't I?" Johnny responded. "Here little boy, start over." He dropped the ball behind wicket #1. Already upset because he sensed his chances of winning weren't good, Arthur bristled at his older cousin's bullying tactics.

Johnny turned and walked towards a table and chairs sitting alongside the house. He intended to take a sip of a now-warm can of soda. Arthur rushed over to where his ball lay, picked it up and threw it at Johnny. The older boy turned around in time to duck as the ball whizzed over his head, just missing him—but not a nearby bedroom window. Crash! The ball continued on into the house.

Henry threatened, "You're gonna get it! My dad is gonna-be real mad!"

For a brief second, Arthur remembered that time Uncle John had intervened on his behalf right after his father had thrown him into the television set. Arthur wasn't as worried about Johnny's father as he was worried about his own.

Arthur panicked. This wasn't a misdeed he could hide—or hide from. He couldn't head for his beloved woods in Suassa Park to seek temporary refuge. He also couldn't tell his cousins exactly how frightened he was of his father. That would be too revealing and unbearably embarrassing.

Apparently, the relationship between August Berndt and his

son wasn't as much of a secret as Arthur thought it was. Johnny took pity on his younger cousin. "Your old man scares me, so you must really be scared stiff of him. Let's go inside and see what happened."

The boys entered the house and hurriedly passed by the four ladies chatting in the living room. They headed for Skipper's bedroom. The ball was nowhere in sight. On Skipper's desk by the window were scattered different sized shards of glass. A model airplane, one of its wings lying beside it, was lying on the floor. A container of pickup sticks had also been knocked off the desk and the sticks lay scattered on the floor as if part of an ongoing game.

Henry chimed in. "Arthur, you're an asshole. You know that?"

Asshole. Having heard that term a number of times at home, it had lost much of its sting. Nevertheless, Arthur protested. "No, I'm not."

Johnny chimed in. "Let's clean this shit up before dad gets back. It's not really that bad." He pulled the curtain across the broken pane to hide it—at least from those inside the house. The four boys carefully picked up as many pieces of glass as they could spot and threw them in a wastebasket. Skipper placed the damaged aircraft back on the desk, putting the detached wing in a drawer for the time being. Henry collected the pickup sticks, jammed them into their container and set it on the desk. Lying on his belly, Henry spotted the croquet ball under Skipper's bed.

Hearing the sound of a car pulling into the driveway, Johnny looked out the window and said, "Dad's back!" Johnny told Henry to leave the ball where it was. The boys left the bedroom and headed for the kitchen where all four ladies had begun preparing snacks. Outside, Joe Berndt arrived with his two daughters. Right behind him were Karl Berndt and his family. Within seconds, twenty-two people were crammed together inside the kitchen, grabbing snacks and beverages and then heading to other, less crowded rooms. In a matter of moments, there were Berndts scattered throughout the house.

Food in hand, Arthur went back to Skipper's bedroom, where several of his cousins had begun watching the Yankee game on a small TV. The minute he saw the pinstripe uniforms, Arthur felt compelled to express his distaste. "The Yankees stink."

Johnny replied, "Oh yeah, how many World Series have your

great Dodgers won?" Without waiting for a response, he answered his own question. "Zero." Henry, Paul, and Skipper, also in the room, all laughed. Arthur realized he was surrounded by Yankee fans. Undaunted, he replied, "I bet you we win this year."

Henry answered, "Yeah, that's what Dodger fans say every year."

Arthur wasn't backing down. "Yeah, well Duke Snider is better than Mantle."

"No way!"

"Is to!"

On the television set, Whitey Ford had just finished striking out the side. The Yankees were leading by a 6-1 score in the seventh inning. The four boys got down to the business of eating in silence while they watched the ballgame.

All the other Berndts were enjoying their food in the kitchen, dining room or living room. All the other Berndts, that is, except John and August. Those two headed outside. They walked over to the table set against the house, made themselves comfortable on lawn chairs and proceeded to drink beer while listening to the final innings of the Yankee ballgame wafting from the television in Skipper's room.

In the course of a debate over who was the better shortstop—Phil Rizzuto or Pee Wee Reese—John noticed the broken window.

He asked himself out loud, "How the hell did that happen?"

August volunteered, "You better get that pane replaced. This weather, you'll have bugs flying all over the house."

The two men got up and headed back towards the house, August finishing off the last can of beer during the journey.

Meanwhile Ella had been attempting to shepherd everyone outside to take a group photograph. As John and August entered the house, most of the Berndt clan was heading into the backyard for the photo shoot. The boys in Skipper's bedroom were stalling in hopes of seeing the end of the baseball game. Uncle John headed there, with August right behind him.

"What happened to the window?"

Johnny responded, "What do you mean, Dad?"

"It's broken. "

"Oh", Johnny said, feigning surprise. He pulled back the curtain. "Yeah, I guess it is."

"Were you boys horsing around in here?"

"Nope!" responded Skipper.

Paul had no trouble volunteering too much information. "I saw it. I know who did it. It was Arthur. He got mad and threw the ball at Johnny and it hit the window."

Arthur shot a menacing stare at Paul. August shot an even more menacing stare at his son. "Well, what do you have to say for yourself?"

Arthur defended himself. "He's lying. He did it!"

Paul shot back, "No I didn't. I wasn't even playing."

John asked his oldest son, "So what actually happened here?"

"We were playing and Art picked up the ball and threw it to me. He's stupid. He doesn't even know how to play croquet. It was a bum throw and it went through the window."

August had heard all he had to. He approached his son and slapped him in the face. The room fell quiet, except for Arthur, who burst out crying.

John tried to placate his brother. "Hey, Gus. It's not that big a deal."

August wasn't having any of it. "He's just a damn troublemaker wherever he goes."

Ella stuck her head in the room and said, "Come on boys. We're all set up outside to take some pictures." She noticed Arthur was crying and asked, "Art, what's the matter?" Arthur was too busy sobbing to answer.

Everyone filed out of the room and out onto the backyard, with Arthur trailing.

Marguerite spotted her son and rushed over to him. "Why are you crying? What happened?"

` "Nothing."

"He's a window breaker now." said a disgusted August. "The law breaker is a window breaker. Doesn't surprise me."

By now, the rest of the Berndts had assembled for the photo shoot. Despite the efforts of several family members to cheer him up, Arthur could not be consoled. The first photo taken was of all the children, with a still-bawling Arthur winding up almost directly in the center of the group.

After more photos were taken of various groupings, everyone but Arthur headed back inside. It was time to enjoy Ella's pastries. Normally, Arthur would have been an eager participant, but not this day. He stayed outside, sitting on a swing and sulking. Physically, he'd received a relatively mild punishment. Emotionally, the embarrassment of having spectators was indescribable. Arthur would rather receive one of his father's brutal beatings in private, than a slap in the face in public.

Chapter 5

A week before returning to school as a sixth-grader, Arthur made plans to go to the movies one last Saturday. After reading in the local newspaper that the Port Jefferson Theater was showing *Pinocchio,* his eyes glanced down to films scheduled at the Brookhaven Cinema, located in Port Jefferson Station. That movie house was showing *20,000 Leagues Under the Sea.* The same film had played in the downtown theater months earlier during the previous school year and Arthur remembered classmates raving about it. This Saturday he faced a dilemma—which theater would he visit? *Pinocchio* didn't interest him half as much as *20,000 Leagues* did.

Arthur weighed his options. All summer he'd gone to the movies without getting caught. If he was spotted in downtown Port Jefferson he'd have some explaining to do, but Port Jefferson Station was a far riskier matter. Both of his parents had made it clear Port Jefferson Station was strictly off limits. That town's movie theater sat over a mile away (much of it an uphill walk) from the one Arthur had been visiting all summer. Arthur hatched a plan. He would set out for downtown, but then go uptown. To make his scheme even more foolproof, he'd stay off the sidewalks and instead take a secret route. That meant walking to the end of the dirt path that lay not far from his house. From there, he'd follow the railroad tracks until he reached Port Jefferson Station. A few times from the family car he'd seen the train station uptown and guessed correctly that the tracks there continued to the spot where he played his imaginary baseball games at the end of the path.

When Saturday arrived, Arthur, as he had all summer, left the house with his thirty-cent allowance and headed down Lowell Place. He made a right onto Hawthorne. However, unlike every other Saturday that summer, as soon as he reached Brook Road, instead of turning left to head downtown he scooted right and ran up to Old Post Road. From there he walked a short distance to the start of the dirt path he knew so well. Would he run into the fearsome old man he'd survived an encounter with months earlier? Today that grizzled spectre was nowhere in sight and not even on Arthur's mind. He was on his way to see another interesting character—Captain Nemo!

He walked towards the south end of the dirt road, knowing that when he reached the tracks he would continue the rest of his journey in unknown territory.

As was his custom when walking this path, he occasionally turned around to see if anyone was following him. Today, somebody—or something—was! It was too far away to distinguish, but moving fast. Seconds later, Arthur made out the rapidly approaching object. It was Rex! While walking the neighborhood, the ever-alert German shepherd had picked up his young master's scent and tracked him down. Boy and dog greeted each other, but now Arthur had to give his dog the brush off. "Go home, Rex!" he ordered.

Arthur proceeded, but Rex followed right alongside.

"I mean it! Go home, now!"

Rex's face took on a scolded look and, as Arthur resumed walking, the dog hesitated, but not for long. He quickly caught up to Arthur and kept pace next to his favorite human.

"Rexy, you can't come with me this time. This time is different. You get it?"

Rex tilted his head to one side, as if trying to understand. Arthur's voice took on a sterner tone. "Get out of here! Go home!"

That didn't work so the next command was "Stay!" That one Rex knew and obeyed, temporarily. Arthur made it about twenty additional yards when again Rex came barreling up alongside him.

The young boy had to make a choice: bring Rex back home or let him tag along. The former would put Arthur behind schedule; the latter would greatly complicate things.

The youngster made his decision. Boy and dog walked on

together. After reaching the tracks, they began walking alongside them in an easterly direction, entering uncharted territory. The train tracks remained the one comforting constant. Arthur had no idea how much farther he'd have to walk to get to the movie house but he had no fear of getting lost. To get back home he'd simply retrace his steps along the railroad tracks.

After traveling a half-mile past woodlands that bordered both sides of the tracks the two came upon a series of rundown houses sitting nearby to the south. Five dogs came charging from one of the properties, rushed up a bluff and came out upon the tracks. Two of the dogs matched Rex in size while three were smaller. They began to threaten Rex, lunging at him and then retreating when Rex replied in kind. Arthur had never been bitten or even chased by a dog in his life. Now he and his dog were being threatened by a crazed pack of five canines—and no one in sight to prevent the soon-to-be bloodbath!

Rex was doing his best to ward off the canine attackers, but how long could one dog bluff five? Arthur feared Rex would soon be killed in a fight and then the dogs would come after him. The young boy had to do something. He called to Rex. Usually obedient, Rex paid no mind. He was too busy standing his ground. Arthur began running, hoping his dog would follow him. Rex was too preoccupied to follow his master's lead. Then, Arthur grabbed some rocks and began hurling them with both hands at the enemy, careful not to hit his own dog. As soon as his hands emptied, Arthur scooped up more ammunition. Though his aim was scattered, several of the rocks hit home. Two of the smaller dogs backed off. All the while, Rex continued his aggressive posturing. Another rock hit one of the larger dogs. He yelped and stopped lunging, as if weighing his options. The other sizable canine, sensing a one-on-one fight with Rex, didn't like his odds and he too lost his enthusiasm for the battle. All three smaller dogs, never eager participants in the confrontation, had long since become bystanders. Arthur began running down the tracks, calling his dog to follow him. Rex felt secure enough to let down his guard. He turned away from his now-disinterested attackers and scooted after his master. Arthur looked over his shoulder as he ran and saw the pack of dogs heading back from whence they came.

Arthur slowed his pace and resumed walking with Rex beside him. They passed another treed area, then the backyards of a few scattered houses. After that, the landscape began to change significantly. Commercial buildings came into view along both sides of the tracks—warehouses, small manufacturers, a few stores. Arthur and his dog had reached Port Jefferson Station.

The railroad tracks continued across Main Street and ended at the Long Island Railroad's last station on its Port Jefferson line. That wasn't Arthur's destination. Arthur made a right turn with Rex onto the sidewalk. He could see the Brookhaven Cinema just up ahead.

Minutes later, Rex and his master arrived in front of the movie house. The lobby was empty. The day's entertainment had already begun. Arthur let Rex in and together they walked up to the ticket cashier.

"That'll be thirty cents."

"Darn. That means I won't have any money for candy. How come it's only twenty cents downtown?"

"Young man, I don't set the prices." The cashier spotted Rex. "Sonny, is that your dog?"

"Yup."

"Sorry, there are no dogs allowed in this movie house."

"Oh, you don't have to worry. He's a really good dog. He watches the TV with me and is real quiet."

"Doesn't matter. Take him home and then get back here if you want to see the movie. And you better hurry—the cartoon's already being shown."

"But I can't take him home. It's too far."

"Well, you got here didn't you? Say, shouldn't you...Hmm...Where are your parents?"

The word "parents" alarmed Arthur. He exited the theater with his dog. The youngster debated with himself whether to head back home with dog in tow or try to send the dog home alone.

Arthur couldn't let go of his wish to see *20,000 Leagues Under the Sea*. He hadn't walked all this distance just to turn around and go back home. He initiated a one-way conversation with his dog. "Rexy, you have to go home. I can't explain it right now. You *have* to go home!" The youngster began retracing his steps toward the railroad tracks, Rex following at his side. After a few minutes, Arthur stopped and looked at Rex. "Now, you keep on going home." The young boy began walking backwards towards the theater while repeatedly commanding his dog to "Go home!" His words didn't fall on deaf ears, but might as well have. Rex stood motionless, whining at his young master.

"Go home! Be a good dog!"

The young boy turned around and began running back to the theater. He looked behind him. Rex was following. For the second time that day, they both reached the entrance to the movie house. Arthur again addressed his dog. "Okay. I'm gonna go in and see a movie. You wait for me out here and then we'll go home together." Cars were whizzing by on Main Street. Arthur worried that his dog might get hit by a car. "Rex, you wait right here by the front door. Don't move. I'll be out in a little while. You wait right here." With his hand on Rex's rump, Arthur forced the dog into a sitting position. "You wait here. Just sit and stay."

Arthur reentered the movie house. He pulled a quarter out of his pocket and gave it to the cashier.

"Okay, Sonny. Hurry in there. The movie's already started."

Arthur glanced at his dog, seated outside at the front door. Tail wagging, Rex was staring at his master. Fighting off pangs of guilt, Arthur grabbed his stub from the ticket taker and entered into the darkened theater. He walked past the concession stand and vending machines located in the cinema's foyer. Short on funds, the youngster wouldn't be conducting any business there today.

There were a number of people staring at the movie screen while standing along a solid five-foot high barrier, just outside the seating area. After walking by them, Arthur headed down one of the two aisles leading to seats and soon realized there were none available. He walked back up the aisle and returned to the foyer. He took a spot between two adults in the SRO crowd and, on tiptoes, was able to peer over the wall separating the seating area from the lounge. He began watching the movie. Every few minutes his calves tired and he had to stand flat-footed, unable to see the action on the movie screen. As soon as physically possible he went back up on his toes to re-engage with the movie. The young boy continued this exercise, all the while thinking about his dog. *Did Rex go home? Was he still out on the sidewalk? What if he wandered off? He might get hit by a car!* His conscious gnawing at him, Arthur walked back out to the lobby and looked through the glass doors leading to the street. There, like a statue, sat Rex staring into the theater. Spotting his master, the dog sprang to his feet and began bouncing on all fours. Arthur scooted back inside, guiltier than ever. Finding another spot among those standing, he resumed watching the movie, but could no longer do so with any enthusiasm. Standing on tiptoes was bad enough, but knowing he had deserted his dog was too much to bear. He walked back out to the lobby's doors and snuck a peek at the theater's entrance door. There sat Rex. Arthur ducked back into the theater before his dog caught a glimpse of him.

Arthur again tried to watch the movie, all the while distracted by thoughts of his dog patiently—or was it impatiently?—waiting for him outside the theater. Minutes before the movie ended, Arthur rushed out of the theater, hoping to keep Rex away from the crowd of strangers that would soon be filing out of the movie house. As Arthur approached the theater's exit doors, Rex stood up and began dancing in joy at the return of his youthful master. Once outside of the theater, boy and dog happily reunited. Arthur petted Rex, in part out of guilt. He knew he should have treated his dog better. After all, no one cared about him like Rex did.

The duo walked briskly away from the theater, avoiding what would soon be a mass exodus of moviegoers.

When the two companions reached the railroad tracks, Arthur had a decision to make. Retracing their steps meant risking another encounter with the same pack of dogs that had ambushed them earlier. The only other way Arthur knew to get home was to follow Main Street toward downtown Port Jefferson. He and Rex crossed over the tracks and began that trek.

As the two headed downhill toward Port Jefferson, Rex obediently stayed close at hand to his youthful owner. Fortunately, traffic was light. Unfortunately, not light enough. At a spot halfway between Port Jefferson Station and Port Jefferson the Berndt family car passed by. Had Arthur been spotted? Yes! The youngster took comfort in the fact his mother—not his father—was driving. She pulled the car over and, with a look of concern on her face, shouted to her son, "Stay right there. Don't move." After waiting for traffic to pass, Marguerite made a U-turn and pulled the car up alongside her son. "What are you doing in this neighborhood? You know what we told you."

"I couldn't help it, Mom. I was playing with Rex and he saw a dog and started running after it. He wouldn't listen to me."

"Arthur... Well, get in the car." Arthur let Rex in the front seat and squished himself alongside the groceries sitting on the backseat. Marguerite made a second U-turn and headed home.

"Mom, I ran and ran. I couldn't catch him. He kept chasing the other dog."

"Did you recognize the other dog?"

"No. All I know is he was big and fast. He was growling at me. But then Rex scared him."

"Thank God, they didn't fight. Or did they?"

"Nope. Like I said, Rex scared him. Rex finally stopped chasing him right where I was when you saw me."

"(Puzzled) I didn't see any other dog."

"Oh, he went behind that dentist's big house. That's when Rex stopped. Right when you saw me." Visualizing the largest dog in the pack of canine attackers he and his dog had confronted earlier, Arthur felt compelled to embellish his story. "Oh, I remember now. The dog was really big and black. He growled a lot. He was real scary."

Marguerite mulled things over and then replied, "Art, I'm going to believe you this time. No need to upset your father. Get in the car and let's go home. Just where were you playing anyway?"

"On the football field."

"Which one—the Blaskowitzes'?"

"No. The high school one."

"Art, that one is a bit too far away from our house. Remember I told you to stay out of the woods behind that old man's house?"

"Yup."

"Well, I'm saying you shouldn't go all the way to the high school football field either, with or without Rex. God, I do wish you could make friends with someone in the neighborhood."

"I tried, Ma."

"I know. Maybe we should have you join the Cub Scouts."

"What's that?"

"It's a group of children that meet and do things together. Louise Howell is what they call a den mother. I'll have to check with her. You might be a little too old. I know you and Warren parted ways... I've never really been sure why. What actually happened between you two?"

"He was bad to Rex."

"Really?"

"Yup, he threw rocks at him and everything."

"Well, I can't blame you for not going to his house. But, in Cub Scouts, Rex will be at home. You should be able to bury the hatchet."

"What's a hatchet?"

"Well, it's something used to chop things with."

"So, where do I bury it?"

Laughing, his mother replied, "Well, that's just a figure of speech. It means you stop holding a grudge against Warren."

"What's a grudge?"

"It means you don't like someone for what they did."

"I really hate him for what he did to Rex."

"Well, sooner or later it's best you put that behind you. Besides, there'll be other kids there besides Warren. I like the idea. I'm going to call Louise when we get home."

Minutes later, the car pulled into the driveway at Twenty-one Lowell Place.

Arthur was struggling with mixed feelings. He had gotten away with going all the way to Port Jefferson Station to see the movie he had wanted to see. But, he'd also forced Rex to wait outside the theater for over an hour. Having done that to a dog that saved his life that same day only made the guilt worse.

He'd also missed the ending to *20,000 Leagues Under the Sea* and never gotten to see the Nautilus swept away by tsunami waves.

Chapter 6

Ten days after Arthur's final summer visit to the movies, it was time to head back to school.

That first day of the new school year started off in a positive way for Arthur. He hadn't wet his bed the night before. Something most other children his age might take for granted always felt like a miracle to Arthur.

The initial day involved getting an assigned seat, receiving textbooks, and then getting to work on arithmetic and reading. As he had in each previous school year, Arthur would prove to be up to this grade's academic challenges. Looking around the classroom, Arthur recognized most of the kids in his class. There were a few newcomers to the Port Jefferson School District. His new teacher, Mrs. Snow, had everybody introduce themselves and tell the rest of the class how they had spent the summer vacation. Arthur judiciously left out his close encounter with a neighbor's car, his introduction to fire starting, and the vast amount of time he'd spent in the woods by himself or with his dog. He did eagerly recount his regular weekend visit to the movie house, embellishing the story by stating that his father took him and bought him "all the candy I wanted".

All in all, Arthur's first day *inside* school as a sixth-grader was uneventful. The excitement awaited him *outside* after school ended.

3 P.M. Arthur shoved the composition he had been working on into his desk and participated in a relatively orderly dismissal from the school building. Like the rest of his classmates, the closer Arthur got to the exit door, the less orderly he became. The

young boy burst out the door into a dazzlingly sunlit day. Some students headed for their buses, some headed for their parents' car. Others, like Arthur, began the walk home.

As was his custom, Arthur had helped himself to some of his mother's money before leaving for school and now he would put that money to good use.

Arthur opted for the Crystal Fountain. It still had the greatest selection of sweets in town and since he was using "other people's money" (making shoplifting unnecessary), the glass case that stood between Arthur and his prized sugary delicacies wouldn't subvert the youngster's sweet tooth.

Gilbert, the owner, warmly greeted one of his staunchest customers. "So, Art, what will it be today?"

As always, the choices were difficult for the youngster. So much candy, such limited funds.

"I'll take a pack of Charms, a box of Chocolate Babies, and Neccos. How much is that?"

Gilbert replied, "That'll come to fifteen cents, son."

After recounting his money, Arthur said, "Well, then I'll take a box of Root Beer Barrels and five of those big Tootsie Rolls too."

"Okay. That'll be twenty-five cents. You must do a lot of chores around the house to get such a big allowance."

"Yup, that's what I do."

The purchase completed, Arthur left the Crystal Fountain and started to walk home. He immediately began sampling his sugary stash, starting with a couple of Tootsie Rolls.

Arthur followed his usual route home, taking the alley next to the Cooper's Stationery store, and then walking through a vacant, sandy lot that led out onto Brook Road. After another five minutes of walking, Brook Road became an uphill trek that passed by the two high school athletic fields. To further energize himself, Arthur opened his package of Charms and stuffed three or four of them in his mouth.

On his way up Brook Road, Arthur passed the intersection with Emerson Place. This was a significant landmark for those on foot. If one dared continue, up ahead at the corner of Brook Road and Hawthorne Street, was the Wellings' residence. The Wellings had no children but they did have a "problem child" named Tar— a huge black Labrador retriever mix with a fearsome and well-earned reputation. Like any other pedestrian, whenever Arthur approached the Wellings' house from any direction, he did so with caution. It was critical to determine whether Tar was inside the house or outside on the Wellings' unfenced yard. If Tar sensed an approaching pedestrian before they reached the Wellings' house, he would rush to the edge of his yard growling fiercely. This amounted to an early warning system that let a pedestrian know he or she was about to enter a no man's land. People who ignored Tar's heads up had paid a bloody price! Whenever Arthur saw Tar in the yard he would backtrack and take a longer, but much safer route to get to his destination. During the past summer, Arthur had managed to get past the Wellings' residence without incident on his way to the movies.

With Tar nowhere in sight, Arthur continued his journey up Brook Road, albeit with his guard up. When the youngster reached the intersection of Brook and Hawthorne he made the right turn, intent on making the next left onto Lowell Place. Arthur was just passing the Wellings' property and happily digging into the remainder of his package of Charms when he heard the unmistakable, throaty growls of a wild animal. He turned around to see Tar racing from the side of the Wellings' house and heading straight for him!

Arthur knew he could never get to the safety of his house before Tar got to him. Instead, with Tar in hot pursuit, he ran into the woods that sat directly across the Wellings' residence and desperately tried to scale the first sizable tree he came to. The trunk was too wide, so, jumping up from the ground, he grabbed the lowest limb and, hanging on with his hands, swung his legs up, wrapping them around the limb. With his back to the ground, his hands and legs were all that were keeping him from his canine pursuer. Just below him, Tar leapt threateningly, attempting to snatch his prey, tantalizingly just out of reach. The youngster held on literally for his life, dangling like a piece of ripe fruit, ready to fall at any moment.

Arthur saw there was another branch above the one he was holding on to. If he could swing himself around and lie on the limb he was clasping to, from there he could reach up and grab the branch above it and more comfortably wait out Tar. But he was afraid to move, fearing he'd lose his grip and fall to the ground where the black monster awaited him.

So there the youngster continued to hang, with Tar less than six feet below him. The dog, tired of leaping and still having the advantage in this waiting game, lay down and made himself comfortable, occasionally growling just to let the youngster know what awaited him should he lose his grip.

Arthur, dangling from the tree branch, cried "Help!" hoping somebody at the Wellings' residence would hear him. He cried "Help!" again, but faintly, fear having temporarily weakened his vocal cords. Even at full voice his pleas would have gone unheeded. Unbeknownst to Arthur, there was nobody inside the Wellings' place. Tar had picked up Arthur's scent and bolted through the unlocked back screen door, with his owners not there to restrain him.

After waiting several more minutes and realizing no one was going to save him, Arthur decided he had to try to stand up on the limb he was holding on to while he still had the energy to do it. Using all the youthful strength and agility he had, he swung himself up and on top of the limb, lying belly down on it and still holding on with his arms and legs as if his life depended on it. As if to convince Arthur it did, Tar took notice of the youngster's movements and acknowledged them with several guttural growls.

In his new position, Arthur was more comfortable than he had been dangling from the limb. But he knew he'd be even more comfortable if he could stand up on the limb he was clinging to. With his left arm he grabbed onto another limb immediately above him. He pulled himself up onto his feet, enabling him to grasp the second limb with both hands. There he was, hands overhead clutching one limb, while his feet balanced on another—a dead boy standing. Below, Tar had also gotten back on his feet due to all of the youngster's activity. Again, Arthur shouted at the top of his lungs for help and, again, there was no response.

Arthur noticed he'd lost a button on his brand-new shirt. His pants were dirty and his shoes scuffed. Would he get in trouble when he got home? This was one time when he'd technically done no wrong. He didn't even have to make up a story. Everybody knew the Wellings' dog was a beast. Several people had been bitten by him, one virtually mauled. No one knew why the Wellings kept such an animal or why there had apparently been no legal consequences to date. In this situation, Arthur didn't have to fear his father as much as he had to fear the four-legged enemy that lay in wait just below him.

Arthur wondered if and when someone would finally come to his rescue. Wouldn't the Wellings come outside and look for their dog? What if they weren't home? In that case, he realized he might have a very long wait. How would his parents react if he was still missing by the end of the day? What if the police had to get involved? Even though he hadn't actually done anything wrong, Arthur could never be sure how his father would react—and he didn't want to find out. The youngster decided to take matters into his own hands.

Do dogs like candy? Arthur hoped the answer was "Yes". If there ever was a time to find out, this was it. The youngster fumbled in his pockets. He still had a few Charms, some Tootsie Rolls and entire packages of Root Beer Barrels and Neccos. Arthur conducted an internal debate—was it worth it to give up all that candy? He didn't even know if Tar had a sweet tooth. Right now he knew no one was at his house. Getting home late could raise suspicions. How about the damage to his clothes? Again, would his parents believe his story about Tar? If they didn't, he'd be in trouble. In Arthur's world, taking whatever chance it took to get home before anyone else did seemed to make the most sense. If he got home now, he could change into other clothes, fix the scuffs on his shoes, clean off his pants and figure out something regarding the missing button on the shirt later. Ultimately, Arthur decided he'd rather take his chances with a mad dog now then his mad father later. As for the loss of all his candy, Arthur consoled himself with the knowledge that in less than twenty four hours he could replenish his supply of money courtesy of his mother's pocketbook and then, just a few hours after that, replenish his supply of candy after school.

Arthur opened his package of Neccos and heaved them as far as he could into the woods. That sparked Tar's interest and he ran over to the nearest wafer. After sniffing it, he grabbed the wafer with his teeth and after a few moments spit it out. Obviously, Neccos were not going to do the trick. Arthur decided to chuck all the rest of his remaining candy at once. He bombarded the ground with Charms and Root Beer Barrels. The youngster briefly hesitated when it came to parting with his Tootsie Rolls. They were one of his absolute favorites, but he concluded this was no time to show favoritism. Arthur unwrapped the Tootsie Rolls and chucked them as far away from the tree as he could. On the ground, Tar eagerly checked each of the goodies and settled on the Tootsie Rolls. He began chewing one with relish, losing all interest in Arthur.

In one seamless movement, Arthur bent down, grabbed the limb he was standing on, lowered his body towards the ground and then let go of his grip on the limb. The sound of the young boy landing on his feet caused Tar to turn around. While putting the finishing touches on a Tootsie Roll, the dog looked at Arthur in an almost grin-like fashion. Arthur picked up another Tootsie Roll that lay nearby and threw it over to Tar who immediately began devouring it. Apparently, Tootsie Rolls had become one of Tar's favorites too.

Arthur took the opportunity to run out onto Hawthorne Road, never stopping until he got to Twenty-one Lowell Place. There, Rex, a man's—and a boy's—best friend, happily greeted him. Arthur didn't have time to exchange pleasantries. He cleaned the dirt off his pants with dish soap and water, and put them in his closet to dry. Then, he used paper towels and his father's shoe polish to un-scuff his shoes. He buried his shirt-sans-button in the dirty laundry already piled in the washing machine. He could claim it came off while being washed.

Following his far-too-close encounter with Tar, Arthur made the decision to avoid going near the Wellings' property altogether, thus making his walks home from school forever far less eventful.

Chapter 7

His near-death experience with Tar was quickly forgotten by Arthur, as was most everything else for a few precious weeks.

As the month of September progressed, the youngster's attention narrowed down to a single source of excitement—the Brooklyn Dodgers. Arthur's (and his father's) favorite baseball team were winding up the greatest regular season in the franchise's history. They clinched the National League pennant on September 8th, with several weeks still remaining in the season. It was clear who they would be facing in the World Series—their arch nemesis, the New York Yankees. In recent years these two teams had faced each other in five championship rounds and the Yankees had won all of them. In fact, the Brooklyn Dodgers had never won a World Series. The Dodgers were baseball's bridesmaids and their fan's rallying cry was "Wait until next year!" With the team's unusually strong showing in 1955 fans couldn't help but wonder if this was finally to be their "next year!"

Arthur had mixed feelings about professional baseball. Rooting for the Dodgers was one of the few things he could do with his father. The downside was his father's ill temper, which flared up whenever the Dodgers didn't perform up to the elder Berndt's standards. Alcohol often was the fuel August Berndt added to his always smoldering fire of poor sportsmanship. One of the most tension-provoking experiences for the youngster was sitting in the living room and watching the Dodgers fair badly on the field while his father was drinking. He never forgot that time his father threw a beer bottle into the television set.

Arthur had long ago developed radar that detected the slightest changes in his father's mood. If things were taking a turn for the worse on the baseball field, Arthur often responded by taking his dog for a walk. If, in addition to his father's mood, the weather had also turned foul, the youngster would head upstairs and read comic books while listening to his father shouting even fouler expletives downstairs. If, by some chance, the Dodgers turned the game around, August would also turn his mood around. August Berndt was the ultimate fair-weather fan.

As a result of his father's predictable unpredictability, Arthur approached the soon-to-be played World Series with mixed feelings of optimism and concern. He desperately hoped the Dodgers would be victorious, not only for their sake, but for his safety's sake.

Because of its proximity to the five boroughs of New York City, Port Jefferson, like all towns on Long Island, had a generous sampling of Yankee, Dodger, and New York Giant fans. Adults and youngsters alike argued over which was the best team. In recent years, it seemed that at least one baseball club from New York participated in the World Series at the end of each season. In addition to arguing over which team was the best, fans debated which individual players were the greatest. Arthur's favorite player was the centerfielder Duke Snider. The youngster got into innumerable arguments with his peers over the relative skills of Mickey Mantle, Willie Mays and the Duke. When the subject of baseball came up at school, students eagerly promoted their favorite team and its players on the playground and, at times, in the classroom. Many teachers openly displayed their fanaticism by acknowledging allegiance to one of the three local teams.

September 28. Finally, the World Series began. It was a school day, but Arthur was at home due to a cold. Before leaving for work, his mother had instructed him to stay in bed, telling him he could listen to the game on the radio. The contest began at 1:00 PM. With no one else home, Arthur headed downstairs and turned on the television. He watched the game with one eye on the television and one eye out the window to make sure he didn't get caught downstairs when he was supposed to be upstairs.

The youngster got so wrapped up in the game he didn't hear the family car until it pulled into the driveway. Off went the television, upstairs scooted Arthur and on went the radio. He was forced to listen to—instead of watch— the last three innings of the game. That meant he only heard and did not see Jackie Robinson's controversial steal of home plate. That play brought the Dodgers within one run of tying the game, but they ultimately lost 6-5.

The following day, Arthur was back in school. In the halls of youthful academia, World Series fever had reached an unbridled level. Despite his teacher's show of disapproval, the principal occasionally interrupted class to give a score update. Arthur got home from school just in time to see the last two innings of a game the Dodgers lost 4-2.

This World Series was turning out to be just like all the others had been for the Dodgers—a losing effort and a huge disappointment for their fans. In the Berndt household, everyone was careful not to bring up any sports issues in general or the World Series in particular. August Berndt himself attempted to tune out what was going on with the Dodgers. However, despite knowing his team was down two games to none, he couldn't resist listening to the sports analysis featured on both television and radio. That analysis only made him more disgusted with his "favorite" team.

With a youngster's optimism, Arthur held on to the dream that his team would come back and win the whole thing. His was a desperate optimism based on fear of what it would be like at home if the Dodgers lost.

That night following the second Dodger loss Arthur went to bed with more trepidation than usual. He always feared his father's reprisal if he wet his bed but he wondered if his dad's ugly mood over the Dodgers' misfortunes would make him even more violent. When he woke up the following day in a dry bed, he was relieved that he wouldn't have to find out. Later that day, the Dodgers won 8-3. Dared a Dodger fan hope for the impossible?

Saturday, October 1. The fourth game of the World Series was a home game for the Dodgers and a home game for the Berndts. Being a Saturday, there was no school and no job for Marguerite and the kids to go to. Secretly, they had hoped to watch the ballgame without August Berndt, but, uncharacteristically and at the last minute, the head of the household gave up overtime work in order to stay home and view the game. August's presence added a measure of unwelcome 'excitement" beyond that provided by the ballplayers.

The game itself was full of ups and downs for each team. The one constant: August Berndt's drinking. He was well into his second six-pack by the time Duke Snider had made several circus catches that prevented the Yankees from scoring runs. On top of that, he hit a three-run homer. The Dodgers held on to win 8 to 5. The World Series was tied at two games apiece. There was also peace in the Berndt household. August Berndt was as happy a drunk as he'd ever been.

Sunday, October 2. The Dodgers won 5-3 in workman-like fashion. Duke Snider hit two more homeruns making him the only player in baseball history to hit four home runs in two separate World Series. Arthur would go to school the following day loaded with ammunition for his argument that Snider was better not only than Mantle and Mays, but maybe even Babe Ruth. As for the Dodgers, they were one win away from clinching their first World Series. For the time being, things remained relatively serene in the Berndt household.

Monday, October 3. Back in school, Arthur had to settle for updates from the principal over the intercom. He could have done without them. The Yankees defeated the Dodgers 5 to 1. The Series was tied three games apiece and the final game would be played on enemy turf—Yankee Stadium.

When Arthur got home, he found his father in a somewhat philosophical mood. "Well, it comes down to one game. Anything can happen." The rest of the Berndts were grateful the head of the household had taken the day's loss so surprisingly well.

Tuesday, October 2. Again being in school, Arthur had to settle for updates provided by the principal. The game Arthur didn't see turned out to be a nail-biter. The Dodgers had a two-run lead entering the bottom of the sixth. The Yankees were up and had a man on first with only one out. Yogi Berra hit a slicing drive into the left-field corner. This had all the earmarks of a double that would make it a 2-1 game with the man on second and still only one out. This scenario seemed all-too-familiar to the typical fatalistic Dodger fan (to quote a favorite expression attributed to Yogi Berra himself "It was Déjà vu, all over again"). At the last minute, Sandy Amoros, the Dodger left-fielder made a spectacular catch and—two great throws later—the runner on first was thrown out before he could get back to the bag. Just like that the threat and the inning were over. Brooklyn fans collected their breath and started to sense that this just might be their year.

The Dodgers hung on to win the game 2-0 and the World Series four games to three. 1955 turned out to be the "next year" that Dodger fans had been waiting for ever since the World Series championship round began in 1903.

Arthur had only heard about the Dodgers winning but that didn't dampen his excitement. He ran home after school, displaying an uncustomary eagerness to reach the house he normally avoided whenever possible. It took a Dodgers World Series victory to mitigate the young boy's fear of the house he was growing up in.

The minute he got home, he turned on the sports news to get a recap of the ballgame. The minute the summary ended on one channel, he turned to another in hopes of hearing the same information again. Since the three or four stations the television picked up were all located in the metropolitan area, a World Series featuring two local teams was indeed big news.

Later, his mom and sister both came home. All three openly celebrated the Dodgers victory; all three left unspoken their relief that the Dodgers had saved the day for the Berndt household.

Finally, August Berndt got home from work. He was smiling!!! This was the first time Arthur had ever seen his father's face fail to betray the rage that seethed within. For the moment, August had his chronic anger cooking on an almost imperceptible low flame.

Father and son sat down to watch continued reporting of the World Series on television. This was a story that would never get old to Arthur.

To top things off, after dinner, August Berndt said, "This calls for ice cream!" August and Arthur drove down to the local delicatessen and Arthur picked out his favorite—Breyers vanilla, chocolate and strawberry.

Two years earlier, Arthur had won his school's medal for academic achievement as a fourth-grader and been treated to ice cream. Back then, getting ice cream proved to be the calm before the storm—a brutal beating at the hands of his father. This time ice cream proved to be the calm before an additional treat.

A week after the World Series ended August took his son to meet Dodgers pitcher Johnny Podres at the high school in the town of Huntington. Podres had won two games in the Series.

There was a mixture of adults and sons in the audience that listened to the Dodger star recount each game of the World Series in detail. Arthur and his father listened with rapt attention. After fielding questions from the audience, Podres made himself available for handshaking and signing autographs. August and his son had come empty-handed, bringing nothing on which the pitcher could sign his name. August hurried out to the car and came back into the school with a roadmap. Father and son waited in line until it was their turn to chat with the Dodger ace. August asked Johnny Podres to sign his name on a small blank portion on the back of the map. Arthur simply stared in awe at the larger-than-life athlete. After his father shook the pitcher's hand, Arthur did likewise, summoning up the courage to blurt out, "You pitch good." Podres replied, "Thanks, son." Arthur basked in the glory of having been thanked by a baseball demigod. Especially since the thank-you included the word "son", a word in short supply in Arthur's life.

That evening in Huntington, August Berndt and his son Arthur gave the best impression they ever had and perhaps ever would of being a truly bonded father and son. Even the car rides to and from the event were relatively tension-free, with father and son preoccupied in their discussion of the relative merits of this or that Dodger player vis-à-vis his Yankee counterpart. Perhaps the two were never more on the same wavelength than when it came to their utter dislike of the New York Yankees.

The following year the Dodgers lost the World Series to the Yankees in seven games. There was no ice cream party at the Berndt residence.

45

Chapter 8

Sunday, October 16th.

The elation of the Dodgers' World Series victory had subsided and the Berndt household had settled back into its more typical pattern of interaction. Arthur was walking through the neighborhood headed nowhere in particular. He'd left his house listening to his drunken father ranting about the cost of groceries, President Eisenhower's foreign policy, the car mechanic he didn't trust—the list went on.

The youngster turned onto Owasco Drive. He passed a wooded lot on his left and then reached a house with #10 on the mailbox. He immediately recognized the Cadillac sitting in the driveway. He eyed the vehicle, not as a car, but as a weapon that had been used by its driver to intimidate him. A deep anger welled up inside the young boy. Per the sign planted in the front lawn, he was facing the Baldwin residence. Now Arthur knew his enemy's name. It was Mr. Baldwin who had threatened him with serious physical harm months earlier.

In Arthur's worldview, August Berndt might have the right to torment him by dint of being his father, but a stranger didn't have that same right. Besides, even if he wanted to, Arthur dared not directly confront the monster he had to live with. That would lead to swift retribution. Mr. Baldwin, a neighbor, was a different matter. The young boy decided to exact revenge the only way he knew how—by setting the Baldwin house on fire.

First, he had to make sure no one was at home. If someone was, Arthur would strike another day.

He decided he'd knock on the door. If someone answered

46

he'd lie and say he was looking for his dog. The young boy walked up the driveway, along the flagstone path, up the steps and onto the front stoop. He rang the front doorbell. Nobody responded. He rang again. Still no response. Just to be sure he rapped loudly with the door knocker. No one came to the door.

Emboldened, Arthur calculated his next move. It had been easy to get away with starting a fire in the woods, but he sensed starting a fire in the middle of a residential neighborhood would be far more challenging. One plus in the youngster's mind: the Baldwin house was flanked on both sides and at the rear by woods and there was a vacant lot directly across from it. Because of that, Arthur could go about his business with little chance of being spotted.

The young boy didn't feel confident that if he started a fire on the outside of the house it would do enough damage. Would he dare to break inside? He had done that before at the Cohen residence and gotten caught. Back then, he'd had a partner in crime. Now, however, he was working solo and was older and more savvy.

Several months ago, Arthur had stashed matches in a dry spot underneath the back steps at home. But he knew he'd need something besides matches to make sure the Baldwin residence would go up in flames. Out of curiosity, Arthur walked over to the detached garage and peered through the window. After a few seconds of searching, something caught his eye. It was a gasoline can sitting next to a lawnmower. Arthur had seen his father at home fill up the lawn mower with gasoline. He had warned his son to leave the gas can alone because it was dangerous. Just as on the can at home, Arthur could see the word "flammable' on the can inside the Baldwin's garage. The side door to the garage was unlocked and Arthur went in. He walked over to the gas can and lifted it up. He got a sudden rush of excitement because the can was full. Now he had to go get his matches.

In order to not be detected by his own family, Arthur cut through the yard of the house behind Twenty-one Lowell Place. He made a mad dash over to the back steps and quickly went under them. Inside the house, he heard his sister Ruth playing the piano downstairs, while he heard classical music coming from his father's radio upstairs. It was not the kind of music August Berndt liked, so Arthur assumed his father was sleeping off his alcohol binge. That accounted for the whereabouts of two family members. Arthur didn't know where his mother was, but he was on a mission and he would just have to take his chances. He located the box of safety matches and to his great relief it was bone dry. He grabbed the box and made another mad dash across the backyard and through his neighbor's property, coming out onto Whittier Place. He then scooted up to Hawthorne Street, made a left turn and then a quick right back onto Owasco Drive.

Time for secrecy. He cut through the woods to get to the edge of the Baldwin property. He was now facing the south side of the garage. Arthur dropped his box of matches on the ground, opened the garage window and climbed inside the garage. He grabbed the can of gasoline, carried it back to the window, and boy and can both exited the garage. After picking up the matches, Arthur scooted around to the back of the garage and sat down on the ground, virtually invisible to the rest of the world.

The young boy briefly considered whether or not he should proceed. The recurring mental picture of Mr. Baldwin threatening him with his car made Arthur ever more resolute to carry out his incendiary plot.

When Arthur had knocked on the front door earlier, he hadn't bothered to check if it was unlocked. Fearing he might be spotted, he hesitated to go to the front of the house a second time. Making his job easier, he found a set of Bilco doors attached to the back of the house that led to the basement. Arthur opened them and, with the can of gasoline and box of matches in his hands, walked down the steps into a dark basement. Normally, walking in the unlit basement of a house owned by an unfriendly stranger would be frightening to an eleven-year-old, but Arthur's anger gave him all the incentive he needed to continue undaunted. Not bothering to look for a light switch, he instead stumbled his way in the dark until he found the stairs leading up to the inside of the house.

It had been several years since Arthur had broken into anyone's house but the feeling remained the same—entering forbidden territory was an experience both frightening and exciting.

When Arthur reached the top of the stairs he put the gas can down and, with both hands, opened the door that led into the kitchen. Then, he picked up his can of flammable ammunition and invaded the living quarters of a neighbor, something he had done several times before. Breaking and entering made up a significant part of Arthur's rap sheet.

Suddenly, fear gripped the youngster. If a car pulled up what would he do? How could he get out of the house without being seen? How would he explain himself if he was found inside the house? Arthur realized he had to act quickly and then make his escape.

The young boy wasn't sure of the ideal place to start the fire. He walked into the dining room and spotted additional fuel for the fire he was about to set—a pile of logs and a stack of newspapers both sitting near the fireplace.

Arthur recalled the way his father started a fire in the fireplace so he arranged the logs and newspapers in a similar way—but on the living room floor, not in the fireplace. Then he had second thoughts. He wasn't sure such an arrangement would cause more than just small local damage. He took a few newspapers and logs and crammed them under the sofa. He took a few more newspapers and spread them on the wooden dining room table.

Arthur heard a car outside! He ducked down hoping not to be seen through the bay window. On his knees, he peered outside and to his immense relief, saw a vehicle pass by and continue on to some destination other than Ten Owasco Drive. Now his nervousness reached a fevered pitch. He had to ratchet up the destructive process and then get out of there!

Arthur scattered gasoline on the logs and the remaining newspapers under the sofa and lit it. He poured some more gasoline on the dining room table and lit that. He splashed some gasoline on a floor model record player with a mahogany case. He emptied every last bit of gasoline on the living room carpet and set that ablaze. Having no more use for it, he threw the gasoline can across the room into the television set, smashing the screen.

Arthur perched himself on a stool in the kitchen and from there viewed his handiwork. The sofa was now ablaze. So was the record player. The top of the dining room table was smoking and flaming. Smoke was beginning to fill the house.

It was time to get out. Arthur found the light switch next to the basement door and turned it on. He'd be able to exit the house via an illuminated basement.

After taking one last look at the conflagration he had created, he scurried down the cellar stairs. On his way over to the Bilco doors he spotted an unexpected surprise—another can of what he thought was gasoline. It wasn't—it was turpentine, but that would serve the youngster's purposes just as well. He poured the can's entire contents on the basement steps from top to bottom and lit the bottom step. He watched in fascination as a flame jumped from step to step right up to the top one.

Sensing it was no longer safe to linger and create more havoc, Arthur shifted his focus from causing destruction to avoiding detection. He sped up the concrete steps that led outside. After exiting, he felt compelled to close the Bilco doors—an odd mannerly gesture from the youthful arsonist. Outside, though Arthur could hear the fire's crackling, there were not yet any visible signs outside the house as to what was going on inside.

As he walked away from the house, again for a split second Arthur was tempted to go back inside and further stoke the "home fires". Spotting smoke escaping from a half-open window, he quickly dropped the thought of doing any further damage and returned to "getting away with it" mode. Still clutching his matches, he scurried through the woods alongside the garage until he came out onto Hawthorne Street. He had hoped to hold on to his remaining matches so that he could continue to feed his fire-starting frenzy in the future, but didn't want to risk detection trying to hide them again at his house. He reluctantly tossed the matches back into the woods and continued home. Not carrying any incriminating evidence, he was able to enter Twenty-one Lowell Place from the front door.

Ruth had finished piano practice and was upstairs doing homework. August was still in his bedroom listening—or sleeping—to music on the radio.

Marguerite was in the living room watching television and knitting. "Well Art. Where did you go?"

"I was just outside walking around."

"You should've taken Rex. He was looking for you."

"Well, maybe I'll go back out. Come on Rex!"

"Just make sure you get back by around five o'clock. That's when we're eating."

"I bet you dad won't be eating." Knowing his father had gotten drunk earlier than usual in the day, the youngster figured his father would spend the rest of the day sleeping his binge off.

That was a plus for Arthur. He always enjoyed dinner more when his father wasn't at the table.

"You're probably right. It'll be you, me and Ruth. Roast beef and gravy."

"Yum. Maybe I'll go to David's house for a while."

"Really? You two getting along again?"

"Yup."

Arthur didn't go to David's house. He took Rex up Lowell Place and across Old Post Road onto the dirt path the youngster went so often without his parents' permission.

Walking along the path, he heard a fire siren sound off in the distance. This was the second time in a matter of months that the fire department's alarm went off due to a fire of Arthur's own making. It wouldn't be the last time.

Chapter 9

Carolyn Marino. Arthur didn't remember ever having seen her in previous school years—and with good reason. Carolyn was a new arrival to the area and to Arthur's sixth grade class. She was a "bus kid", coming from a faraway land called Coram. She was petite, with thick eyebrows, black hair cropped a la Moe Howard, and just the slightest beginnings of a mustache. Arthur definitely knew how to pick 'em.

Though Carolyn hadn't caught the young boy's eye until well into October, he was determined to make up for lost time. Unfortunately, the would-be twosome sat three rows apart in the classroom. Arthur would have to content himself with gazing at Carolyn from afar. Alas, love unrequited.

Then, one magical day the desk immediately ahead of Carolyn's became vacant after its former occupant transferred to another school. Arthur implored his teacher to let him relocate under the pretext that he "would be able to see the blackboard better". That same day he found himself sitting in front of his heartthrob.

How did their romance officially begin? Though usually a boy of few words, Arthur made the first overture. One day prior to a spelling test, Arthur offered to let Carolyn see his paper so she could copy his answers. Her response was noncommittal. Undeterred, during the exam the young boy graciously placed his answer sheet on his desk in such a way that Carolyn could easily see it. The young girl had not asked for his help, but, trusting Arthur's spelling skills more than her own, decided to change "moosic" to music and "stayshun" to station on her test paper.

Perhaps she should have made a few more changes. While Arthur scored a ninety-five on the test, Carolyn limped in with a seventy.

As the weeks progressed, Arthur and Carolyn became quite the item, at least in Arthur's mind. Carolyn played it close to the vest, not committing totally to the serious relationship Arthur thought they already had. She did, however, continue to take advantage of Arthur's testing skills.

Due to Arthur's persistence-bordering-on-insistence, Carolyn eventually relented and the two began exchanging heartfelt love notes. Since she sat behind him, the two lovebirds didn't have to rely on their classmates delivering the mail and likely compromising their confidentiality. They put a lot of thought into their responses to each other's questions. Sometimes the written exchanges got very deep. Arthur initiated this one:

Do you like Mrs. Snow [their teacher]?
Yes.
Why?
She is nice.
What bus do you take?
Number three. What one do you take?
I don't. I'm not a bus kid.
Do you have any pets?
Yes.
What kind?
Rexy.
What's a Rexy?
A dog, my dog. His name is Rex, but I call him Rexy a lot.
I have a hamster and a cat.

All in all, the kind of conversation dreams are made of.

Arthur and Carolyn seemed a match made in heaven, or at least in Port Jefferson. In the classroom, notes were soon being passed between the two at a feverish pace. On the playground, Carolyn became Arthur's favorite target during games of Elimination. Brenda Watson, his flame in the fourth grade, was now only a distant memory.

***

As the school year progressed, Arthur felt Carolyn's affection begin to wane. What made him come to that conclusion? Let's just say sixth grade boys can sense these things. Besides, he had plenty of proof her love had soured. In the classroom, she had become painfully slow in responding to Arthur's notes, now suddenly expressing concern she might get caught by the teacher, a fear that had never interfered with her passionate letter-writing before. Out on the playground, she was playing much less Elimination and spending much more time with her friends on the swings.

This was a first for the youngster. His affair with Brenda Watson had never weakened; she had simply been forced to leave town, undoubtedly against her wishes. On the other hand, Carolyn's inexplicable change of heart befuddled the youngster. Arthur decided he had to do something to regain her attention before all was lost. But, how to bring the magic back into their fast dwindling relationship? Arthur thought long and hard.

The young boy had a liking for items found in the trick and novelty section of a local store—the fake doo-doo, hand buzzer, phony spilled ink bottle, whoopee cushion, a pen with invisible ink, etc. A few weeks earlier, the youngster had obtained a pack of hot gum (disguised cleverly to look like Wrigley's Doublemint). The gum had grabbed his attention—not enough to pay for it, so he stole it. At the time of the theft he felt he just had to have the gum, though he actually didn't have the slightest idea what he'd ever do with it. Since then, he carried the gum with him constantly, waiting for the opportune moment to use it, all the while having no clue what that moment might look like.

Why would a person want to set someone else's mouth on fire with chewing gum? Until now, Arthur hadn't been able to think of one good reason. Then, one day in class, while deep in desperate thought inspired by a flickering romance, it dawned on him. The perfect plan to regain Carolyn's attention—he would put hot gum in her lunchtime sandwich when she wasn't looking! What better way to regain her attention and show his love at the same time?

On school days, some of the kids in class purchased lunch in the cafeteria, but others brought their lunches from home. Carolyn did the latter. These lunches were kept in the cloakroom until noon, when students retrieved them and ate at their desks. Arthur usually ate the cafeteria lunch. That was about to change.

Arthur spent a whole weekend pleading with his mother to start making him a bagged lunch on school days. When she asked what had brought on this sudden need to change his eating habits, Arthur concocted a story about the lunch line being too long, a seat in the cafeteria being too hard to find, and so on and so on. His mom took the bait.

The following Monday, Arthur arrived in class with a homemade lunch. The youngster cheerfully put it alongside the other bagged lunches already sitting on a table in the cloakroom. Why was he so upbeat? Because, having brought his lunch had allowed him entry into the cloakroom, where he could put his plan into operation. Arthur couldn't be bothered with trial runs. Why wait? Today would be the day! Another reason for the youngster to be so upbeat? He was totally oblivious to the potential downside of his venture.

After sitting down at his desk, he watched as other kids entered the classroom to begin their school day. Then *she* arrived—his fallen idol. Carolyn came into the classroom carrying her lunch. As luck would have it, she brought her meal in a white paper bag, making it easy to find among all the other brown bags. Things were working out better than planned. However, the young boy still had to figure out a way of getting back into the cloakroom without raising his teacher's suspicions.

An hour or so before lunchtime, Mrs. Snow was called out of the classroom. She gave the students a reading assignment and instructed them to keep at it in her absence. Opportunity knocked and Arthur quickly answered the door. This was becoming too easy. Seconds after the teacher left the classroom, he got up from his seat.

A classmate immediately warned him, "Oh, you're gonna to get in trouble."

Another student quizzed Arthur, "Where you going?"

Arthur's terse, but honest reply: "I left something in my coat jacket."

Arthur opened the door to the cloakroom and stepped into it. He immediately got down to business. The "something" he had left in his jacket was the pack of hot gum. He retrieved it and, after taking out a couple of sticks, put the remainder of the pack back into his jacket and headed over to the table covered with bagged lunches. Once there, he opened up Carolyn's lunch bag and found a square-shaped object covered in aluminum foil.

After unwrapping what turned out to be a tuna fish sandwich, Arthur proceeded to tear the two sticks of gum into tiny pieces and bury them inside the tuna fish. By the time he was done, Arthur had shoved ten blazing bits of gum into the fishy part of the sandwich. He slammed the two halves of the sandwich back together, haphazardly resealed the foil around it, and put the sandwich back in its bag. If this didn't get her attention, nothing would. What a clever way to get his former flame's flaming attention. He congratulated himself on his romantic creativity.

Arthur exited the cloakroom and reappeared in the classroom wearing an air of confidence. He stuffed the empty gum wrappers he was clutching in his hand into his pants pocket. Then, he sat back down in his seat. None too soon, as Mrs. Snow returned just seconds later.

For the rest of the morning, Arthur could barely keep his mind on the schoolwork in front of him. He was too distracted by the big clock behind Mrs. Snow. All he could do was watch its hands march inexorably forward.

High noon.

The cafeteria kids lined up at the door and were given the okay by the hall monitor to leave the classroom and head for the dining area. The other students, Arthur and Carolyn included, headed for the cloakroom to get their respective lunch bags. Back to their seats they went, ready to dig into their homemade goodies. Arthur opened his bag and found one of his favorites— ham salad on rye, especially appreciated by the young boy as the extracurricular activity that morning had built up a bigger than usual appetite. He also had an apple and three Fig Newtons as a chaser to stave off his never-say-die sugar cravings. A silence fell over the classroom as the students got down to the business of eating.

"Oh!" Carolyn was holding the side of her face and wincing. "Ow! Mrs. Snow!"

"What is it?"

"My mouth hurts. My sandwich is... it tastes funny." Her eyes started tearing.

"Don't eat any more of it."

"My mouth burns." Carolyn began gulping her milk to put out the fire. Mrs. Snow rushed over to the young girl's desk.

The teacher picked up the sandwich. A couple of pieces of gum stuck out from between the two slices of bread.

With a quizzical look on her face, Mrs. Snow asked no one in particular, "Why, whatever is this?" She put what remained of the sandwich back onto Carolyn's desk, and, after lifting off the top slice of bread, probed at the tuna fish with a pen. She extracted a few bits of gum from the sandwich.

"What in the world is this? Carolyn, are you okay?"

Carolyn's eyes were still watering. "My mouth is sore. It hurts."

"Can you make it to the nurse's office?"

"Yes."

Writing a note, Mrs. Snow sent Carolyn down the hall to the nurse. Turning to the rest of the class she asked angrily, "Who's responsible for this? This is outrageous!"

No one said a thing, though a couple of kids snickered.

"This is not one bit funny! Who did this? This class is going nowhere until I find out. This is completely unacceptable. You will not be going outside for recess until I find out who did this."

Peter, the classmate seated in front of Arthur, turned around and said, "Tell the teacher what you did!"

"Shut up!"

Mrs. Snow turned her attention towards Arthur. "Tell me what, Arthur?"

"Nothing."

Richie, a nemesis of Arthur's going back to the second grade, kept the ball rolling, pointing at Arthur and declaring, "He did it."

Other kids took turns chiming in.

"Yup."

"I saw him."

"It's his stuff."

Still more students offered testimony against the culprit.

"He went into the cloakroom when you were gone, Mrs. Snow."

"He showed me the gum before class. It's some kind of bad gum. He had it in his jacket."

Arthur remained dead silent. He didn't understand. He had only been trying to win back the girl of his dreams and now the whole classroom had turned against him.

Glowering directly at Arthur, the teacher asked, "Young man, why don't you tell me exactly what happened."

Arthur answered defensively. "Nothing happened. I didn't do

nuthin."

"Anything. Are you telling me the truth?"

"Yes."

Once more without prompting, Richie spoke up. "No he isn't, Mrs. Snow. Ask him what's in his pockets."

Arthur's stomach sank to the floor. He remembered the empty wrappers he'd shoved into his pockets in front of twenty-four young witnesses all too eager to testify.

"Arthur, what's Richie talking about?"

"I don't know. He should keep his big mouth shut."

"Now Arthur, that's no way to talk! Don't be fresh! You have nothing to worry about, if you're telling the truth." He wasn't, so he had plenty to worry about.

Mrs. Snow stood in front of Arthur, weighing her options. Finally, she asked, "Well, *do* you have anything in your pockets?"

"No."

"Okay then, would you have any problem emptying them in front of me?"

"Nope."

Confidently, Arthur jammed closed fists into his pockets, then quickly pulled them both out, waving his open palms in front of his teacher, as if proving his point.

"Arthur, that won't do at all. Please pull your pocket liners out completely so I can see them."

Again the young boy shoved his hands back into his pockets. He confidently pulled out the liner of his right pocket. Nothing to see there. He dawdled with the left pocket. While the teacher kept a watchful eye, Arthur attempted to show just enough of the left pocket liner while using his fingers to hide the gum wrappers. A mission impossible.

"Arthur, please pull your left pocket out all the way. Come on, let's get this over with."

The young boy complied, and the wrappers fell to the floor. He picked them up and sheepishly stuffed them back in his pocket.

"I've seen enough. Now, where is the rest of the gum?" His cover blown, the young boy walked into the cloak room and came back out with what was left of the pack of gum.

Mrs. Snow took it from him and, after looking it over, asked, "Do your parents know you have this?"

"Not exactly."

"I'll take that as a 'No.'" The teacher shook her head in disgust as she looked at the gum and muttered "What nonsense!" After putting the evidence in her pocketbook, she began writing something on a piece of paper while Arthur stood next to her desk. At that moment, Carolyn returned to the classroom.

Mrs. Snow signaled her to come over and asked, "How do you feel?"

"Okay, I guess. Mrs. Cagney made me swish a lot of cold water in my mouth. It still burns a lot."

"Arthur, I want you to apologize to Carolyn right now."

Disappointed and embarrassed by the fact that his act of love had been rejected by its intended beneficiary, Arthur was also confused. Why should he apologize for what he had done? He looked at Mrs. Snow and asked, "I don't know. What should I say?"

"Well, are you sorry?"

"I guess so."

(Nodding toward Carolyn) "Then tell *her* that, don't tell me."

Arthur turned to his estranged heartthrob and resentfully blurted out an insincere, "I'm sorry."

Carolyn didn't reply. With the teacher's permission, she returned to her seat. The kids that sat near her wanted to see the inside of her mouth, but she refused to satisfy their curiosity. Meanwhile, Mrs. Snow put the finishing touches on her note and handed it to Arthur with a stern order. "Take this to Mr. Tolleson's office, right now!"

Arthur, feeling already convicted, glumly headed out of the classroom and down the hall toward the principal's office, where he would receive his sentence. He hadn't been able to hide his crime. Could he minimize his punishment?

On a handful of occasions during his scholastic career this or that teacher had threatened to send Arthur to the principal's office, but the only time he ever wound up there was by invitation from Detective McIntyre following a burglary the youngster had participated in as an eight-year-old. Now it was happening—a teacher was sending him to his doom. As he reluctantly headed there he envisioned the paddle Mr. Tolleson had hanging on the wall outside his office, in plain sight to all the students passing by in the hall. Mr. Tolleson was beefy and over six feet tall, which made him humongous to a sixth-grader. He rarely ever cracked a smile, purposefully maintaining a stern look throughout the school day—apparently a requisite for his job.

Arthur walked into the principal's office and gave the note to the secretary. She had always seemed like a warm lady until today. Now he saw her as nothing more than an executioner's henchwoman. She read the teacher's note and then folded it back up and got out of her seat. She gently rapped on the partially open door leading into a room where, out of sight, sat Mr. Tolleson at his desk. The secretary walked in and handed him the note. Arthur heard a stern "Tell him to wait!" The secretary returned and conveyed that same message to Arthur.

The anxiety built. Would a paddling in school be as bad as what he endured at home? Might it be worse? Then, a thought crossed his mind that filled the young boy with outright panic— what if the principal called his parents?

Arthur sat and waited. Was the principal purposely delaying their meeting to heighten the youngster's fear? If so, his tactic was working. Though Arthur was all-too-well acquainted with this type of anxiety, it never got any easier to handle.

After a seemingly interminable wait, the young boy heard his name being called.

"Arthur Berndt, get in here, young man."

Arthur got up from his chair and walked into the principal's private quarters.

"I'm looking at this note from your teacher and I don't like what I'm reading. What do you have to say for yourself?"

"Nothing."

"Nothing? No explanation? Why in the world would you do such a thing?"

Arthur wouldn't answer because he couldn't answer. This was a personal matter that he was convinced no one would understand, so why waste time spelling out his lovesickness and leave himself open for ridicule?

"Mrs. Snow says you apologized to the young lady. That's the first step. The second step is to never pull a stunt like that again. Do you understand?"

Even though he didn't, the youngster replied, "Yes, sir."

"All right. There are consequences for misbehavior. I want you to put your hands on my desk and bend over."

A question Arthur had been carrying inside his head for a long time was finally being answered. His father *wasn't* the only one capable of hitting him, after all.

60

The young boy knew this was going to hurt badly; his father had long ago taught him that. Arthur considered making a deal with Mr. Tolleson: the principal could hit him as hard and as long as he liked if he promised not to tell the young boy's parents. The youngster thought better of that idea. Such a proposal might lead to questions, questions that could make public family secrets.

As he usually did in such a situation, Arthur tried as best he could to visualize his world after the punishment was over. He imagined himself surviving this just as he had survived all his father's beatings.

Arthur began lowering his pants. Somewhat shocked, somewhat confused, Mr. Tolleson said, "I didn't say anything about taking your trousers off. Pull them back up and lean over my desk. Put your hands on the desk. I'll be right there."

Arthur did as told and bent over, his hands placed on the principal's desk. He took a quick peek and saw the principal reaching for the hard wooden paddle hanging on the wall in the secretary's room. He came back into his office, paddle in hand. The young boy braced himself.

"Hopefully, this will be the first and last time for this, young man!"

Whack! The paddle struck Arthur's butt. Whack! It landed again. Something didn't make sense to Arthur. Was he imagining things or did these blows not really hurt? Another whack. Again, Arthur felt little pain. The youngster thought it might be because he was wearing thick corduroy pants. He began crying, not because he was in pain, but to convince the principal he was. A couple of more strikes of the paddle and the disciplining was over.

"And let that be a lesson to you."

What lesson? Arthur felt that delicious feeling of getting away with something. Had Mr. Tolleson only intended to scare him straight and, accomplishing that, eased off during the actual physical punishment? Could it be the principal didn't have his heart into administering physical punishment like Arthur's father did? Arthur quickly dismissed that possibility. He preferred to smugly gloat over the thick trousers that he was sure had fooled the principal and literally saved the youngster's hide. He thanked his lucky pants all the way back to Mrs. Snow's classroom.

Upon arriving, he found his fellow students were busy writing down spelling words as Mrs. Snow wrote them on the board. Arthur got to his desk and joined in. The teacher made no mention of the hot gum incident the rest of the day, or ever again.

As Arthur walked home from school that day, he couldn't believe how lucky he had been. Of course, his relationship with Carolyn was in shambles; nothing could be done about that for the moment. But, he'd survived a paddling unscathed! In addition, his misdeed had gone unreported to his parents, an even bigger break for the young boy!

Chapter 10

Several weeks went by. Both the principal and Arthur's teacher had forbidden him to interact with Carolyn for the time being. To make his task easier, Mrs. Snow moved the young boy two rows away from his one-time belle. He was not to approach her on the playground. The problem? Arthur found he didn't know how to get through a school day without Carolyn. Plus, Carolyn herself sent mixed messages. Every once in a while Arthur caught her sneaking a glance at him from across the classroom. He was certain he wasn't imagining things—the hot gum had worked after all! Now, what to do since they had been torn apart by adults? At school, talking to her would be too risky; sending her a note, taboo. In the name of love, Arthur racked his brain as he never had before.

One day in class, he hit mental pay dirt! When school ended, Arthur hotfooted it home. When he got there, he figured he had about fifteen minutes before Ruth would arrive following her school day. The youngster grabbed the phone book in the dining room and sat down on the floor. He began leafing through the pages until he got to the "M" section. He ran his finger down the page until he got to the name Marino. There were two listings for the name Marino. He got up, went to the phone and dialed one of them. What he was doing—calling a stranger's home—was scary enough, but to make matters worse, he was under a time limit. If his sister came home before he was done, she would ruin everything. She ratted him out every chance she got. As far as Arthur was concerned, that's what his parent's favorite child did for a living.

After a few rings, the phone was picked up on the other end and answered by a female.

"Hello."

"Uh, hello."

"Who's calling please?"

"Um, my name is Arthur. I ...is Carolyn there?"

"You mean my granddaughter?"

Though he didn't know exactly what a granddaughter was or if Carolyn was one, he answered with a "Yes."

"She doesn't live here. She lives with her parents over on Forest Lane. Can I give her a message? What is this all about? You sound like a nice young boy."

"Well, Carolyn's in my class and I have to talk to her about something."

"Oh. Can you tell me or is it something secret?"

That question rattled the young boy. He decided he'd better get off the phone and, without saying another word, promptly hung up.

Arthur ran over to the phone book he'd left lying on the floor, bent down and memorized the other Marino number. He scooted back to the phone and dialed it. Time was running out.

"Hello, this is Cheryl."

"Does Carolyn live with you?"

"Why, yes. Is anything wrong? Who is this anyway?"

"Can I speak to her? I want to."

"Well, not until you tell me your name."

"I'm Arthur."

"Are you that Arthur boy she's mentioned, the one in her class?"

She'd told her parents about him! The youngster's heart went aflutter.

"Yes."

"Well, she's not here yet. You know, young man, she has to take a bus home all the way from Port Jefferson." Arthur had forgotten that little detail in his plan. "Why don't you call back in about a half-hour to be on the safe side?"

Arthur said he would, though he knew he wouldn't. From the dining room window he saw Ruth, walking with school books in hand, turning onto the driveway. Arthur ended the second phone call as abruptly as he had ended the first.

Because she had spoiled his well-laid plans, Arthur greeted

his sister with a surly "What are you home so early for?"

"None of your business. If you have to know, I got let out early to come and get my flute." Translation: *Unlike you, I get special treatment, at home and in school.*

His sister was a musical whiz. Though only a ninth grader, she was qualified to play multiple instruments in the high school band. Piano, flute, clarinet, drums, school chorus—Ruth did it all. Arthur swore she "did it all" to make him look bad by comparison. Or maybe he just resented the fact he was the designated underachiever in the family.

After his sister left the house, flute case in hand, Arthur flirted with the idea of calling the Marino residence again, but thought better of it because he knew his mom would be coming home any minute. His scheme had been delayed, but the youngster was determined not to be totally thwarted. Arthur was a never-say-die kind of kid.

***

School became Arthur's torture. There the youngster sat, in the same classroom with his dream of dreams, barely allowed to acknowledge her existence. Every once in a while the two would exchange glances, which only lifted the young boy to an even loftier cloud in heaven. The same hot gum that had caused their separation had now taken their relationship off life-support and propelled it to a higher level. Or so Arthur thought.

Chapter 11

Jolted out of a deep sleep by a dreaded discomfort he knew far too well, Arthur sat up in his bed. He was drenched—in his own urine. He knew that at any moment his father would be coming in to check on him. This monitoring had been going on his entire life. If his father found him soaked, it usually meant a beating and always meant an uncomfortably steaming bath followed by a trip to the basement where he'd have to wash his soiled sheets by hand. If his father found him dry, the youngster felt as if he had gotten a stay of execution—at least until the following evening when the nightly drama repeated itself.

Every evening, Arthur went to bed fearing what might happen during the night. Though for years he endured an ongoing ritual of punishment for his bedwetting, it never got easier for the youngster to handle. When rousted out of bed by his father, he did his best to avoid his father's hands-on treatment by scurrying to the bathroom to take a-middle-of-the-night bath. If his father watched, he had to fill the tub with hot water only. If his father was less attentive, he could take the chance of running some cold water to take the edge off what otherwise would be a boiling cauldron.

This night, like so many others, Arthur lay awake in his bed dreading the moment the alarm clock went off in his parents' bedroom. He knew that, when it did, within seconds his father would barge into his room and, finding his son had wet the bed, all hell would break loose. Tonight he simply couldn't muster up the fortitude to endure the ritual that his father and he participated in on a far too regular basis.

Arthur dragged himself out of the bed and stood by the door, considering his options. If he went downstairs he knew his father would eventually find him there and perhaps be even angrier that his son had been trying to dodge his "just" punishment.

The alarm clock went off! Arthur heard his father turn it off and mutter something indecipherable. The youngster had only seconds to act! In a moment of sheer panic, Arthur headed for the bedroom window. He opened it up and climbed out onto the slanted roof that sheltered the extended living room on the first floor. Closing the window behind him, he lay down on his belly and, with little to hold on to, carefully climbed up the roof to its peak. Once he got there, he clutched the peak with both his hands to keep from sliding off and dropping thirty feet to the ground.

Arthur heard his father enter the bedroom. The bedroom light came on.

"What the hell?" Arthur heard his father open the bedroom closet door in search of his missing son. "Shit! Where the hell are you?"

Arthur had no intention of giving his whereabouts away. He heard his father storming down the stairs to the first floor. August Berndt went from room to room, but found no one. The silence of the night was broken by an occasional "Dammit!" and "Jesus Christ!"

Still hanging on to the roof's peak, Arthur saw the front yard suddenly become illuminated. His father had turned on the outside light to inspect the premises for his missing son. Tiring of the exercise, August decided that now that he was up, he might as well stay up. He went to the kitchen, made himself a cup of coffee and then went to the living room. He turned on the television set, only to find nothing but test patterns on all the stations, so he sat in his recliner and reread the previous day's newspaper.

Marguerite got up and after checking her son's bedroom, came downstairs. While still adjusting her bathrobe, she walked into the kitchen and opened the door that led to the basement. Finding only darkness, she turned on the basement light and descended into the cellar, calling her son's name. Finding and hearing nothing in reply, Marguerite came back up the steps and entered the living room. There, she found her husband studiously reading the sports pages of Newsday.

67

"Gus, what exactly is going on? Where is Arthur?"

"Damned if I know. He pissed in his bed. I'm guessing he didn't want to face the music."

"Well, I think it's time we saw Doctor Mills about this again. He's going to be twelve in February and it just doesn't seem like he's getting any better."

"What the hell is a doctor going to tell you? 'He'll grow out of it.' Isn't that what they told us what...five, six years ago?"

"Well, I think it's fair to say that your way isn't working either. I'm going outside to look for *our* son. I could use your help."

August grumbled something under his breath, then reluctantly accompanied his wife out the door. Both were still in pajamas, but wearing winter coats. Each was armed with a flashlight. They walked the property calling Arthur's name and then went out onto the street. They had taken Rex with them in hopes he might locate their missing son.

A neighbor across the street, Mr. Guschel, opened up his front door and called out, "Something going on?"

Somewhat sheepishly, Marguerite responded, "Well, we're looking for our son."

"What?"

"He's not in his bedroom and doesn't seem to be in the house."

"He picked a hell of a cold night to go for a walk. Want some help?"

August chimed in. "Don't know how you could. I have no idea where the hell he might be. I'm sure he'll show up when it's breakfast time. He doesn't like to miss meals."

"Well, hope it's nothing serious. I'll keep an eye out for him when the sun comes up."

After thanking their neighbor, Marguerite and August headed back inside.

"Gus, I know I've said it before, but I have to tell you I'm uncomfortable with your checking up on Art the way you do. Look at the situation we're in tonight. I'm sure he doesn't wet his bed on purpose. So I just don't see how punishing him for something he doesn't want to do makes sense."

"Well, if he really didn't want to do what he does he wouldn't do it—that's my opinion. Makes sense to me."

As they entered the house they were greeted by a sleepy-eyed

Ruth who had been awoken by all the activity. "What's going on Ma?"

"Well, it's Arthur. We can't find him. I'm not sure what to do."

"I guarantee you he will show up for breakfast. You know how he likes his Wheaties and brown sugar."

"That's what your father said. I hope you're both right." It was now 5:30 in the morning. August went about getting ready for work. Marguerite made his lunch for him and then cooked some eggs for breakfast. Not able to go back to sleep, Ruth joined her parents at the breakfast table. All meals were uncomfortable at the Berndt household, but this one featured a discomforting twist—the Berndt's son was missing in action.

Marguerite suggested, "Gus, maybe you should stay home from work today."

August responded, "You know I can't afford to miss a work day. Nobody's going to pay the mortgage for us. I get to work about quarter after seven. Call me if he doesn't show up."

August turned to his youngest daughter and gave her a backhanded compliment, "Well Ruth, *you* don't wet your bed. At least we have one normal kid."

The three Berndts finished breakfast. At 6:30, August left for work. He took the family car as it was his turn to be the driver in his carpool. Ruth practiced on the piano, then got dressed for school and, at 7:30, headed out the door for her short walk to the high school.

Employed as a high school cafeteria food preparer, Marguerite had already made up her mind she would not be going to work that day if her son did not reappear. Holding on to a thin thread of optimism, she got herself ready to go to work.

Marguerite had just finished putting on her work uniform when the phone rang.

"Marguerite?"

"Who's this?"

"Louise Sinclair."

"Oh Louise, hello!" There was surprise in Marguerite's voice. Since the drainage ditch incident last summer the Berndts and Sinclairs had not been on speaking terms. August Berndt had claimed Mrs. Sinclair to be crazy for so long that he had the rest of his family convinced she was. In fact, Louise Sinclair had suffered a nervous breakdown a couple of months earlier and had mysteriously been sent "someplace" for several months. She had only been back home for a week, so what she said next was difficult for Marguerite to believe.

"Your son is on your roof."

"What? What did you say?"

"I said 'Your son is on your roof'. I'm sitting at my window and I can see him from here."

"Where? What part of the roof?"

"The part that's right above the big window in your living room. Why is he out there?"

For just a few brief moments, Marguerite acknowledged to herself why her son had done what he had—he was that terrified of his father. Not only couldn't she reveal that fact to Mrs. Sinclair, she refused to continue thinking about it herself.

"Thank you so much Louise for your call. I'm going to check this out right now. Thanks again."

Conversation over, Marguerite went upstairs and into Arthur's bedroom. She opened up the bedroom window and, craning her neck, saw her son still hanging onto the roof.

Marguerite began crying. "Oh, Arthur. Why oh why...?"

"Can I come in now?"

"Of course. Be careful. "

Marguerite was able to grab her son's ankles. "Let go of the roof with your hands. Slide down real slowly. I'll hold on to you while you do."

Arthur relaxed his grip on the roof and began slowly edging his way down the roof on his stomach. Leaning out the window, Marguerite lent support by holding on first to his legs, then his waist, and finally his chest.

She pulled Arthur up onto his feet and he grabbed the window sill. With his mother's assistance, the youngster climbed back into his bedroom.

"I'm sorry Ma. I didn't know what else to do."

"I don't ever want you to put yourself in danger like that again. We're going to have to do something about your bedwetting. Things can't go on like this. *That's* for sure! I'm calling up your father to let him know you're okay."

Talking aloud to herself while in her son's presence, Marguerite said, "Guess I'll have to think up something to say. Maybe not. Maybe it's time to handle things differently. "
Turning to her son she said, "Right now, we have to get you ready

for school. I'll take care of the sheets. You take a bath and brush your teeth. You're going to have to skip breakfast this morning. I'm sorry."

Arthur did as told and, by 8:30, was headed out the door and walking to school. His mother also set out on foot for her job.

Arthur arrived late for school. His mother had given him a note to show his teacher:

Dear Mrs. Snow,

Arthur was late for school today because he was up all night with a stomach ache. I didn't have a car so I couldn't get him to school on time.

Thank you,

Marguerite Berndt

The second part of Marguerite's note was truthful. The Berndt family was one of lies mixed in with the occasional half-truth.

Compared to how he had spent the night, Arthur's day in school was relatively uneventful. But something of significance *did* happen while the young boy was standing on the lunch line at noon.

As children waited their turn to enter the cafeteria, those that had already finished eating walked by, heading back to their respective classes. While Arthur was calculating which dessert he would choose, he detected an unmistakable smell, a smell he recognized all too easily. Someone had just walked by, leaving a waft of urine behind them. Arthur turned around and spotted suspects marching down the hall. Was it Peter? Sal? Larry? Or maybe Becky? He immediately eliminated Becky from his calculations, assuming that a girl simply wouldn't wet her bed at such an advanced age. Besides, he couldn't imagine Becky getting beaten up by her father like he did by his.

He would never be able to determine who was the bed-wetting culprit that had passed by him that day, but in some small way, Arthur found cold comfort in discovering he wasn't the only one who wet his bed. That had been an illusion fostered

71

by his father and his own imagination for years. It was no more than cold comfort because though he now knew he was not the only child who wet his bed, he still remained the only one that had to endure August Berndt's brutal punishment.

Chapter 12

His mother's reaction to Arthur's desperate and daring escape onto the roof ignited a flicker of hope in the youngster. Maybe his terrifying middle-of-the-night meetings with his father would be coming to an end. He dared not get his hopes up too much, and, as it turned out, with good reason. Over the following weeks his father's late-night visits continued and, in the process, extinguished whatever hopes Arthur had had that his bedwetting would cease having such dire consequences. The young boy responded by praying even more fervently before going to bed— not for a new bicycle, a bigger allowance, or a chance to see the Brooklyn Dodgers, but just to wake up in a dry bed the following day.

Despite the rougher side of his life, there was one person who continued to lift Arthur's spirits even from afar—Carolyn Marino.

***

Several weeks had passed by since Arthur had made his unsuccessful attempt to reach his beloved fellow student by phone. Arthur decided to wait for more favorable conditions before making another stab at talking to her. His patience was rewarded. One Saturday in early November, while his father was at work putting in extra hours, his mother took Ruth to a doctor in Riverhead. Arthur didn't know exactly how far away that town lay, but his mother told him she'd be gone a few hours, long enough for his purposes. The young boy watched excitedly from a window as his mom pulled out of the driveway and headed up the street. Just to be sure he was "home free," Arthur ran outside onto the lawn and, craning his neck around an oak tree that hid the rest of him, watched the family car turn onto Old Post Road, heading for the great beyond.

The youngster sprinted back into the house. This time he could get down to the business at hand without having to worry about getting caught in the act. Only his dog was at home and, unlike Arthur's sister, Rex would never snitch on him.

Out came the phone book. Now knowing Carolyn had told her folks about him, and certain she had spoken of him in glowing terms, Arthur confidently dialed, ear to the receiver. Miles away, an adult male answered the young boy's call.

"This is Ralph. Who's calling?"

"My name is Arthur. I'd like—"

"Oh really? And just what would you like?"

Put off by the tone of the man's voice, Arthur struggled for words.

"Well...well, sir, I have to speak to Carolyn about something."

"Yeah, and just what might that 'something' be? Weren't you told to stay away from my daughter?"

In the middle of this unfriendly inquisition, Arthur found something to be grateful for. He was being scolded long-distance over the phone; there was no way Mr. Marino could hit him. That fact gave the young boy the courage to keep pressing his case, and his luck.

"Yes, but..." Arthur had been about to explain his feelings for Carolyn to her father, but he suddenly realized he couldn't even explain them to himself. He was left speechless.

"Listen you... you're to keep away from my daughter, in school and out! You got that?"

"Yes...sir..."

"Do you have any idea how stupid that little trick of yours was? In fact, let me talk to your old man. Or, is your mother there?"

"No, it's just me and Rex. He's my dog." For once, Arthur wasn't lying.

"Well, I'd been thinking about giving your parents a call. I'm telling you right now. You make one more stupid move and I will. Do you understand?"

"Yes sir. But does that mean I can't talk to her on the phone either?"

(Totally exasperated) "Hey kid, how thick are you? *Yes! That means you can't talk to her on the phone!* Now listen, I'm going to hang up. If I hear from my daughter that you are in any way bothering her, I'm going to show up at your house. Sounds like you're not getting enough discipline at home." *Click.*

The young boy put the phone back in its receiver, struggling to absorb this latest setback. No new plan of action came to mind, so he went outside with his dog to play.

***

While in his classroom the following Monday, Arthur briefly gazed over at his beloved sitting two rows to his left. Two rows? More like worlds apart. The youngster's mind drifted away from his surroundings and began rummaging for a new tactic, something he could get past all those meddlesome grownups in his life. His wheels were making so much noise he failed to hear his teacher.

Mrs. Snow yelled louder. "Arthur... *Arthur!*"

Shaken out of his introspection and back into reality, Arthur looked up to see Mrs. Snow staring at him from her desk. "Young man, I shouldn't have to call your name incessantly to get your attention. Where were you? You certainly weren't paying attention."

"Nowhere, Mrs. Snow."

"I'll say! I want you to pick up the reading where Susan left off. Any idea where that might happen to be?"

"Not exactly."

"I'd think not. Page seven, the third paragraph down."

Arthur hurriedly flipped to that page and began reading. To avoid more such encounters with his teacher, he temporarily postponed his scheming.

Later that day, on the way home from school, Arthur resumed his feverish search for a way to talk to Carolyn, the elusive object of his affection. His mental machinations accompanied him all the way to his house and then out into the woods, where he went with Rex. He picked a fallen tree trunk to perch himself on as he continued his search for a stratagem. Then it hit him! He'd write her a letter, not a note in school but a *real* letter, officially mailed by the U. S. Post Office. That way she'd get it for sure. Arthur raced back home and went directly to his bedroom, Rex accompanying him the entire trip. As his dog made himself comfortable on the floor, Arthur took out some note paper and a pencil and began pouring his heart out:

Carolyn,

Hello. I'm Arthur. I used to sit near you in class. I got in trouble so now I can't. I won't put gum in your sandwich ever again. I promise. Will you play Elimination at lunch time with me?

Art

P.S. Do not tell your dad or mom.

A short missive, but oh so sweet!

The following morning, as was his custom, Arthur secretly helped himself to some change from his mother's pocketbook. This time he took a bit extra to pay for an envelope and postage.

Off he went to school. All day long he fought the urge to just hand the letter to Carolyn. If the teacher saw him do that, he would be in big trouble. Even if he wasn't spotted by Mrs. Snow, he wasn't sure how Carolyn would react. She might tell the teacher. For Arthur, the hardest part of this romance was dealing with Carolyn's mixed messages. Love was such a complicated and dangerous minefield.

After school, Arthur had two missions to accomplish. The first was a familiar one—visiting the Crystal Fountain, his favorite emporium for sugary treats. The second was a brand-new one. He'd been to the post office a few times with his mom, but today he was going there alone to conduct personal business. After completing his candy purchases, Arthur took the short walk to the post office, entered, and approached the service counter where Mr. Floyd, a neighbor from Suassa Park, was waiting.

"Why Arthur, what brings you here?"

"I have to mail a letter."

"Really? Where is it going?"

"All the way to Coram."

"Wow. That far, huh? Can I ask what the occasion is?"

"I can't tell you. It's a secret."

"Oh, I see. Sorry for asking. Well, just drop the envelope... Better yet, just give it to me."

"I need to get an envelope."

"Oh, okay. Need a stamp?"

"Yup."

"Tell you what. I'm going to give you one of our special envelopes. The stamp is already on it."

"Neat!"

"Sure is. But I need five cents."

Arthur let his fingers fumble in a pocket full of candy until he found a dime. He was glad he'd fought off the temptation to spend all his money at the Crystal Fountain.

"Here you are, Mr. Floyd."

"Pleasure doing business with you, son."

Arthur wondered why Mr. Floyd had called him "son" when the older man wasn't even his father. Then, it dawned on Arthur—his father never called him son either.

Arthur took the envelope and headed for the counter used by postal customers. When he got there it became obvious the youngster was just a tad too short to accomplish his task. He looked for something to stand on. Spotting a waste basket, he grabbed it and brought it over to the counter. Wobbling as he stood inside it, the young boy still came up short. He had Mr. Floyd chuckling from behind him.

"Get over here, young man. I'll fill it out for you." Arthur walked back to the counter and handed the postal clerk a piece of paper that had Carolyn's full name and address on it.

As he wrote on the envelope, Mr. Floyd sounded out the name of the addressee. "Carolyn Marino. A friend?"

"Yup."

While writing, the postal clerk continued talking. "I already know the return address. I live right around the corner from you. How's your dog doing?"

"You mean Rex? He's the best dog in the world!"

"Well, he sure gave Joe a run for his money a couple of years ago. Glad that got straightened out. Joe almost quit the mail delivery business."

Done filling out the envelope, Mr. Floyd offered further assistance. "Okay, Art. Give me your letter so I can put it in the envelope and make sure it's sealed properly."

Arthur hesitated. "You have to promise you won't look."

"Scout's honor."

Mr. Floyd was a man of his word. He placed the letter in the envelope, sealed and postmarked it, and put it in the basket of mail sitting behind the counter next to him.

Arthur immediately said, "Hey, don't throw it away! I want to *mail* it."

"Oh, I didn't throw it away. It'll go out first thing tomorrow morning."

"But, *I* want to mail it."

"All right, I won't fight with you." Mr. Floyd reached down and pulled the letter out of the basket and handed it to the young boy. Pointing, he said, "You just go over to that slot there where it says "out of town" and drop it in. It'll still go out first thing in the morning."

"Okay, sir." Arthur walked over to the mail slot and dropped it in. He left the post office filled with the certainty that his former and flickering flame would soon be re-kindled. That feeling was quickly dispelled by a flash of fear that shot through the young boy. He had second thoughts. What if this whole scheme backfired? What if his parents found out? Was he doing something wrong? He turned around and went back inside the post office.

"Mr. Floyd, can I have my letter back?"

"Uh, why would you want to get it back?"

"I don't know."

"I don't either. You know, once it's postmarked, it's the property of the U.S. Postal Service. It's our duty to deliver it. Besides, you wrote a nice letter, right?"

"Yup."

"You want her to get it, right?"

"Yup."

"So, don't worry."

"Okay."

Once again, Arthur exited the post office. Mr. Floyd had convinced him he was doing the right thing. It didn't take much to convince the love-smitten youngster.

Arthur had decided he'd do whatever it took to win back the love of his life. For the first time in his life, he let his judgement be blinded by infatuation. It wouldn't be the last time.

He did his best to convince himself he had nothing to worry about. Even if he did, which was worse, having to face his dad or

78

losing Carolyn forever? He decided he'd do whatever he had to keep her in his life, even if that meant risking the wrath of *two* fathers—Carolyn's and his own.

Arthur headed home, soothing his anxiety with some M&Ms.

The following day was a Friday. Mistaken in his belief that the letter had already been delivered, Arthur sat at his desk, waiting with great anticipation for some kind of sign from Carolyn as soon as she entered the classroom. Not only would there be no sign, there would be no Carolyn. She was absent that day. Arthur would have to struggle with his emotions until the following Monday.

Over the weekend, he busied himself by mentally painting the ideal scenario. He convinced himself Carolyn would read the letter and resume playing Elimination at lunch time. That didn't seem like much to ask for, but it would mean *oh so much* to Arthur.

***

Monday morning arrived and, when Arthur walked into the classroom, Carolyn was already at her desk. To his surprise, she was looking directly at him. He assumed the letter had arrived and their relationship was back on track. She looked away as he purposely walked by her on the way to his desk. Oh, those mixed signals!

After wolfing down lunch, Arthur headed out to the playground for recess as sides were being chosen for Elimination. Arthur spotted Carolyn heading his way. It worked! The letter worked! He decided he'd be nice and not hit her with the ball until late in the game.

Arthur was mistaken. Carolyn wouldn't be playing Elimination. She had walked over to her one-time heartthrob with a more sinister purpose.

"My father is really mad at you."

"Why? What did I do?"

"He said he told you to leave me alone and you didn't."

Arthur was suddenly embarrassed he had written the letter, yet anxious to know what Carolyn thought of it. "Well, anyway, did you read my letter?"

"No. My dad ripped it up. Then, he decided to pick up all the pieces and put them back in the envelope and hide it somewhere. He said he's calling your parents."

Carolyn went over to her friends at the swings. A downcast Arthur sat on the sidelines during the Elimination matches.

Recess over, all the students headed back into the school. While walking toward their classroom, Carolyn turned to Arthur and said, "I *really* have to stay away from you now."

Arthur's world collapsed. To stay connected with Carolyn, he had risked his father's ire. Now, not only was his relationship with Carolyn over, but the young boy's mind was quickly filling up with that all too familiar dread that so often swamped him prior to getting punished by his father. He began the search for something to get optimistic about. Maybe Carolyn's father wouldn't call. Maybe he would, but no one would be home. Maybe only Arthur would be at home to answer. In that case, maybe he'd be able to convince Mr. Marino to drop the whole matter. Maybe Mr. Marino would talk to Arthur's mom and she'd keep the conversation to herself. If his father did find out, maybe he wouldn't get too mad. If he did, instead of the belt, or getting kicked, or being punched, maybe the punishment would go no further than a spanking. Arthur's uncertain world was filled with "maybes".

For the rest of the school day, Arthur was a distracted student, preoccupied with his latest relationship setback and, even more so, the trouble he was in. Arthur sat in class trying to figure out the gravity of his crime and the punishment he was in for. In a childlike way, the youngster rated his current misdeed on an imaginary scale of his own creation that assigned different antisocial acts their degree of severity. He had done wrong, but optimistically concluded his infraction didn't rise to the level of what adults called a felony.

By the time school ended, Arthur changed his plans. He'd been looking forward to stopping by the Crystal Fountain, but his current predicament turned his usually mammoth sweet tooth sour.

Arthur dawdled on the way home from school that day. He just couldn't work up much enthusiasm for showing up to his own execution in a timely fashion. He considered heading into the woods to temporarily escape from his life, but instead bravely marched onward to face his fate.

Upon entering the house, Rex greeted him with typical canine exuberance. The thought crossed Arthur's mind that his dog's life was far less troublesome than his own.

Normally, Arthur would go to the kitchen and make himself a peanut butter and honey sandwich. Instead, after going to the bathroom, he decided to head for the woods after all. Just as he was getting ready to leave the house with Rex, the phone rang. Though fearful of answering it, he figured if Mr. Marino was calling, this would be his chance to intercept the older man's anger before it got into the wrong hands. Arthur picked up the receiver and answered with a tentative "Hello!"

His heart sank when Ralph Marino's deep, threatening male voice replied, "Well, I don't want to speak with you. Is your mother or father home?"

"No."

"You're not lying, are you? If I have to, I'll drive to your damn house." That would be the worst that could happen in the young boy's life. He pictured himself taking a beating from not one, but two, adult males.

"No. Nobody's here right now. But my mom will be home soon."

"How soon? I want to get this over with."

Craning his neck to look at the clock in the kitchen, Arthur responded, "She'll be here in about ten minutes, sir."

"She better be. I'm going to call back at four o'clock sharp. If she's not there, I'm going to come to your house and wait until your parents get home. Got that?"

"Yes, sir."

"So, if she's there right now, you might as well get it over with."

"She's not. I promise."

"Okay." Mr. Marino abruptly hung up.

Arthur put the phone back in the receiver. Never before had he prayed so badly that his mother would get home before his father did. If *she* got the phone call from Mr. Marino. Arthur clung to a flimsy thread of hope that he'd be able to convince—if necessary, beg—his mother not to report this matter to his father. If August Berndt was to get that call, the young boy knew he would be in for it.

What if Arthur simply denied everything? That rarely, if ever, worked, especially when it was an adult's word against his. A kid simply had no clout in a system run by "big people". His only hope was to catch a reprieve from his mom.

Rex's scratching protestations on the inside of the front door were a sign he wanted to go outside to take a walk with his young master. Arthur let his dog out alone. Occasionally, he looked at the phone, seeing only an instrument of doom—his. The youngster's mind wandered. If no phones existed, Mr. Marino couldn't have called. But then he'd have driven to the Berndt home. Cars became the enemy. If there were no automobiles, Mr. Marino couldn't drive to Arthur's house. But, then Mr. Marino could have written a letter. The young boy realized there were just too many ways to get in trouble. Arthur traded in his always shaky childlike optimism and wrapped himself in a black cloak of fatality.

His morose thinking was interrupted by the sound of a car pulling into the driveway. His mother was home. Rex was the initial welcoming committee, dancing around Marguerite as she made her way up to the house. She found Arthur sitting in the dining room, an unusual spot for him at this time of the day.

"Art, why aren't you outside with the dog? Not feeling well?"

He wasn't, but it had nothing to do with his physical health. Arthur decided to prep his mom for the impending phone call.

"Mom, I have to sort of tell you something."

"'Sort of?' Should I be concerned?"

"What does 'concerned' mean?"

"Worried."

"No. I didn't do anything wrong. It's just that..."

"Yes....?"

"Well, there's this girl in my class. All I wanted to do was to be friends with her and her father yelled at me for that. It's not fair."

"A girl? What's her name?"

"Carolyn. Carolyn Marino."

"Does she live around here?"

"No. That's the problem. She lives way far away. Some town called Coram. Anyway, I wrote her a letter and her dad saw it and called and said he was going to call you."

"Well, this sounds like something that—"

The phone rang. As Marguerite picked up the receiver, Arthur's heart began pounding, not out of love for Carolyn, but out of fear of his father.

"Hello. This is Marguerite."

"Hello, Mrs. Berndt?"

"Yes?"

"Hello, my name is Ralph Marino. I'm Carolyn's father. Your son and my daughter are in the same class, though I wish to hell they weren't. I want your boy to stay away from my daughter and stop calling my house."

"Why, what's been going on? What's Arthur been doing?"

"You're not aware of what he's done?"

"Well, he told me something about writing your daughter a letter. I hope it wasn't inappropriate."

"It was, because he did it after I told him to stay away from Carolyn."

Marguerite pulled a nearby chair over by the phone and sat down. "Was he bothering her? I hope not. That's not the way we raised him."

"Just how *have* you raised—" Mr. Marino stopped himself and collected his thoughts. "I'm sorry. You know... that Italian temper of mine."

"I understand. My husband has a German one. But, what is it that has you so upset? And when did you speak with my son? I wasn't aware of that."

"No doubt he didn't tell you. Listen, you sound like a nice lady so I'm going to make this as short and sweet as possible. My daughter said they were friends and then they weren't. So, then he put some kind of damn hot crap—I mean, gum or candy—in my daughter's sandwich. Right in the classroom, mind you. Your son's got some nerve. Geez, I did a few things when I was a teenager but he's only what—ten, eleven?"

"He's ten. He'll be eleven in February."

"So, he's ten. You know what I'm saying. The school told him to leave her alone. I called your place and told him the same thing. I told him to tell you I called."

"Oh, he didn't."

"Not surprised. I told him if he pulled anymore stunts I'd call back. So, he goes and sends her a letter after I told him to stay away from my daughter. Did he get you to find our address?"

"No, he didn't. Mr. Marino, this is the first I'm hearing about any of this, the letter, the hot—what was it again?"

"Some kind of trick gum or candy that burns the mouth. I don't know where or how he got it and I'm sure he's not supposed to be bringing that kind of nonsense to school. With all due respect, you folks have got to keep your son on a tighter leash."

"We do the best we can, I assure you."

"Well, I don't really care what he does, as long as he stays away from my daughter. I mean, if he doesn't, I don't know what I'll do next, but I'll do something—get the school after him, get the cops after him... it'd be kind of ridiculous, getting the cops after a sixth grader. You just make sure he stays away from Carolyn and that'll be that."

"I appreciate your concern. We'll have a very serious talk with Arthur. I'm glad you called."

"Sorry I had to make the call. Good day." An uncomfortable conversation came to an abrupt ending.

Marguerite let the phone fall into the receiver. She turned to her son.

"Well, that's quite a story Mr. Marino told me. Anything to say for yourself?"

Arthur knew he'd never be able to lie his way out of this situation. Carolyn's father had exhibit A—Arthur's letter—as proof of his crime. He felt completely exposed and at the mercy of whatever his mother might decide to do next. He scrutinized her face for any signs—positive or negative. He braced himself for whatever she was about to say, clinging to the faint hope he might escape his father's rough hands.

"Arthur, I think it was very commendable you were trying to make a friend in school. Someone better than the troublemakers you've gotten mixed up with around here. Why would you ruin her sandwich? Why would she want to be friends with someone that did something like that?"

"I don't know."

"I don't know, either. And I don't know why the school never called us about this. I think they should have. Now you can't talk to her even though you're in the same classroom. That's a shame."

"It's not fair. I didn't do anything."

"Do you really feel that way?"

Though he did, the young boy sensed it would be better to act remorseful. "I guess I made a mistake. But, I still don't see why I—"

Arthur stopped himself. He detected a hint of empathy coming from his mother. Why risk throwing cold water on it with his half-hearted apology? He let her talk to see if his optimism was built on a solid foundation.

"Arthur, you know if I don't tell your father about this, in a sense I'm not being truthful."

"Mom, I didn't do anything real bad. At least there weren't any policemen this time, right?"

Her son's rationalization left Marguerite briefly at a loss for words. Rather than try to explain how the presence or absence of police was not the only measure of a child's conduct, she said, "Why don't you go outside and play with Rex?"

Arthur looked at his mother and asked, "Mom, are you gonna tell dad?" Afraid of the answer he'd get, he exited the house with his dog before his mother could respond.

Then began a battle Marguerite fought with herself far too often. Should she withhold information from her husband to protect her son? There was always the chance August would find out and that might spell trouble not only for her son, but herself. This day her maternal instinct trumped her fear of being discovered. Another secret kept by a member of the Berndt family.

Chapter 13

Arthur's attempts to get back into Carolyn's good graces had failed, but his mother hadn't failed him. Thanks to her, his ill-fated affair with a classmate came and went undetected by his father.

Just as Arthur's relationship with Carolyn ended, a special time of the year was beginning. It was now late November, 1955. Thanksgiving week unofficially initiated the holiday season which extended through December, Christmas and New Year's. There always seemed to be a little bit more magic in the air during that time of the year.

Some of that magic even found its way into the Berndt household annually. Every year, for a little over a month, it was as if the Berndt family came to its senses. This temporary ceasefire unofficially began during the last two weeks of November and ended without ceremony January 2 of the following year. Within that time frame there was a lessening of tensions as the holiday spirit flexed its muscles and took over life at Twenty-one Lowell Place. Even August Berndt got caught up in the spirit of the holiday season, allowing himself a time out from his customary tortured thinking and violent behavior. The days right before and after Christmas especially provided smooth sailing on calm waters for all the Berndts. The reprieve from the fear, coldness and criticism that typically permeated the Berndt residence never lasted past New Year's Day. Those precious weeks of relative peace would never be the standard fare of life for the Berndts. The entire family tacitly understood that fact and savored the calm while it lasted.

Thanksgiving dinner was the first big event kicking off this special time of the year. Marguerite roasted a turkey with all the trimmings including her classic stuffing. Dessert consisted of homemade pumpkin and cranberry-apple pies. Liz, who stayed away from home as much as possible ever since she had gone away to college, now lived and worked in the town of Hempstead. She, too, got into the spirit of things and suspended her voluntary and unofficial exile from the house she grew up in. Thus, on Thanksgiving Day the family was reunited physically, if not emotionally. Although during the rest of the year altercations often broke out at the dinner table, Thanksgiving dinner was usually tranquil and this year's proved no exception.

***

Until this year Arthur had always taken for granted the gifts he received at Christmas time. Despite threats that gifts would be withheld due to his misbehavior, he was never disappointed with the presents he received on Christmas Day. At eleven years of age, Arthur had become old enough to fully appreciate how generous his family—and particularly his sister Liz—were at Christmas time. In prior years, his mother had given him a few dollars that he used to buy a single inexpensive gift for each family member. Earlier in the fall, he'd decided he wanted to match everyone else's generosity—and perhaps even surpass it. In a misguided attempt to improve his image at home and thus feel better about himself, the young boy planned to earn his family's approval by way of prolific gift-giving.

The problem was, apart from his weekly allowance of thirty cents, the only income he'd have before Christmas was the couple of dollars his mother typically provided him. Whatever money he'd earned doing chores for neighbors and turning in deposit bottles had already been spent on candy and comic books for himself. With that in mind, he started another income stream in mid-October—one that flowed on an intermittent basis from Ruth's piggy bank into the young boy's hands. Every once in a while, when he was home alone, he would enter his sister's room and extract coins from her not-so-strongbox, which was a pig-shaped piece of ceramic. Arthur secreted his ill-gotten goods in a drawer in his bedroom underneath T-shirts and shorts. He'd practiced the art of thievery in such a subtle manner that Ruth had not noticed the loss of her funds.

The Saturday after Thanksgiving was spent by the Berndts as it usually was every year. Marguerite and her two daughters drove to Patchogue and Babylon to begin Christmas shopping, August worked overtime as a maintenance man at the RCA plant to help defray the upcoming holiday expenses and Arthur was left to his own devices.

With everyone out of the house, Arthur entered his sister's bedroom and went straight for the piggy bank. Thanks to her own weekly allowance and the money she made babysitting, Ruth's piggy bank was flush with coinage despite the withdrawals that Arthur had been making for more than a month.

The youngster grabbed the piggy bank, turned it upside down and began shaking it. As he did, a coin or two occasionally dropped out. Arthur knew the value of money so he was always more excited to extract a quarter than he was a nickel or dime. Pennies were reinserted for two reasons: they weren't worth much in stores, but they did add weight to the piggy bank, camouflaging the fact that Ruth's savings were being systematically decimated. He continued shaking the piggy bank until he had "withdrawn" three dollars and twenty-five cents. He put the piggy bank back in place and took the money to his bedroom, immediately hiding it with the rest of his substantial pilferage.

Savoring a jaded sense of accomplishment, he went downstairs and turned on the television set. Rex hopped up on the sofa next to him and they both watched *Popeye* cartoons. Normally, Popeye and Brutus would have kept the young boy's attention but he couldn't keep his mind off his sister's piggy bank. He knew there was a small fortune in it ripe for the taking and convinced himself he hadn't taken enough. Back upstairs he went and, after jiggling the piggy bank for several minutes, scooped up the loose coins and stuffed them into his pocket. Then, he sat on his sister's bed and stared at the piggy bank for several minutes. Though Arthur entertained the thought of taking even more money, he decided not to push his luck any further. He resisted temptation and walked out of his sister's room. After adding another two dollars and seventy-five cents to his hidden stash of coins, the youngster went back downstairs. Rex, still on the sofa, was waiting for him and they watched the rest of the *Popeye Show* and then all of *The Little Rascals*.

Later that day, both Ruth and Arthur received their allowance. Ruth went upstairs and deposited hers into her piggy bank. She came back downstairs and announced to anyone who would listen, "I've really saved up a lot of money. And the Drakes want me to babysit every Saturday. I bet I'll have money left over after Christmas." Her mother praised Ruth's industriousness and thrift. Arthur silently praised *himself* for having gotten away with this day's heist and rejoiced in learning that his sister would be bringing home more money with which he could continue to fill his coffers.

Chapter 14

A few days later, Arthur was looking through several of the mail-order magazines that were sent to his mother on a regular basis: Miles Kimball, Breck's of Boston, Sears, and B. Altman. Until this year, he had never had any interest in these magazines, but now he was scanning them in search of gifts to give to his family members. Never before had he given much thought to the gifts he bought at Christmas time since his tight budget made his choices for him. Now that he had ramped up his purchasing power at his sister's expense, he could pick and choose his purchases from among more expensive gifts. He went out to the kitchen, magazine in hand and opened up to a page, and pointed to a mixer. He asked his mom, "Would you like that for Christmas?" Marguerite laughed. "Well, that's a very nice gesture, but the mixer I have works fine. And look at the price—$14.95. Actually, that's not a bad price for a G.E., but that's way too much for you to spend on me. Maybe next weekend we'll go to Woolworth's and you can pick out some gifts there."

"Nah."

"No? Why not?"

"I dunno."

"I'm sure you'll change your mind by Saturday."

Arthur's non-answer was the best he could come up with. He couldn't tell his mother that Woolworths no longer measured up to his standards. He decided he'd go about his shopping privately. He might not be able to purchase the most expensive merchandise in the catalogs but he was sure he would discover items that were better than anything he would find at a five-and-dime store. Operating alone and without consulting anyone's Christmas wish list, *he* would decide what to get each family member based on what the magazines offered. After all, the best presents are surprises.

Later that same week, Arthur was at home alone following school. Before he did anything else, the young boy took some more money out of his sister's piggy bank. This time the haul was a hefty $3.93. Make that $3.90 after he re-inserted three straggling pennies he deemed not worthy of his consideration. Then, on Saturday, Arthur again found himself the only one at home for a few hours and it cost Ruth $2.60. Arthur was now stealing from his sister with the same reckless abandon he had stolen from his mother some years earlier. Unlike then, he wasn't stealing to satisfy his sweet tooth. He had a much more noble purpose—gift giving. The thought occurred to Arthur that he felt less guilty stealing from his sister than from his mother. After all, his mother was—well, his mother. Ruth was just a pesty, over-achieving sister that made him look bad at home and in school. Arthur contemplated the possibility of continuing to dip into his new-found cash cow—in the form of a pig—long after the holidays were over.

***

By the middle of December Arthur had amassed over twenty-seven dollars, most of it garnered from the bedroom down the hall from his. By now, he had already sent away for and was awaiting the arrival of treasures from such faraway places as Boston and Kalamazoo. He had ordered an oval sponge rug and Zippo clothes pin bag for his mother, a customized shaving cream brush for his father, and for Ruth (primarily with her money) 45 RPM records of some of her favorite tunes such as "Mockingbird Hill" and "Rock Around the Clock". He'd gotten his sister Liz, a chain smoker, a carton of Chesterfield cigarettes from the local grocery store.

Saturday, December 17th. Only nine days before Christmas. Arthur sat on his bed and pondered. Though his closet was stuffed with gifts for his family members, the young boy felt the need to purchase even more presents. Shopping via mail, he'd have to send his order immediately for it to arrive in time for Christmas. He had to make one last piggy bank withdrawal and had to do it right now! The trouble was Marguerite and Ruth were also home.

In the privacy of his bedroom, Arthur filled out an order form he'd detached from the Miles Kimball catalog, slipped it in an envelope and addressed it. He knew the post office closed early on Saturdays. He checked his own supply of money and found he was almost four dollars short of the amount needed to send a money order that would cover his final purchase for this Christmas season. Arthur went to his door and conducted vital reconnaissance. Ruth was downstairs playing the piano. Marguerite was sewing in the bedroom across the hall from where Arthur was standing, but she had the door closed. Desperate times call for desperate measures. He brazenly walked into his sister's bedroom and began shaking money from the piggy bank. He told himself this would be the last visit to the bank before Christmas so he wanted to make it a worthwhile effort. He shook out $6.75 worth of coins, including two fifty-cent pieces. He shoved the money in his pocket, put the bank back into place on the dresser and hustled back to his bedroom. Now, he could conduct business at the post office and even have some money left over.

After getting permission from his mother to go bike riding, he did just that—conveniently not revealing his destination. He rode his bike down to Main Street in Port Jefferson and entered the post office. Mr. Floyd was at the desk. "Well Art, let me guess. You want a money order. "

"Yup. How did you know?"

"You've been in here several times looking for money orders. You're a wealthy kid."

"Wealthy?"

"Yeah, you know. You have lots of money."

"Yup. I do."

"So how much is the money order for this time?"

"$4.98."

"Gotcha!"

After concluding business, Arthur left the post office and headed back home. The youngster was relieved that his Christmas shopping was done and even more relieved that the pressure to steal money was no longer so overbearing.

He walked into his house, and before one word was spoken by anyone, Arthur sensed he had entered a hostile environment, one more unfriendly than the customary unfriendliness that festered inside Twenty-one Lowell Place. Arthur had long ago developed a sixth sense for sniffing out danger and at this moment the house reeked of it.

"Ask him, Mom! Make him tell the truth for once!" Ruth was in the living room with her mother, demanding justice.

"Arthur, your sister says you've been taking her money. Is that true?"

Lying being his customary first line of defense, Arthur replied with an emphatic "No!"

"He's lying. I emptied out my whole piggy bank. I had three fifty cent pieces and now there's only one."

Arthur was quick to reply. "Well, maybe you thought they were fifty cent pieces and they were only quarters."

Ruth remained unconvinced by her brother's explanation. "There's a lot of money missing. I know it."

"Prove it! Ma, she's lying and trying to get me in trouble. That's what she always does."

"Arthur. I noticed you've had some packages coming to you in the mail over the last few weeks. What did you buy and where did you get the money to buy whatever it is?"

"Mom, I can't tell you what I got because it's a surprise. It's for everybody at Christmas. It's my own money. My allowance and stuff I saved up. Remember those times I raked leaves for the Harmons and the Marshalls? And I collected all those bottles. I got all those bottles and got the deposit money for them?"

"Yes, Art I remember. Are you telling me that you've saved that money all this time? You don't usually hold on to money for very long."

"I know Mom, but this time I did. This Christmas is different. You'll see."

Marguerite was not completely convinced her son was telling the truth. However, she didn't want to get her husband involved so she played the role of peacemaker. "Okay, Ruth I'm going to give you three dollars. Tomorrow, I'm going to the store and I'm going to get you some kind of piggy bank with a lock on it. "

Turning to Arthur, she said, "Arthur, since you seem to have so much money I'm not going to give you any Christmas shopping money this year. Wherever you're getting the money from, I have a feeling you've spent way too much already. And I'd better not catch you in your sister's room, do you understand? "

Though Arthur was disappointed he'd be losing out on the

money he traditionally got from his mother for Christmas shopping, he knew he had gotten way more than that from his sister. Fuming, Ruth marched upstairs to her room shouting, "It's unfair! He's a thief! He always gets away with things!"

For his part, Arthur remained silent. He was the only one who knew exactly what he'd gotten away with and that suited him fine. The only downside to his months-long crime spree? A piggy bank with a lock dashed all hopes he'd had of continuing in perpetuity unmonitored withdrawals from his sister's small fortune.

The remaining days prior to Christmas proved far less uneventful. On the 22nd of December, Arthur received a package from Miles Kimball. He had added a pressure cooker to the gifts he was giving his mother. He also bought his father a bottle of cologne. In an attempt to assuage his sister Ruth, who had mentally convicted him of robbery and rejected all appeals, he bought her a stuffed dog. He also purchased personalized stationery for his sister Liz. In a final grand gesture, he purchased for the entire family two large boxes of Whitman's Samplers from Grammas's Sweets in downtown Port Jefferson.

Chapter 15

The day before Christmas, Marguerite was busy preparing homemade German-style cookies and fruitcake. Liz had come home the Friday before Christmas and had the following week off from her job as a schoolteacher. Christmas was on a Sunday and August Berndt had foregone working overtime on Christmas Eve in order to stay home all day Christmas Eve.

Normally, the Berndt children would have been disappointed that their father took off any day. When he was out of the house, they felt graced by his absence. But this was the day before Christmas and they were dealing with a different kind of August Berndt. True to form, he was doing his share of drinking, but the Christmas spirit was suppressing his tendency to get ugly when under the influence. At one point during the day, he began taking turns with his two daughters playing on the piano. He also sang several Christmas carols in his once tenor and now baritone voice—a voice that he long ago had hoped would carry him to the heights of operatic fame.

While the other members of the family had already wrapped their presents and placed them under the Christmas tree, Arthur had waited until the last minute to wrap the ones he was giving. Upstairs and behind a closed bedroom door, he had gift wrap, tags, scissors, and scotch tape all spread out on his bed. He began methodically taking one present at a time out of his closet and wrapping it before removing another from the closet and giving it the same treatment.

Not only was this Christmas a first in regards to the amount of gifts Arthur purchased (and how he got the money to buy them), it was the first year in his life that he took it upon himself to do his own gift wrapping. When he finished with the final gift, his bed and floor were covered with uniquely covered packages. The youngster eschewed style in favor of function. Though his gifts were not attractively wrapped, each one was completely covered, many with an overabundance of wrapping paper.

When younger, Arthur was unsure as to the existence of Santa Claus, but this year clinched it. In the past, when his mother had gone shopping around Christmas time he'd assumed that meant she was going to visit Santa. He himself had seen Santa Claus at the Macy's in Babylon when he was six years old. In his elementary school, there was a tradition. The day before school closed for the holidays, Santa Claus visited each classroom to deliver a box of candy to each student. The last couple of years Arthur couldn't help but notice that "Santa Claus" bore a striking resemblance to the school custodian.

This year, the fact that he himself was buying gifts convinced him once and for all that Santa Claus was simply a trick—albeit a pleasant one—played on kids by their parents. Despite all this, Arthur still had enough childlike spirit in him to sign each of the gift tags on the packages he had wrapped with the name "Santa".

Having to make several trips from his bedroom to the living room, Arthur placed all the presents under the Christmas tree. Meanwhile, his two sisters and his father continued entertaining themselves around the piano.

Watching her brother carry the final batch of gifts to their destination, Liz remarked, "Wow! You must've visited Santa Claus a lot this year!"

Arthur replied proudly, "No. Santa didn't get these—I did."

Ruth said, "Yeah, with my money!"

"Did not!"

"Did so!"

August Berndt, sitting at the piano, stopped playing and, resting his fingers on the keys, asked, "What's all this bickering about? Doesn't sound very much like Christmas to me."

"Well, it's not very nice to buy Christmas presents with somebody else's money," said Ruth.

"What's your brother been up to?"

"Ask him, Dad. He knows."

Thanks to the fact that August was having his drinks with Christmas spirit as a chaser, his mood was more pleasant than it would typically be with alcohol alone. Though Arthur had drifted into his father's crosshairs, August's sight was blurry. In fact, the head of the household had reached a state of inebriation that the rest of the family wished he'd reach more often—slaphappy.

"Well, son..."

Arthur wasn't sure if he'd ever heard his father call him "son" before this day.

"Let me rephrase that. What is Ruth talking about?"

Since his father was in a relatively good mood and not threateningly suspicious—at least not yet—Arthur decided to be a bit less brazen in his self-defense. Instead of accusing his sister of lying, the young boy implied she was mistaken. "I don't know. I think she didn't keep track of her money. She thought she had more than she did."

Arthur couldn't completely maintain a diplomatic stance. "Maybe when she found out she didn't have as much as she thought she did, she ran to Mommy." The words "ran to Mommy" were uttered in such a disparaging way they left little doubt what Arthur was really saying: *My sister is a snitch*!

Ruth seethed. "You are such a liar. You know you took my money."

"Dad, I already proved to mom that I got the money all by myself. Mom agreed."

Ruth begged to differ. "That's not true. You didn't prove anything. You're a thief and a liar."

In an odd turn of events, it was August Berndt who worked to defuse the situation. "All right, all right. It's goddamn Christmas Eve. Let's have some peace and quiet. New Year's is coming up. Turning to his son he said, "You ever hear of New Year's resolutions?"

"No, Dad."

"Well, those are what people make at the beginning of the year, promises they make for the upcoming year. Maybe you can make a New Year's resolution to stop stealing and lying." August laughed at what he thought was a joke.

Ruth was unconvinced. "He's never going to change."

Liz was getting tired of the entire conversation. "Hey Dad. Are you ready for another drink?"

He was and so was she. Liz had developed a drinking habit in her teens that had continued ever since. This day, she had gotten a late start imbibing but she was doing her best to catch up to her father. Though August Berndt's drink of choice was normally beer, every once in a while he'd drink scotch and soda. That's what he'd been drinking today and Liz made two of them. Insincerely, she clunked glasses with her father and said "Cheers!" and then followed that up with, "Or as they say in the old country, Gesundheit!" She then turned on the television. At the same time, Marguerite came out of the kitchen to take a break and everyone sat down to watch a Christmas-themed variety show. Everyone except Ruth, who went up to her room, still seeking justice. She remained convinced her brother had gotten away with robbery in broad daylight.

The following morning—Christmas morning—began in a spectacular way for Arthur. He woke up dry. That was never a guarantee that the rest of any day would go smoothly for the young boy, but it was at least a step in the right direction. And this was Christmas after all, a day the Berndt's were as peaceful a family as they could ever be.

At 6:30 A.M. Arthur rushed downstairs. The only living creature there to greet him was Rex. The two of them sat on the couch—Arthur staring at all the gifts impatiently and Rex just glad to be next to his pal. In short order, the rest of the Berndt's came downstairs. In a rare show of unanimity, all the Berndts agreed to open the presents first before having breakfast. That suited Arthur fine as he was bursting at the seams to see what he was going to get. For the first time in his life, he was also eager to see how everyone else would react to the gifts he had gotten them.

Liz became the designated gift hander-outer. Though Arthur wasn't aware of it, the gifts he had purchased via catalogs were not of the highest quality. His family did its best to camouflage that fact. After unwrapping it, Marguerite looked at the sponge rug quizzically as if to say *"What in the world do I do with this?"* But she tactfully remarked, "This is perfect for me to use in the basement by the sink." When August took a whiff of the cologne his son had gotten him, he stifled his repulsion and said "That's a new one on me." Liz opened a package and found a collection of cheaply made pens she less than wholeheartedly exclaimed, "Great! I can definitely use these. I'll use them when the pen I have stops working."

Ruth, however, did nothing to hide her continued resentment towards her brother. She half-heartedly opened the gifts he gave her and immediately put them to the side. She did note that the stuffed dog didn't have matching ears.

As for Arthur, he got new shirts and pants, two new model airplanes to assemble, and a View-Master, complete with several reels featuring national parks, famous actors and actresses and professional baseball players. His favorite gift of all was a football. It featured the autograph of Johnny Lujack. Arthur had no idea who Mr. Lujack was but assumed having his signature on the ball made it even more valuable.

After all the presents had been unwrapped, the family enjoyed a relatively amicable breakfast together. Following that, each family member went about his or her business. Liz took a long bike ride, Ruth went over to the Regalmutos, her other "family," Marguerite began preparing Christmas dinner, and August listened to classical music on the radio. After watching a bit of television, Arthur began to assemble a B-52 jet bomber, one of the models he received for Christmas. An casual observer might have confused the Berndt family with the Andersons of TV's *Father Knows Best*.

Later in the day, August surprised his son. "Why don't we go down to the high school field and kick your football around a little bit? "

Arthur was surprised by his father's suggestion. He said "Okay!" for two reasons. For one thing, he didn't dare decline the offer and, for another, he jumped at the rare opportunity to improve his shaky relationship with his father.

After putting on their jackets, the two headed out of the house and took the short walk to the high school's sports field. Arthur kicked the football as one would expect an eleven-year-old to. August let go some boomers. Many years earlier, August had been an excellent scholastic soccer player and some of that athletic expertise had survived many years later. Father and son alternated between kicking and throwing the football to each other. While savoring this opportunity to interact with his father, Arthur was afraid things would turn negative. To his surprise, his father didn't criticize any of his less than stellar kicks or passes. This experience reminded Arthur of the occasional pleasant experience his father and he two had watching baseball on television. However, the quality of their interaction while watching baseball was in great measure dependent on how the Dodgers were doing. The quality of interaction they had kicking a football to each other depended solely on them—and they were doing fine. Several hours went by. The only thing that brought their activity to an end was the fact it was beginning to get dark. As they walked off the field and onto Brook Road, Arthur said, "Thanks, Dad. That was fun."

"Well, I didn't know I could still kick like that. Your father was a damn good soccer player—once."

"What happened?"

"The war. That's what happened."

"Oh... Why were they fighting?"

"That's a long story. Germany and England were at each other's throats for a long time before the war broke out. Archduke Ferdinand got shot and that got the war started. If he hadn't been shot, I'm sure something else would've happened to get the war going."

"What's an Archduke? Is that like Duke Snider?"

August laughed. "Not at all. For Snider, it's just a nickname. For a real Archduke it's a title. He must have belonged to some royal family, you know, like a king and a queen?"

"I guess I get it."

"When you get older, you'll study history. I've studied history, but the more facts I have, I don't know... Can you really trust what you read to be the truth?"

"Do I learn the truth in school, Dad?"

"At your age, probably yeah. Arithmetic, English, what else do they teach you?" "

"Well, spelling, penmanship, health and stuff."

"Not much to fool around with in those subjects. When you get older, it gets more complicated."

August cried out. "Ow! Goddammit!" Arthur wondered if he had said something to touch off his father. Then he noticed how badly his father was limping. As long as he could remember, his father had always had a bad knee.

"Is it your knee dad?"

"Yeah. Kicking that damn football around didn't do it any good."

"How did it happen? You know, your knee. How did it get hurt?"

August started to respond, then stopped himself. He looked off in the distance and then turned and, with anger in his eyes, admonished his son. "Don't ask me that again. That's none of your business. That's none of anybody's business. You got that?"

Just like that the subject was dropped and the two continued their walk home, Arthur slowing his pace so that his limping father could keep up.

Shortly after the two arrived home, dinner was served. Roasted ham, scalloped potatoes and string beans. Everyone was in attendance. Even Ruth had returned from her sanctuary, the Regalmuto residence. No one wanted to miss out on Marguerite's baked ham. For dessert everyone feasted on German butter cookies and fruit cake.

On Christmas Day, the Berndt family held it together as they had every Christmas before. There were no fights and no one was hit. This year no one even got drunk. August and Liz held off until December 26th.

One week later, a new year began. The end of the holiday season also marked the end of the seasonal cease fire at Twenty-one Lowell Place.

Chapter 16

The New Year started off predictably. Recognizing the holiday season had ended, Arthur resumed his strategy of keeping a safe distance from his father. Usually, he did that by staying out of the house. Since he hadn't had any steady friends in the neighborhood for several years and there were none on the horizon, he spent the time outdoors either bike riding or wandering in the woods near the railroad tracks. Often, his soulmate Rex would accompany him. When in the house, he gravitated to his room, where he read or constructed plastic model planes and boats. Other times, he'd play on a less-than-official-sized pool table in the basement.

Arthur's bedwetting continued. He soiled his sheets several times each week. His father still checked on him every night. If he found his son had wet the bed, the follow-up procedure remained the same as it had always been.

Although Arthur would soon be twelve years old, he still rocked and hummed himself to sleep. Experts believe such activity is often the result of an obsessive-compulsive disorder and a need for self-soothing. Whatever the reason, Arthur had tried to stop himself from rocking but found the effort too discomforting. The young boy wouldn't give up his rocking and humming anytime soon.

Marguerite contacted Louise Howell and found out that Arthur was too old to join the Cub Scouts. She'd suggested the Boy Scouts to Arthur, but her son was unenthusiastic about joining that organization. Arthur had become a loner.

The one place where Arthur had the least difficulty

functioning around people was in school. In a classroom filled with twenty other children, it was physically impossible to isolate. Socially, the youngster interacted well enough to pass for normal. His fellow students were not aware of what was going on in his home and had no idea that he spent so much of his free time alone in the woods.

In school, Arthur acquitted himself well academically, despite making sure not to be the top student in his class. He wanted no part of winning another medal like the one he'd been awarded—and thrown away—years earlier. On the playground, he excelled in athletic activities. On one occasion, Harold, a fellow student, invited Arthur to his house. Harold lived in Wading River which meant one of Arthur's parents would have to drive him there. That might entail a long, uncomfortable ride for the youngster if his father were to take him. In addition, Arthur was becoming more self-conscious about his family. Both his parents spoke with accents and that was a source of embarrassment for the young boy. He refused Harold's invitation.

Starting at age of five, Arthur had unwillingly gone to Sunday school at the First Presbyterian Church on a regular basis. Often, he would hold on to the contribution envelope and, after school was over, walk directly across the street and spend it at Cooper's Stationery store. His fear of incurring God's wrath was overridden by his ever-present sweet tooth.

At age eleven and at his mother's insistence, Arthur became the youngest member of his church's choir. That meant he'd have to attend formal religious services every Sunday. Facing more scrutiny than he had in Sunday school, he reluctantly handed over his tithing as the bowl was passed from choir member to choir member.

Arthur had always felt out of place in church and the minute the Sunday service ended, he rushed to hang up his choir robe and head for the street.

Although Arthur hadn't had any formal run-ins with the law in several years, that wasn't due to any lack of effort on the young boy's part. He had set two fires in the past year, but hadn't been caught. He continued to shoplift on a regular basis, always going undetected in those efforts.

Chapter 17

February 13th. Arthur turned twelve years of age. His last year as a preteen. As a birthday present, he received a model kit of the HMS Bounty. His mother baked his favorite cake—devil's food with white icing. Marguerite remarked that he was becoming such a big boy. That night Arthur wet his bed.

Chapter 18

Near the end of February, Mrs. Snow announced that the entire elementary school was going to be putting on a talent show scheduled for March 15th. Volunteers were needed to perform on stage. Gina said she would dance ballet. Sal said he could do magic tricks. Andy claimed to be a juggler. No one else in Mrs. Snow's class felt confident enough to disclose their talents. Mrs. Snow let the class know that there could only be one representative from each class. With that, Andy admitted that he couldn't really juggle that well and he dropped out of the competition. Mrs. Snow asked Sal to prepare his magic tricks for an audition the following day. The teacher had already seen Gina dance and been impressed by her skill.

The next day, Sal stood before the class and attempted a card trick that didn't work. He then pulled a fake rabbit out of his hat. The problem was the class saw the rabbit long before it was supposed to appear as a surprise. Rather than hurt Sal's feelings, Mrs. Snow said she felt his act would be difficult for students sitting in the back of the auditorium to see.

Gina was selected as the class representative for the talent show.

***

On March 7th, Mrs. Snow made an announcement. "Class, I just found out that Gina will not be able to participate in our assembly program. She has come down with the measles and won't be coming to school for a while. I hope nobody else here comes down with it."

Ellen said, "I had the measles. It's yucky."

Nancy asked, "Mrs. Snow, will Gina die?"

Mrs. Snow answered "I certainly hope not. That's not usually what happens but she does have to stay quarantined."

A student asked, "What's a quarantined?"

"It means she has to stay by herself so she doesn't give the measles to anyone else. Hopefully she'll be back in school in a couple of weeks. Right now, we have to decide on something else. Who is going to be the representative from our class at the talent show?"

Nobody's hand went up.

"Well, I'm going to have to think of something."

From the back of the classroom, Harold blurted out, "I know. Let Arthur sing."

Arthur's face turned beet red. He didn't want to have anything to do with the talent contest. Was Harold volunteering him in good faith or because Arthur had turned down his invitation to visit him and he was jumping at the chance to put his would-be friend on the spot? Whichever the case, Arthur feared the idea of performing in front of a huge audience.

Mrs. Snow was intrigued. "Harold, how do you know Arthur can sing?"

"Because he told me he has to sing in church every Sunday."

Mrs. Snow turned to Arthur. "Why Arthur, is that true?"

Reluctantly, Arthur nodded his head.

"Well, would you be willing to display your talents next week?"

"Nah."

"I'd hate to have to stand up at the assembly and announce that my class was not fielding a representative."

A couple of students sitting near Arthur began encouraging him.

"Come on, Art."

"You can do it."

"Let's hear something now."

Feeling the pressure from his classmates, Arthur had been thrown into the position of being a hero or a goat.

Mrs. Snow asked him, "If you were to sing, what kind of song would it be?"

"I don't know. It couldn't be church stuff. That stuff is too hard."

"I don't know what kind of musical accompaniment we could give you. There isn't much time left. Let me see what I can come up with."

The following day Mrs. Snow chatted with Arthur before class started. "Arthur, I know this is all late notice, but I think I've come up with something that you'll be able to handle and will still be entertaining for the students. You know, the big thing with youngsters these days is Rock 'n Roll. Why don't you pick out a popular tune, one that is popular right now? We'll have you pretend you're singing it. Wouldn't that be easy enough?"

"I guess so, Mrs. Snow."

"You have any records at home?"

"I don't, but my sister does."

"So go home tonight and pick one out. Please bring it into the class tomorrow."

When he got home later that day, Arthur told his sister what his teacher had asked him to do.

"If I give you a record to bring to school, how do I know you won't break it? You probably will."

"My teacher will keep it until the assembly and I promise I'll bring it right back home. If it breaks, I'll buy you another one."

Ruth couldn't resist. "With what—my money?"

"No, smarty-pants! With my allowance."

"Do you know what a record costs these days?"

"Nope."

"About seventy cents. And I *don't* want a 78 rpm."

"So that's three weeks allowance. Not even"

"Yup, and if I give you the record, I'm telling mom what we're doing so you can't get away with anything."

"All right."

Her voice tinged with skepticism, Ruth asked, "And you're going to sing along with the record? You don't even know the words."

"I think I just have to kind of stand there and pretend."

Ruth fished through her record collection and pulled one out. "Keep it in its sleeve so it doesn't get all scratched. When is the assembly?"

"Next week Wednesday."

"Okay. I want this record back right after school that day."

The following day, Arthur handed over to his teacher the record in a large sandwich bag

Mrs. Snow took the record out and, after examining it, said, "This is a very popular one right now. A lot of the older kids are going to recognize it. Art, I appreciate your cooperation at the last minute. You helped me pull an iron out of the fire."

Unsure what that expression meant, Arthur responded with a simple, "Okay, Mrs. Snow."

***

March 15th. Port Jefferson Elementary school was abuzz with excitement. Much of the regular school day schedule had been canceled for what would be a lengthy program. At nine o'clock in the morning, all the classes from first grade to eighth filed into the auditorium. Mister Tolleson, the Principal, briefly addressed the students, reminding them today's event was not a contest but rather a chance for students to showcase their various talents. Then, the ceremonies began.

Arthur was sitting behind the stage curtain with the other participants, waiting his turn. The ceremonies began with the first grade, then the second and so on in order. The first grader was a tap dancer. The second grader recited a poem she had written. The third-grader played the xylophone—poorly. As each student completed their performance, it got closer and closer to being Arthur's turn. He was experiencing that anxiety that had always been an issue for him. As the fifth grade student finished his act—an amateurish demonstration of bird calls—Mrs. Snow began coaching Arthur. "Okay, Art. Put this on for size." The teacher opened up a case she'd had lying beside her. She took out a guitar and draped it around the youngster. "I borrowed this from my brother. I think it's going to really add something to your performance."

The curtain closed in front of the bird caller. While Principal Tolleson was congratulating that performer and warming up the crowd for the next act, Mrs. Snow set Arthur up on a chair with his guitar. As the teacher dashed off the stage, the curtain opened and there sat Arthur, guitar in hand, in front of one hundred twenty-five students. Immediately, *Heartbreak Hotel* began pouring out of the auditorium's loudspeaker system. Since Arthur hadn't had time to learn the words, his lip-synching was out of sync. He mumbled a stream of disconnected words totally unrelated to the lovesick lyrics Elvis Presley was crooning on the record. Despite that, the audience was enjoying his performance.

Halfway through the song, Arthur got up and began to walk around with the guitar, awkwardly strumming it. That got an even bigger rise out of the audience. By the time the record ended, Arthur was so into what he was doing he continued lip-synching and strumming to dead silence. The students—especially the older ones—were now really whooping it up, applauding and laughing simultaneously. From the side of the stage, Mrs. Snow signaled to Arthur to take a bow. He did and then, at Mrs. Snow's coaxing, reluctantly walked off the stage. After conquering his stage fright, he had been enjoying the show—his show!

Mr. Tolleson came back out on the stage and quipped, "Well, it's going to be hard to top that performance but we must move on. Here's John O'Reilly playing Chopsticks on the piano."

Arthur stayed backstage until the talent show was over. Then, like all the other students, he filed out of the auditorium.

When he got back to Mrs. Snow's classroom, all his fellow classmates—even Carolyn Marino—greeted him as if he had been the winning contestant on *Ted Mack's Original Amateur Hour*. He wasn't sure how he had pulled it off, but without singing a note or playing a chord on the guitar he had brought down the house.

Arthur had also just become the first Elvis impersonator in history.

Chapter 19

Later that day, Arthur returned the Elvis record to Ruth. Despite her painstaking inspection, she couldn't find any damage to it. Arthur was free to spend his upcoming weekly allowances as he saw fit.

For weeks following his performance in the talent show, Arthur rode a wave of celebrity in school. Students from other classes addressed the youngster as Elvis when passing him in the hall. Even Carolyn Marino gave the young boy a smile now and then, though still keeping her distance.

***

The month of March gave way to April and on a warm, spring day Arthur was walking through Suassa Park with Rex. He passed the Howells' house, a residence Arthur had years ago sworn to never again visit—and hadn't—after Warren Howell, his one-time friend, had mistreated Rex. Arthur continued walking and came to a halt in front of the house immediately to the left of the Howells'. There was a moving van parked in the driveway and workers were carrying furniture and other objects into the house. A lady standing with a teenaged boy was monitoring the workers' activity. Arthur watched for a bit and then began to move on. Before he got far, a voice cried out to him. "Hey, where ya going?"

Arthur turned around and saw the teenager running up to him. "Hey, do you live around here?"

Arthur answered, "Yes."

"Well, my name's Johnny. Johnny Stefano. What's your

name?"

"Arthur Berndt."

"What's your dog's name?"

"Rex."

"I like dogs." With that, Johnny stooped down and stuck out his hand for Rex to sniff. Taking that as a sign of friendliness, Rex wagged his tail and licked Johnny's hand. Johnny stood back up.

"My mom and me just moved here."

"Where did you used to live?"

"Brooklyn."

"That's real far away, right? "

"Lots of miles from here. It's part of the city."

Arthur felt compelled to ask, "Do you like the Dodgers?"

"You better believe it. And I hate those effin Yankees. "

"Me too! We beat the pants off them last year. "

"Damn right. So Arthur... It's Arthur, right?"

"Yup"

"Great. What grade are you in?"

"Sixth."

"I'm in the ninth. I start at the high school Monday. What are kids like around here anyway?"

"Oh, they're okay, I guess."

The older boy's mother called to him from the front stoop. "Johnny, come on in and give me a hand."

"All right, Ma." Johnny turned to Arthur. "I gotta go. You could come in but my mom doesn't like dogs like I do. I'll see you around."

Johnny entered the house with his mother. Arthur continued on his walk with Rex to nowhere in particular, unaware of how fateful his meeting with Johnny had been.

Chapter 20

A few days after meeting Johnny Stefano, Arthur took Rex for a walk following a day at school. When he got back home with his dog, it was time for dinner. American Chop Suey, one of Arthur's absolute favorites. It was also one of the few meals that August Berndt, a picky eater, ate with any relish. By Berndt family standards, the meal was consumed in relatively stress-free fashion.

After watching a bit of television with his family, Arthur went to bed, praying as always that he wouldn't wet it.

Later that evening, Arthur awoke with a start. Not because he'd wet the bed—he hadn't. He had left his bedroom door ajar and coming from somewhere in the house he heard what sounded like crying. Not being soaked with urine, he got out of bed without any fear of being punished and, basking in his dryness with an air of accomplishment, decided to investigate. He walked out into the hallway and realized the sobbing was coming from downstairs. He also realized who was doing the crying—his father!

Arthur hesitated. He wasn't sure how to proceed. He'd never once in his life seen or heard his father cry. Did the young boy dare approach the older man when he was in such an atypical and emotional mood? The safer option would be to get back in bed and celebrate the fact he was dry. At the same time, the young boy felt an instinctual need to console his father. Summoning up all his courage, Arthur descended the staircase. Reaching the first floor, he entered the living room. There he saw his father sitting in the rocking chair, the same rocking chair he had threatened to hit his son with years earlier. August held a crumpled piece of paper in his hand. Arthur saw the man that so often terrorized him wiping tears from his eyes with the back of his hand.

Arthur sat down on the sofa, closer to his father than he would typically choose to be. Not knowing what else to say, Arthur asked, "What's wrong, Dad?"

"Life's wrong—that's what's wrong. Let me tell you something. This life is a pile of shit. The sooner you realize that the easier it will be for you to get through it."

"Why, Dad? "

"Because of this letter I'm holding in my hand. That's one reason." He began to unravel the crumpled paper he had in his hand but then stopped. "It's in German. You couldn't read it anyway."

"Who is it from?"

"My goddamn mother. I guess I should say my former mother. She doesn't want to have anything to do with me. This has been going on for years but now she's making it official."

"What is she doing?"

August let out a bitter, halfhearted chuckle. "I guess you could say she's divorcing me. I came over here and I married a Protestant and she can't forgive me for that. Your mother tried to do little things like... You know why we eat fish every Friday?"

"No."

"Because that's what Catholics do. Your mother even offered to convert, but I told her not to bother. I hate the Catholic Church. I hated going every single stinking day of my life when I was your age. Yeah, when I came over to this country I was looking for a job, but I was also looking to get away from my mother and get away from the Catholic Church. And now I guess I'm really 'away from my mother.' She's pretty much told me to never contact her again."

"What about your dad?"

"He's been dead now a few years. He was pretty much dead even when he was living. She ran the house. And for some reason she picked me out of all the brothers. Well, maybe because even though they came over here, they all stayed in the Catholic Church."

"Do you think she would ever change her mind?"

"Not the way she wrote this letter. She's not going to be

around that much longer either. Right now, I don't think I'd even go to her funeral. Bitch."

The two sat there in silence, August done talking and his son unable to think of something to say.

As if on cue, Rex came in from the kitchen. He walked over to Arthur who gave him a few gentle pats.

"Well Dad, is it okay if I go back up to bed?"

"Yeah and don't talk to your mom about this. She didn't read this letter. I have to figure out how I'm going to handle this. Maybe I won't do anything. With any luck, my mother will be dead soon."

Arthur rose to his feet and headed upstairs. Rex was eager to follow, but rules were rules and his young master directed him to stay downstairs.

Arthur continued up to his bedroom. It was now 3:45 in the morning. The young boy was tired and needed more sleep but worried that if he wet the bed, his father would be in a worse mood than ever. The youngster closed the bedroom door and began working on his model of the HMS Bounty in an attempt to stay awake. Despite his best efforts, he could not keep his eyes open sufficiently to focus on assembling the ship's sails. The youngster walked to the bathroom and forced himself to urinate. Then, he walked back to his room, lay down on the bed and quickly drifted into a heavy slumber.

Downstairs, August Berndt, still seated on the rocking chair, called out to Rex, who had returned to the kitchen. An uncustomary gesture from a man who was generally standoffish around the family pet. This night, the normally stoic August Berndt briefly let down his guard and sought the same comfort that canine companionship so often provided his son. August fell asleep in the rocking chair, Rex lying at his feet.

A few hours later, Arthur woke up and to his great relief he was still dry. It was 6:30. When he came downstairs, he found his mother and sister eating breakfast. August had already left for work. Nothing seemed out of the ordinary. Had the young boy only dreamt of the emotional conversation he thought he'd had with his father?

Later that afternoon, when August came home from work he made no mention of the letter and his son knew better than to bring the subject up.

The following Sunday, while at home alone watching

television in the living room, Arthur spotted something lying underneath the lamp table next to him. He bent down and picked up an envelope. He couldn't read the words on the envelope, but guessed they were written in German. The young boy had his proof. The letter his father had received and their middle-of-the-night conversation about it were both all too real.

What to do with the envelope? Because of what his father had told him, he felt he had to get this envelope to his father without his mother knowing. For the time being, he stashed it in a safe place—underneath his clothes in a dresser drawer where he kept his money, both earned and unearned.

CHAPTER 21

Arthur slammed his social studies book shut and stuffed it into the storage area of his desk. Peter, a fellow student sitting in front of him, turned around and asked, "Do you wanna play softball? We're gonna have a game after school."

"Nah. I have to go home."

Normally, Arthur would be interested in playing softball, but he had been planning all day to make a visit to the Crystal Fountain. He hadn't been there in several weeks and today his sweet tooth was getting the best of him. He had stolen seventy-five cents from his mother's pocketbook earlier in the day to supplement his own savings. Today there would be a hefty purchase of candy.

The school bell rang. Before Arthur could leave the classroom, Mrs. Snow called him to her desk. "I won't keep you too long, Art. I just wanted to let you know you're a very good student, but I think you can do even better. I just get the feeling that if you tried a little harder..."

Arthur defended himself. "I'm trying, Mrs. Snow."

"Sometimes you hand in a spelling test and I see you've crossed out your first answer which happens to be correct and then misspelled the word. Just seems odd to me. You were the top student in your class a couple of years ago and I'd like to see you reach that level again. Wouldn't you?"

"Yeah, I guess so. Well, maybe I will."

"I certainly hope so. Okay, Art. I don't want to hold you up. I'll see you tomorrow."

"Yes sir—I mean, yes ma'am."

Arthur walked out of the classroom, through the hall and down the stairs to the exit. Passing the playground in front of the school, he saw that sides were already being chosen for the softball game. He was tempted to change his plans but then, as they had been doing all day long, visions of sugary treats began dancing in his head.

The young boy walked down Tuthill Street, made a right turn on Main Street and, shortly thereafter, strolled into the Crystal Fountain. Minutes later, he came back out, loaded with $1.30 worth of goodies. He unwrapped a Tootsie Pop, stuck it into his mouth and continued his walk home. Taking his regular itinerary, he walked from Main Street to Barnum Avenue, crossed Barnum to get onto a path that led through a wooded area and then came out onto the private, unnamed road that led to the high school. Arthur continued onto a sidewalk, passing the school on his left and basketball courts on his right. Then, he headed up a slope and proceeded onto a dirt path that began behind the high school and led to Brook Road.

While on the path, Arthur finished his Tootsie Pop. He came to a stop and, out of his pockets bulging with candy, pulled another treat. He went to work on a box of Good N Plenty while resuming his walk. As he did, a voice startled him.

"Hey kid, you got some for me?"

Arthur looked into the woods and saw a familiar face. It was Johnny Stefano. He was sitting on a fallen tree trunk, smoking a cigarette.

"Well, do you?"

The last thing Arthur ever wanted to do was share his candy, but he felt it best not to disappoint someone older and bigger than he.

Arthur walked into the woods. After Johnny put out his cigarette and cupped the palms of his hands, Arthur poured a generous helping of candy into them.

"Good N Plenty is plenty good!" joked the older boy.

"They're okay. I like Tootsie Pops better."

Johnny patted his hand on the tree trunk and said "Have a seat. We have business to conduct."

As he sat down, the younger boy asked, "Business? What do you mean?"

"You didn't tell me you like to break and enter."

"Break and enter what? What is that?"

"You know, break into homes?"

"Well, I don't."

"I was talking to that Warren kid that lives next to me. He told me you wrecked somebody's house when you were a real little kid."

"Did not. He's a liar. I don't like him."

"He told me your dog bit him."

"Warren started it. Anyway, I didn't do what he said."

"Hey, I get it. You always gotta plead innocent."

"I don't like to get in trouble."

"Me either. That's why I want to talk to you about something."

"What?"

"I've been checking out a house. It's a couple of blocks away from me. Think it's on Michigan Avenue. No one lives in the house. I don't think anyone owns it anymore. There's stuff in it. It's first come first served."

"What does that mean?"

"Well, since nobody lives there, you can take what you want and won't get in trouble. If we don't take it, somebody else will. Might as well be us."

"I'm afraid of the police."

"But I'm telling you, there won't be any police. First of all, we're not gonna wreck the joint like you guys did. That's stupid. We might get stuff that we can sell and make money from. You like money, right?"

"Yeah."

"So, we go into the house, figure out where the good stuff is and take it. We won't break anything."

"I don't wanna get in trouble."

"What if I promise you ya won't?"

"Well, what do I have to do?"

"Just help me pick stuff out. We won't take anything. I'll do that later with my friend."

Johnny lit up another cigarette.

"I'll tell you what Art. Let's just walk over to the house and look at it."

"I have to get home and walk my dog."

"Why don't you go home and get your dog. What's his name again?

"Rex."

118

"Yeah, Rex. Get him and... Do you know how to get to Michigan Avenue?"

Pretending he didn't know how to, Arthur said, "I'm not sure."

"Well, you know where I live so after you walk your dog come over to my house," Johnny said, more as a demand than a request.

"Well, just as long as we don't do anything."

"We won't, I promise. And you know what? Definitely don't bring your dog."

The boys proceeded to walk the rest of the way home. At the intersection of Hawthorne and Lowell, Arthur turned to go to his house while Johnny continued on Hawthorne to get to his.

"Okay, kid. See you in a few minutes. Hey, thanks for the Good N Plenty."

Arthur didn't respond. He was too troubled by a situation he didn't want to be in. If he failed to show up at Johnny's house, the youngster knew sooner or later the two would run into each other and he'd have to explain his failure to appear. Worse yet, he feared Johnny might show up on the doorstep of Twenty-one Lowell Place. Out of self-consciousness Arthur never wanted anyone from the outside world anywhere near the house he was growing up in.

He took Rex for a short walk, brought him back home and then headed over to Johnny's house hoping that the older boy had dropped his plan to invade the vacant house.

When Arthur showed up at the Stefanos' house, Johnny was sitting on the stoop waiting for him. "I like a kid that follows orders. You and me are friends." Arthur wasn't so sure.

The two boys proceeded to walk over to Michigan Avenue and proceeded to the house Johnny had his sights set on. The yard was overgrown with weeds, the garage door featured two broken panes of glass, there were numerous old newspapers lying on the property, and the front screen door was ajar and hanging on for dear life. All in all, 42 Michigan Avenue was the proverbial worst house on the block.

"Let's keep going. We don't want people to see us standing in front of this house."

The boys walked a bit farther and then into a small wooded lot where they both sat down on the ground to plot strategy. Or rather, Johnny Stefano sat down to plot strategy.

"Listen, if we come up from the back of the house on the right side we can get in through the back door.

"What if somebody sees us?"

"That's where you come in. You're smaller than me. Less to see. If you crawl up to the back door on the grass no one can see you."

"I don't want to do it. Besides, if nobody owns the house, why do we have to sneak in?"

"Because it's my idea. Right now it's my—uh, our secret. If someone else sees us going in, they might look to see if there's good stuff and take it first. You get it?"

"I guess so. I still don't want to do it."

"I'll give you half of all the money."

"What money? How much?"

"Well, I don't know how much yet. Have to see what's in there."

"Why don't you just do it yourself?"

"You're smaller. Besides, I already know you're an expert."

Arthur was experiencing that same ambivalence he'd felt with Ronnie Simpson, Peter Stanton, Warren Howell and Buddy Towle: the desperate need for acceptance and the price he feared he'd pay trying to fulfill that need.

Sensing the hesitation in his younger would-be cohort, Johnny tried to reassure him. "It's easy. All you have to do is go in there and look around and see if there's stuff worth taking. Just go from room to room looking for stuff. Television, radio, silverware, you get it, right?"

"I'm not good at doing that. "

"Well, now's the time to get started. Besides, it's easy."

"I don't wanna get into trouble. It's not worth it."

"Will fifty bucks make it worth it?"

Arthur responded in a questioning voice mixed with equal parts of hope and disbelief. "Fifty dollars?"

"You heard me. Maybe I'll make it a C-note."

"What's a see (sic) note?"

"One hundred dollars, my man."

Even with his years of stealing at home, Arthur had never had more than $35 in his possession at any one time. He pictured himself having all that money. His greed was quickly tempered by skepticism.

"And what do I have to do?"

"Get inside that goddamn house and figure out if there's any good stuff in there."

"What about the 'No Trespassing' sign?"

"That's only to keep anybody from moving in and living here. We're not doing that."

"Hey Johnny, why don't we just look through the windows to see what's in there?"

"Don't be a jackass. You can't see everything inside that way. And someone might see us."

"So what if they do?"

"Stupid! They might steal our idea and get stuff before we do!"

Johnny reached into his pocket and pulled out a small pad and half of a pencil. "I want you to go room to room. You can spell , right?"

"Yup!"

"So write down what you see in each room. Got it?"

"I think so."

"Don't 'think so'! Go in the living room, write down what you see—radio, TV, record player, whatever you see. Then go in the kitchen. Go from room to room."

A look of disappointed exasperation came over Johnny's face. "This isn't gonna work. You're just too chicken." Arthur's lack of protest at being insulted convinced Johnny he was correct. The younger boy stood up, anxious to leave. The older boy, too busy calculating, ignored him.

Suddenly, Johnny had an *Eureka!* moment. "You know what? I have a way better idea. Remember that car in the driveway in the front?

"Yeah?"

"Let's go check it out."

The two boys walked through a treed area bordering the property until they got to the side of the garage. Parked immediately in front of the garage was a 1950 De Soto.

"You see those round things on the tire?"

"You mean the hubcaps, right? Isn't that what they're called?"

"Exactly. You know those are worth money, right?"

"How much?"

"Well, that depends. Depends who's buying them. I'll tell you what. You take them off and I'll give you a quarter right now."

"But don't they belong on that car?"

"I bet that car doesn't even run anymore. That's why they left it here. Might as well take the caps before they get junked along with the rest of the car."

"I'm not sure how to take them off."

"Just go around the outer ridge of the cap and pull with your fingers."

"What if somebody sees me?"

"No one can see you on this side of the car. Get those two off and then we'll figure out something for the other side. I'll keep lookout. If anyone comes along, just duck behind the front of the car. They won't see you there."

"I'm not sure…"

"Twenty-five cents!"

Arthur had turned down the opportunity to make fifty dollars, never really believing Johnny would pay him such a huge amount of money. Now the twelve-year-old was staring at a chance to make—in a matter of seconds— the weekly allowance his parents gave him. The young boy couldn't resist the temptation.

Arthur wasn't so sure how effective Johnny would be keeping watch from the woods but, ignoring that concern, the young boy got to work. He walked out onto the property until he reached the car. Once there, the young boy knelt down by the front left tire. He pulled on the hubcap, but it wouldn't budge.

"Try this," said Johnny, throwing a pocket knife that landed near Arthur's feet. The youngster grabbed the knife and opened it. He was able to wedge the blade between the hubcap and the wheel, loosening the hubcap and pulling it off with his fingertips. He then went to the left rear tire and repeated the process. With a warped sense of pride, Arthur scurried into the wooded area holding a hubcap in each hand.

"Good job. Now let's get the other two."

"Can you just pay me for these?"

"Hey, a deal's a deal. Twenty-five cents for four caps, not two."

Having mastered the technique, Arthur was less hesitant to attempt extracting the remaining hubcaps, even though he was more exposed to prying eyes. Oblivious to the thought of being caught, he quickly removed the remaining hubcaps and returned to the woods with them.

Johnny congratulated his protégé. "Perfect. That was easy, right?"

"Can I have my quarter now?"

"Well, you know I didn't think I'd have to pay you today." The older boy fished through his pockets and came out with two dimes. "Is this good enough?"

Arthur was disappointed in being shortchanged, but wasn't prepared to challenge the older boy. He took comfort in the fact that he had twenty cents more than he'd had just minutes ago.

Stuffing a couple of the hubcaps under his shirt, Johnny gave the other two to Arthur. "Here. Stuff these under your shirt." The two then started walking back to Johnny's house. To make sure their precious cargo didn't fall out, the two delinquents held their hands against the front of their shirts, making it look as if they both were suffering from stomach aches.

Arthur thought about the money he'd been promised if he broke into the house. With that in mind, he asked Johnny, "I could have made more money going inside the house, right? A lot more money, right?"

Johnny said, "Yeah, you and me both. But, I don't know, I just got a bad feeling about that whole thing. It's too complicated. Hey, I know you just made chicken feed today. But this can become a regular thing. I did all right with it back in Brooklyn."

"You mean the hubcaps?"

"Absolutely."

The fact they were hiding the hubcaps on this walk through Suassa Park canceled any doubt in Arthur's mind that what they had just done was wrong. That wouldn't stop him. For years, Arthur had been honing his criminal skills while dulling his conscience.

When they got to Johnny's house, the older boy took the four hubcaps and threw them in the back of his brother's car. He then turned to Arthur and said, "You and I have a lot of business to do. You like money, right?"

"Yup."

"Stick with me pal, and you'll see lots of it. Is that a deal?"

Not daring to disappoint his older friend, Arthur simply said, "Yup."

"One thing. Don't tell anybody what we're doing. Don't say anything at home. You got it?"

"Yeah."

"I mean it. Keep your lips zipped! Got it?"

Arthur nodded his head. He got it all right. Long ago, he'd become a master of lies and cover-ups.

Walking back to his house, Arthur silently debated with himself whether or not he was heading his life down another wrong path. Twenty-cents told him he wasn't.

Chapter 22

On a Saturday afternoon in late May, Arthur was watching a baseball game with his father and mother. Thankfully, the Dodgers had a commanding lead so neither Marguerite nor her son had concerns about August's mood taking a turn for the worse.

As the eighth inning was beginning, Rex trotted over to his favorite person. He began nudging Arthur with his snout.

"Looks like Rex wants to go outside to do his business. Art, will you let him out?" said Marguerite.

"I think I'll go with him, Ma."

August chimed in. "Don't you want to see the rest of the game. Snider is coming up in the bottom of the eighth."

Duke Snider was Arthur's all-time favorite player. Nevertheless, something else had popped up in the youngster's mind that took precedence.

"Nah, I already know he is going to hit a homer."

August laughed. "Yeah, right. It's not that easy."

Rex continued pestering Arthur.

Marguerite said, "Well if you go out with him, make sure you're back by six o'clock. We're having that roast beef and noodles you've been begging me for and I want you at the dinner table."

"Okay, Ma."

Arthur loved his mother's roast beef in particular, but disliked dinnertime in general because it forced him to sit in close proximity to his tormentor. For Arthur, the job of eating supper came with a significant occupational hazard—his father.

Boy and dog charged out the front door and began patrolling the neighborhood. For Arthur, this walk had a purpose. While watching the ballgame on TV earlier, Arthur's mind had wandered back to his successful hubcap caper of weeks earlier. Since then, he'd been looking at automobiles more as a source of revenue and less as a source of transportation. Per Johnny's offer, Arthur would earn a quarter for every set of four hubcaps he stole. If he wanted to make a dollar, he'd have to "de-hubcap" four cars. The youngster wanted to find out if Johnny's offer still stood.

When he got to the Stefano residence, there were no signs of life and just one car in the driveway. Arthur walked up to the car and peeked inside. In the backseat, a tarpaulin lay over unknown merchandise. However, at one end of the tarpaulin a small part of the rim of what looked to be a hubcap jutted out.

Arthur walked up to the front door and knocked a couple of times but there was no answer. As he peeked into the front window, a car pulled into the driveway. In it were Mrs. Stefano and her two sons. Johnny jumped out of the car and joked, "Hey kid. What are you doing? Casing the joint?"

Rosemary Stefano criticized her son. "Johnny, I fail to see the humor. Think about where you just came from."

"Aw, c'mon Ma. I was only joking."

"Well that's the kind of joking I can do without." Rosemary turned her attention to Arthur. "What brings you by? I don't mind you visiting, but please leave your dog home in the future. Nothing personal. I got bit badly a few years ago and I'm just uncomfortable around dogs, even ones that behave themselves like your dog seems to."

"Okay, Mrs. Stefano. I'll take him home."

"No, you don't have to do it this time. Just remember in the future."

After going to his own car, Salvatore Stefano, Johnny's older brother, joined everyone on the front stoop.

"Hey Johnny, is this the kid you were telling me about?"

"Yeah."

Rosemary Stefano glanced at her son and then looked at Arthur. Skeptically, she asked, "John, isn't Arthur a bit young for someone your age?"

"Heck, he's a Dodgers fan and that's good enough for me. It's not so easy to make friends in school when the year's almost over. Besides, I'm a city kid."

"What does that mean?"

"There's a bunch of potato pickers in school. This kid Art has more smarts than most of them do."

"Well, I don't know how Arthur's parents would feel about him associating with somebody so much older. Turning to Arthur she asked, "What do you think your parents would say?"

Without missing a beat, Arthur answered with an air of braggadocio, "Oh, I've hung out with kids a lot older than Johnny."

Rosemary laughed. "Oh, aren't we precocious?"

Arthur wasn't sure what precocious meant, but he took it as a compliment.

"So Arthur, if you didn't have your dog with you I'd invite you in to watch television."

Johnny was quick with an answer. "That's okay, Mom. Arthur was probably walking his dog." He turned to Arthur and with a subtle wink of the eye that his mother couldn't see, said, "Right?"

Arthur agreed.

"Hey, I'll take a walk with you for a couple minutes."

As Rosemary and Salvatore entered the house, Arthur and Johnny set out on a walk through the neighborhood.

"So Art, how the hell ya been?"

"Okay I guess."

"Why did you come to my house?"

"Well, it was that hubcap thing."

"Yeah, it was fun right?"

"Yup. I was thinking I could do it for a while until I saved up for a new bicycle."

"What kind?"

"A Schwinn Tiger."

"Yeah, that'd cost you some bucks. Maybe fifty or sixty. You'd have to do some serious work. Besides, what the hell would you tell your parents if you suddenly pulled into the driveway with a brand-new bicycle?"

"I didn't think about that. I guess I would just keep the money and spend it in secret—you know, comics, candy and stuff I could hide."

"So where you going to get all the hubcaps from anyway?"

"Well, there's cars all over the place."

"Did you ever hear that saying that a dog doesn't lie down where he shits?"

"Nope."

"Well what it means is you don't steal where you live."

Arthur did, but he chose to keep that knowledge to himself.

"What I mean is if a lot of hubcaps start missing around here, the cops will start coming around. That's not good."

"So what if I ride my bike and go real far away. I have a basket on my bike I can keep the hubcaps in."

"Yeah, and you'd be pedaling down the road with all those caps in broad daylight."

"I can put something over them."

"And what? Come pedaling up to my house with them?

Arthur was applying for a job and was determined to get it.

"I could leave them in a secret place in the woods and then you could pick them up."

"Hmm... Now maybe you're beginning to use your noodle. The trouble is you have to do it in the daytime 'cause you're a little kid. Anyway, do you have something to take them off with?"

"Well, I don't have a knife like yours. I could get a knife like the one you use for butter."

"A screwdriver is better. Can you get a real thin screwdriver?"

"I think so."

"I'm not gonna ask any more questions. You bring me four caps, I'll give you twenty-five cents. Do not bring them to my house, you understand?"

Arthur nodded his head. Then he had another idea. "You know that big tower on the street behind your house?"

"You mean that Ground Observer Corps thing?"

"Yup. (Pridefully) I climbed up it once by myself."

"What the hell did you do that for?"

"I don't know. Well anyway, there's a hole dug in the woods next to it. I could put them in there and cover them up."

Johnny gave it some thought and said, "Nah. That's no good. Too many people going up and down the tower. They might see you put stuff in there or me taking it out."

Then it occurred to Arthur—the perfect spot! The dirt path leading to the railroad tracks. He'd never run into anybody there except that one time when he met the old man. His enthusiasm renewed, Arthur did an about-face and convinced his new business associate to accompany him back up Hawthorne Street. "Follow me!"

"Where the hell are we going?"

"You'll see."

Arthur led the older boy onto Whittier Place, which they walked on until reaching Old Post Road. There, they made a left and twenty yards later, turned onto the dirt road Arthur knew so well. Just thirty feet along the way Johnny came to a stop. He veered off the path, walked through a patch of not-yet-in-season wild blueberries and came to a thick, fallen tree trunk.

"Perfect! You can put the crap you steal behind this tree. Cover it with something. Man, this might turn out to be too easy!" Maybe it would be for Johnny. He wouldn't be doing the dirty work.

"So Arthur, you go about your business. I'll check once a week to see what's behind that trunk. If you get caught, play dumb. You're still a little kid. Just say you saw something on TV and you thought you'd try it—some kind of bullshit like that."

Then Johnny got a menacing look that reminded Arthur of his father. "Just remember, you don't know me and I don't know you. So that means you stop coming by my house. You got it?"

"Yes, Johnny."

"You better get it. Nobody likes a snitch and you know what happens to snitches?"

"What's a snitch?"

"Something you better not be. A squealer. Don't get caught and you won't have to worry about it. But if you do, just remember you were working on your own."

"But if I can't ever see you, how will I get paid?"

"Easy. After I count up the hubcaps, I'll leave the money in an envelope. It'll always be coins so it won't matter if it rains." Johnny started rubbing his hands. "This is going to be good. I'm glad I bumped into you, buddy."

"Me too. So who do you give them (the hubcaps) to?

"That's for me to know and for you not to find out. Secrecy, remember? You do your job and I'll do mine."

"Yeah, OK."

"I guess I can tell you this much. Me and Sal were making decent money doing this in the city. That's one reason I didn't want to move out here. Not enough people and action here. But my old man is in jail in Riverhead. We went to see him today. My mother moved out here because she wants to keep me and Sal out of trouble, doesn't want us to wind up like our father. Hell, I don't want to get in trouble, do you?

"Nope."

"Right. So it's about being smart. If you're gonna take hubcaps, ditch your bicycle in the woods or somewhere so nobody sees it. When you take off the caps, make sure they don't hit the ground. No noise! Get some kind of bag you can put all four in at once. Then, get your ass out of there. If you have to, throw the bag in the woods and come back and get it later when it's safer. You know how to tie your shoes right?"

Arthur nodded his head.

"Make sure they're good and tight. You don't want them loosening up when you take off."

The two boys walked back out onto Old Post Road. Arthur took a right and Johnny a left, each headed back home. The two boys, one fifteen and the other eleven, were in business together. Due to the nature of their business there was no written contract.

Chapter 23

As the school year neared its end, it became clear that despite Mrs. Snow's pep talk Arthur was not going to win the medal as the best student academically in his class. He remained solidly entrenched in second place—exactly where he had finished in four of his five previous school years. His scholastic performance was good enough to satisfy his parents without being great enough to provide them the positive recognition as parents that Arthur was determined they would never get again.

As it did every year, the Port Jefferson Elementary School held its annual field day during the final week of the school year. Among this year's events was a half-court basketball game between teams consisting of a mix of sixth and fifth-grade boys. That contest would have to wait until the lower grades completed their events.

Along with his fellow classmates, Arthur watched the various contests—potato sack race, softball throw, three-legged race—offered by the lower grades with great enthusiasm. When the fourth grade completed its relay race, the race that Arthur had battled so fiercely, and unsuccessfully, to win two years earlier, it was time for the basketball game. Mr. Wade, the gym teacher, lined up the boys from the two classes and randomly selected members for each of the two teams. It was then that it dawned on Arthur. He would be playing either with or against Ronnie Simpson. He couldn't decide which would be the worst scenario.

Arthur and Ronnie had become fast friends in the fifth grade. That friendship lasted until a meeting at school that included both of Arthur's parents and Ronnie's father. That was when

August Berndt found out that his son had been fraternizing with a black boy. Upon learning this, he expressly forbade his son to ever associate with Ronnie again. The two boys had an uncomfortable parting of the ways and, obeying his father, Arthur avoided Ronnie throughout the most recent school year. That avoidance was made easier by the fact that Ronnie had been forced to repeat the fifth grade. They rarely were in each other's company. Even when passing in the hall, they ignored each other.

When Mr. Wade was done putting together the two teams, Arthur and Ronnie wound up as opponents. Arthur felt a sense of relief, concluding it would be easier to keep his distance by not being Ronnie's teammate.

Each team consisted of fourteen players. Mr. Wade made it clear everyone would get a chance to play in a game lasting fifteen minutes; there would be no favoritism shown towards the better athletes on either squad. For Arthur, fifteen minutes suddenly seemed like a lifetime as he was growing increasingly uncomfortable at the thought of having any interaction with his one-time friend.

Ronnie Simpson had been by far the biggest kid in the fifth grade during the previous school year. This year, he again was the biggest kid in the fifth grade—and bigger than any sixth-grader. Normally, when Ronnie was in any athletic contest, he would dominate the game for his team's benefit, but Mr. Wade was sticking to his guns and did not pick Ronnie to start this game.

Arthur started for his team. Rather than conduct the customary tipoff that begins a basketball game, two opposing players did odds/evens with their fingers to decide which team would get the ball first. Determination made, seconds later a fellow teammate passed the ball from out of bounds to Arthur who began awkwardly dribbling the ball. Immediately from the sidelines Ronnie began harassing his one-time friend. "Arthur, you can't dribble. You never could."

Arthur immediately passed the ball to another teammate but, in his anxiety to get rid of the ball and shut up Ronnie, he threw it out of bounds. The other team took possession. Ronnie wouldn't ease up. "What's the matter, butterfingers?"

While Mr. Wade cautioned Ronnie to stop the heckling, Arthur anxiously awaited being replaced by another teammate so he could avoid Ronnie's taunting scrutiny.

Peter, on the opposing team, dribbled the ball until he stood ten feet away from the basket. Thinking he couldn't reach the basket shooting overhand, Peter made an underhanded shot. The ball went up, but never reached the basket. Instead, it came down into Arthur's hands. The rule was that if one team gained possession of the ball at the other team's expense, the team with the ball had to pass it at least once before attempting a shot. Arthur forgot that rule and made a two-handed shot that hit the backboard and, after rolling around the rim for what seemed like forever, dropped in. Arthur's elation was quickly dashed by Mr. Wade's whistle. "No good. Ball goes to the other team." From the sidelines, Ronnie mocked, "He doesn't even know the rules."

Never known for his good sportsmanship, Arthur was inwardly seething. Sensing that, but not wanting to single the youngster out, Mr. Wade sent in substitutes for Arthur's entire squad. A few minutes later, he sent in replacements for the other squad, giving Ronnie Simpson his chance to shine. Ronnie immediately took control of a game that had been scoreless. He completed a one-handed set shot. Then, he stole a ball from an opponent, dribbled past the defense with ease and completed a layup. Suddenly, Ronnie's team was leading 4-0. In a show of sour grapes, Arthur muttered on the sidelines to anyone who would listen, "Ah, he's not that good."

With the game halfway over and the score remaining 4-0, Arthur reentered the contest as Ronnie sat down. The two had still not spoken directly with each other, limiting their comments to sideline barbs.

Shortly after reentering, Arthur took a pass from Sal and sunk a two-handed set shot. The score was now 4-2. During the next five minutes the shooting on both sides improved so that the score stood at 10-6 in favor of Ronnie's team.

Just then, Arthur spotted his mother sitting among a crowd of adult onlookers. He was surprised and excited to see her there. She had said earlier in the morning she wasn't sure if she could get out of work early but she made it to his game! Arthur was relieved that his father had decided to put in a full day's work. The young boy didn't know for sure that anything would go wrong during the game, but, no matter what was going on in his life, he always felt safer when his father wasn't around.

With three minutes to go, both Ronnie and Arthur entered

the game. Ronnie took a shot and, following a rare miss, the ball wound up in Arthur's hands. This time, he remembered to pass it and sent the ball over to his teammate Stan. Stan looked like he'd caught a hot potato and immediately threw it back to Arthur who, without thought, immediately whirled around and let fly a long distance bomb. It hit high on the backboard, but instead of bouncing back into play, dropped like a medicine ball through the basket.

Ronnie approached Arthur. "You're just lucky."

"Am not."

With the score at 10-8 and a little over a minute remaining, Ronnie initiated a face-to-face confrontation that brought the game to a halt. "Your old man is a jackass, and you are too."

"So?"

"You're a chickenshit, too!"

"Yeah, prove it!"

Ronnie shoved Arthur in the chest with both hands. "Well, ya gonna do something?"

Ronnie suddenly stuck his foot behind Arthur's leg and tripped the youngster, who landed hard on the ground. Then, Ronnie jumped on top of him and started throwing punches.

By this time, Mr. Wade had run up to the boys. He pulled Ronnie off of Arthur. A crowd of children and adults all watched in stunned silence.

"I don't know what this is all about and I don't want to know. This is no way to conduct yourselves. Either of you."

Mr. Wade turned to Ronnie, "Are your parents here?"

A booming voice behind Mr. Wade said, "I'm his father." Leroy Simpson, a mountain of a man, had introduced himself. Mr. Wade asked him to take his son home. As father and son walked away, Marguerite hurried over to Arthur, who was now back on his feet. "Art, what happened? Are you okay?"

"Yeah, it was nothing. Ronnie started it."

Mr. Wade apologized to Arthur's mother. "I knew they had some issues last year. But I didn't think there'd be a problem in a basketball game. I guess I was wrong."

Marguerite turned to her son. "What were you boys fighting about?"

"Nothing."

Looking her son over, Marguerite couldn't find any signs of battle other than a small scrape on his elbow. Turning to Mr.

Wade she said, "I'll take my son home now."

"That's fine, Mrs. Berndt." As Marguerite turned to leave with her son, Mr. Wade added, "I will say this. From what I could see, Ronnie was doing most of the agitating."

"Thank you for letting me know that. That does make me feel better."

As mother and son walked to the car, Arthur said, "Mom, please don't tell dad. He would get real mad."

"Thank God this happened at the end of the school year and not at the beginning. No doubt there would've been another meeting with the principal. Your father doesn't handle those well."

"Well, dad told me to stay away from Ronnie no matter what, but I couldn't help it. It was a basketball game. Just please don't tell dad."

"I don't see any reason to. School's over. You two managed to stay out of each other's hair all year long right?"

"Yup."

"So, in the fall you'll be in the seventh grade. There'll be no field day to worry about. Seventh grade. You know what Art? You're growing up."

While Marguerite and Arthur got into the family car, Marguerite praised her son. "You did a great job out there playing basketball. I'm very proud of you."

Swelling with pride from his mother's unexpected compliment, all the youngster could say was a heartfelt, "Thanks, Mom."

"Let's get home and clean up that scrape on your elbow. If your father happens to ask about it we'll say you hurt yourself playing basketball. After a pause, Marguerite continued, "Come to think of it, that technically *is* the truth."

Mother and son headed home.

Chapter 24

A weekday in mid-July, 1956. Arthur's father was at work and his mother was grocery shopping. Arthur was at home with his sister.

Ruth came downstairs and announced she was going to start practicing the piano. She and her parents had hopes of her becoming a classical pianist. It was understood that her practice sessions took precedence over anything else going on in the house. This particular day, Arthur especially resented her intrusion since he was watching a baseball game on television. With grudging deference, he turned the volume down and continued to watch the game in silence as his sister played scales on the piano.

The score was 6-3 in favor of the Cardinals. With two men on and two out, Duke Snider came to the plate. He failed to hit the ball with two exaggerated uppercut swings and misses. It was obvious he was trying to tie up the game with one swing of the bat. The next two pitches were way inside, the second one causing Snider to hit the dirt. He got up, glowered at the pitcher, and, on the next pitch, proceeded to hit what appeared to be a long fly ball. The camera fanned out to deep centerfield, but the ball was not visible on the screen. The centerfielder, already playing deep due to Snider's power, was backing up as if ready to make a catch and end the inning. Disappointed, Arthur figured his favorite player had just flied out. Then, he saw the outfielder retreating farther and getting closer and closer to the centerfield wall. Finally, the camera fanned into the stands where a man reading a newspaper put the paper down and made a barehanded catch of Snider's home run. The man nonchalantly put the ball in his pants pocket and resumed reading. Arthur started screaming in delight, which earned him a "Shh!" from Ruth. Resentfully, Arthur let out one more shout in celebration of the home run before stifling himself.

Try as he might, the young boy couldn't fully savor the fact his team had tied up the contest. Arthur bristled at the thought of having to watch the rest of the game in such a restrictive environment. "This stinks!"

With larceny on his mind, the young boy got up and headed down into the basement. Something had been on his mind for several weeks and this seemed as good a time as any to take action. He rifled through his father's collection of tools, knowing exactly what he was looking for. August Berndt was extremely orderly and Arthur found a collection of screwdrivers conveniently together in one drawer. He picked out the one with the thinnest tip and stuffed it into his pocket. He realized he needed something else. He went upstairs and then out to the garage. Hanging on the wall were three burlap bags. Arthur took one. He stuffed it into his bicycle basket, hopped onto the seat of the bike and began pedaling down the driveway out onto Lowell Place. Rex stood at the front screen door looking to join his youthful friend. Arthur was smart enough to know Rex could only complicate things today.

Arthur pedaled up to Old Post Road and made a right. He headed west with no destination in mind. He was out to steal hubcaps, but had no idea where to start. He passed a number of houses, some with automobiles in the driveway. With every car he spotted, the young boy's enthusiasm for breaking the law increased. He got more and more excited at the prospect of getting away with something and making money for it. At the same time, he had trouble shaking the fear of getting caught. *"The trouble is you have to do it in the daytime 'cause you're a little kid."* Johnny Stefano's words reminded Arthur that his chances of getting caught were greater in the daytime than they would be at night, but at his age, he'd have to be in bed by the time the sun set. He bolstered his courage by giving himself a mental pep talk: *Don't I steal stuff from stores in the daytime?*

He continued riding his bike until he came to the outskirts of Setauket. He turned onto Hulse Road. This was brand-new territory for the youngster. The houses were few and far between, which would make for less witnesses. He rode a bit more before coming upon a house that caught his eye. The house was set far back from the road, but there was a detached garage just ten yards in from Hulse Road. A car sat in front of the garage and Arthur saw another vehicle parked inside it. Adrenaline coursed through the youngster's body. He was in it for the money, but also looked forward to the impending thrill of doing something taboo and not only having his misdeed go undetected but, even better, not getting hit by his father for it. The latter had its own value, one only Arthur could fully appreciate.

The youngster rode past the house in question, then did a U-turn and went by it again. He got off his bicycle and rolled it into the woods. He grabbed the burlap bag out of his basket and walked through the woods that abutted the south side of the target property. It was a short walk thanks to the fact the garage sat so close to the road. The young thief sized up his task. He decided the hubcaps on the driver's side of the vehicle would be easy pickings. The car itself blocked any chance someone in the house might see him at work on the left side of the automobile. Arthur crept out of the woods and, with screwdriver and burlap bag in hand, crawled on his belly like an advancing soldier over a narrow patch of grass until he reached the dirt driveway. He squatted down and quickly removed both hubcaps. Panicking at the thought of trying to get the remaining two, he scrambled back into the woods, leaving the burlap bag, now containing two hubcaps, and the screwdriver lying on the ground next to the car.

The young boy sat in the woods working up the courage to complete his task. At the very least, he had to summon up the nerve to retrieve the bag. Would two hubcaps be good enough? At the house on Michigan Avenue the older boy had pushed him to take all four. He pictured Johnny calling him a chicken for not fully completing the mission.

There continued to be no signs of life in the house from the onset. That gave the youngster the courage to reemerge from the woods. He picked up the screwdriver and, in a crouch, duckwalked his way over to the passenger's side of the car. In rather adept fashion, he scrambled to remove the two remaining hubcaps. He tucked them both under his armpit and, still in a crouch, waddled back to the left side of the vehicle. There, he shoved the two hubcaps he was carrying and the screwdriver into the burlap bag, stood up, and ran back into the woods. He heard a screen door slam. Someone had come out of the house!

Arthur ran for his bike. On the way, he tripped over a tree root dropping his bag but quickly got back onto his feet, picked up the bag and got to his bicycle. Then, he heard something that was cause for comfort. A lawnmower! Someone in the house had come outside to cut the grass. While they were busy doing that, Arthur would have plenty of time to get away. He wheeled his bicycle back out onto Hulse Road and headed back to Suassa Park. Occasionally, the young boy dared to sneak a peek behind him. To his great relief, he had no pursuers.

Reaching "his" dirt path in Suassa Park, Arthur pedaled onto it and up to the designated drop off spot for his hot goods. He started to pull the hubcaps out of the burlap bag but then decided it would be better to leave them in the bag behind the fallen tree trunk. That's what Johnny had told him to do. Plus, it was better to hide an instrument of crime out in the woods than constantly have to take it out of the garage at home and risk detection.

His mission accomplished, Arthur rode his bicycle back to Twenty-one Lowell Place. There was Rex, sitting at the screen door, having loyally waited at home throughout his young master's criminal operation.

Chapter 25

For an entire week Arthur fought the urge to check the burlap bag lying in the woods. To resist that temptation, he avoided the dirt path entirely.

Since he also had been warned by Johnny Stefano not to visit his house, Arthur spent the week playing imaginary baseball games in front of his house with only Rex as a spectator, watching TV, reading comic books and riding his bike throughout Suassa Park.

***

Eight days after his first unsupervised hubcap theft, Arthur was at home watching a cartoon show on television. At least, he was trying to. He had fought off the urge all week but now had to satisfy his curiosity—and greed. With Rex, he bolted out the front door with nothing more than "I'm going out to play, Ma!" as an explanation for his exit.

In reality, Arthur wasn't going out to play. He was going out to complete an illicit business transaction.

With Rex alongside him, the youngster rode his bike up Lowell Place, made a right onto Old Post Road and then a quick left onto the dirt path. For years this path had been a haven for the youngster, providing him solace he found nowhere else. Today, for the first time, he hoped it would provide him a financial benefit, too.

Arthur pedaled his bike up to the point from which he could see the fallen tree trunk under which lay the burlap bag. Bursting with anticipation, he eagerly jumped off his bike, letting it fall to the ground. He ran over to where the tree trunk rested, and pulled out the burlap bag. The hubcaps were gone! That was a good sign, but only if they had been replaced with twenty-five cents. The youngster stuck his hand into the burlap bag and fished around in search of his reward. His hands found something hard and metallic. He grabbed it and pulled out a quarter. Though he would've been happy to get his payout in any combination of pennies, nickels and dimes, getting paid with one fat quarter signified something more official and grown up to the young boy.

Arthur shoved the quarter in his pocket. His first impulse was to search for more hubcaps waiting to be stolen. He envisioned a newfound income stream to add to his weekly allowance and his chronic pilfering from his mother's pocketbook. However, today would not be the day for a hubcap caper because he had Rex with him and everybody in the neighborhood knew to whom Rex belonged.

Instead, Arthur decided to ride his bike to the end of the dirt road. The young boy parked his bike at the edge of the bluff that overlooked the Long Island Rail Road tracks. He grabbed one of the several wooden sticks he had fashioned from tree limbs and kept stored under some brush. Then he scrambled down the hill to where the tracks lay and began playing a fantasy baseball game using his stick as a bat and rocks as baseballs. Today, his beloved Dodgers were playing the hated Yankees. To the best of his memory, the youngster attempted to reenact one of the previous season's World Series games in which the Dodgers defeated the Yankees. While Arthur was doing this, Rex, as he always did, roamed the countryside exploring and examining all around him.

The game went on for some time, interrupted only once by the passing of a train. Arthur customarily greeted trains by waving to the engineer. Typically, the engineer waved back and also blew his whistle. Today, Arthur scurried up the hill and hid behind a huge ball of dirt held together by tree limbs. He didn't want to be seen by anyone on the train. For the first time in his life, the young boy openly acknowledged what had been a slowly growing self-consciousness about his unhealthy use of the woods as an escape. From this day on, he could no longer use childlike thinking to justify spending untold hours in the woods. The woods would continue to serve as an escape from his painful life, but now that came at a price—an increasing sense of isolation and a feeling he didn't fit in anywhere else.

The train passed by. No wave to the engineer and no whistleblowing in response. Arthur rushed down the hill and resumed exactly where he'd left off. Gil Hodges was at bat and Whitey Ford was pitching.

Finally tiring, Arthur saw to it that the game ended with a Dodgers victory. He called for Rex who appeared at the top of the bluff on the south side of the tracks. Though tempted, Arthur had never once climbed the hill on that side and explored further. There was something ominous about what awaited on the other side of the tracks, even to a youngster with Arthur's bravado.

Today, perhaps because he was now twelve, Arthur decided to broaden his horizons. He shouted "Stay!" to his dog. Rex waited obediently in place on the edge of the bluff while his young master clambered up the slope to meet him.

The two then walked into the thick woods that spread out before them. About fifty yards later, they walked onto a well-worn path. Arthur turned onto the path and headed in a westerly direction. Both sides of the trail were thickly treed, creating the impression that, apart from Arthur, there was no other human life for miles.

The day was sunny and warm, with an occasional light breeze adding a dash of comfort. Since dinnertime was still hours away, Arthur dared venture on. This was territory that Rex may have very well covered during his young master's lengthy baseball contests, but it was all new for Arthur.

Continuing their walk, Rex suddenly bolted into the woods. Arthur thought nothing of it and continued on. Five minutes later and with his dog nowhere in sight, Arthur stopped.

"Here Rex! Good boy! Here Rex!" He waited for his dog to appear. The woods offered nothing but stillness, broken by the occasional chirping of a bird.

Arthur backtracked on the path and reached the spot where his dog had run into the woods. The young boy called for his dog and, again, got no response.

Arthur began to worry. His dog was not of a disobedient nature and unlikely to ignore the young boy's calls. Arthur feared Rex may have wandered so far away he was out of earshot. If so, that meant the youngster would have to sit and wait until his dog decided to come back. Not content with staying put, Arthur walked deeper into the woods with hopes of finding his dog sooner rather than later.

Then, Arthur spotted his dog—and a pair of human feet! As he got closer, the young boy saw his dog was busy sniffing the body of a man. At first glance, it appeared the man was sleeping. In a low voice, Arthur called to his dog. The youngster wanted to get out of there—quickly! Rex was having none of it. He was too engrossed in smelling the motionless body lying on the ground. Arthur inched closer and saw the man's face was swollen and discolored. His neck was covered with blood. He was fully clothed wearing a long sleeve flannel shirt, dress pants and shoes with dark socks. His black hair was matted with dried blood. Had Arthur stumbled onto the scene of a crime? Was the perpetrator still in the area? The young boy didn't want to find out. Inching even closer to the body, Arthur grabbed his dog by the collar, hoping to pull him away from the corpse.

Arthur worked up the courage to take one last look at what he was leaving behind. The youngster's eyes met the cold, blank stare of a dead man. Having paid a youngster's version of last respects, Arthur wasted no further time. He yanked his dog, reluctant to end his forensic investigation, back out onto the dirt trail. Boy and dog then broke into a sprint that didn't stop until they both had run down the south side bluff, over the tracks, and up onto the north side bluff. As Arthur scrambled to get back on his bike, he looked across the tracks to see if anyone was coming. Spotting no one, he wasn't taking any chances. He pedaled his bike as if his life depended on it, and maybe it did. While pedaling, the youngster continually turned to look behind him. There had been times in the woods Arthur's imagination had played tricks on him and he'd fled to escape what were no more than his own self-induced phantoms. Today, what the youngster was fleeing from was all too real.

At one point, while Arthur was looking behind him he rode into a low lying branch that whacked him on the back of the head. He lost his balance and fell off his bike. Impervious to the throbbing pain in his skull, the youngster quickly got back on and resumed riding as hard as he had ever ridden in his life. Boy and dog reached Old Post Road in record time. From there, they continued home at a more leisurely pace.

Reaching home, Arthur was greeted by his mother. "Well, did you have a nice bike ride?" Unnerved by what he had just seen, but uncertain what to do about it, Arthur answered with a nonchalant, "Yeah, it was okay."

"Don't forget to clean your hands, Art. We're going to eat dinner in a little bit."

"Okay, Ma."

The young boy went upstairs. After putting the quarter he'd temporarily forgotten about in with his other money, he washed his hands in the bathroom. Then, he came downstairs and watched television before eating supper. At the dinner table, the youngster was so distracted that for once he barely noticed his father sitting at arms-length from him.

After supper, the entire family was together in the living room watching *You Asked For It*. Arthur pretended to watch but, in fact, he was deep in thought. The young boy had a secret and he had to share it with someone. He couldn't tell his father and mother. His parents didn't know Arthur was going into the woods by himself, though by now his mother had her suspicions. He had begun consummating shady business deals along the dirt path. The fact that he had crossed the railroad tracks today only would make matters worse. All were reasons for the youngster not to let his parents know where he had been and what he had just seen. He didn't trust Ruth. He was sure she would go running to their parents the minute he made his disclosure to her. Liz, at home for the summer, was his safest bet. She had always stuck up for him as best anyone could in a house run by a tyrant. Plus, she was in her mid-20s. Arthur was confident anyone that old would know what to do.

To gain the opportunity to speak with her in private, Arthur challenged his older sister to a game of pool. She accepted and they both headed down to the basement. Before the first shot was taken, Arthur said, "I have to tell you something. But you have to promise you won't tell anybody else."

Liz responded jokingly, "Well, if you killed somebody, I can't promise I won't tell anybody else."

Arthur answered with a straight face. "Well, *I* didn't kill him."

Liz broke the rack and a game of Eight-all was on.

"What exactly are we talking about, anyway?"

"There's a dead man in the woods."

Liz looked at her brother and said, "Come on, be serious. Is that what you had to tell me?"

"Yup! I saw him with my own eyes, and so did Rex."

"Where exactly was this?"

"You know the dirt path?"

"The one you're not supposed to be going on?"

"Yeah. That's why you have to promise not to tell anybody. Well anyway, I went all the way over to the other side of the tracks and I was walking with Rex and then I saw these feet."

"Just feet or anything more?"

"It was a whole man."

"And this was over there in the woods? Today?"

"Yup. I saw him just before I came back home."

"Were you scared out of your wits?"

"Nah. It wasn't too bad."

"Yeah, I'll bet…. Well, if you weren't scared then I know it didn't happen. This is just something you're making up right?"

"No Liz, I promise. Scout's honor."

His sister laughed. "You're not even a Boy Scout. Now, I *really* can't believe you!"

"Stop it! I'm telling the truth, I swear!"

"Well, before I do anything I have to see the corpus delicti."

"The who?"

"Corpus delicti. That's Latin for proof of a crime. A dead body would certainly qualify. We'll tell mom and dad we're going to go for a bike ride. I don't really feel like walking over to the other side of the tracks so if you're lying just tell me right now."

"I'm not. I swear."

Liz lay her cue stick on the table. As badly as Arthur wanted his sister to see the body and believe him, he also didn't want to end a game of Eight-ball he was winning. Having sunk a few more stripes than Liz had solids, he announced, "If you quit, I win!"

"Art, you are without a doubt the world's worst sport. I want to get this dead body thing resolved before it gets too dark, so yes, I'm quitting. Go ahead and gloat!"

Arthur gloated as he followed his sister upstairs. After telling their mother they were going bike riding, Liz and Arthur set out for the scene of the crime. Rex tagged along. Once they passed the extensive patch of wild blueberries, Liz entered what was for her brand-new territory, territory that her younger brother had by now explored for years. They continued up to the bluff overlooking the train tracks. There, they parked their bikes and made their way over the tracks and up the cliff on the opposite side of the tracks. Arthur led his sister through the woods and onto the east-west trail. They headed in the same direction Arthur had just hours earlier. After walking for several minutes, Arthur said, "It's going to be right there, up ahead a little bit on the right. I remember that tree with the broken branches. The guy is just past there."

Liz and Arthur passed the tree Arthur had pointed out and walked on a bit farther.

"Well?"

Arthur looked around. "I don't get it. He was right near that tree. I'm not kidding."

"Yessiree, Bob!"

"I'm not kidding. I swear." Arthur held out his hand so his sister could see his fingers weren't crossed.

In the meantime, Rex was engaged in a feverish sniff down in one particular part of the woods. He was smelling everything within a six foot long area on the ground.

"See? Rex knows." Arthur called to his dog. "Hey Rex, where is he? Go find him!"

Rex briefly looked at his young master and then went back to smelling the ground. Eventually, Rex followed the scent back out onto the trail and then lost interest.

"You know Art. Either you have a great imagination or you're a great liar—or both."

"I swear I'm telling the truth."

"You know that story about the boy who cried wolf?"

"Yeah, I know it. But that's not me. Not this time."

"Well, maybe someone was here. Maybe he wasn't dead. Maybe after you left, he got up, dusted himself off and left."

"But he was all beat up and bloody."

"Maybe somebody left him for dead and he wasn't. All I know is there's nothing here and I want to get home in time to watch *The Steve Allen Show*."

"I don't get it. All I know is, I saw someone and he wasn't moving. Even Rex couldn't wake him up."

"Well, the only advice I can give you is maybe you shouldn't hang out in the woods so much."

With exhibit A no longer on the premises, there was nothing for Arthur and his sister to do but head back to their bikes and then on to their house.

Whether or not this mystery would forever remain unsolved, the experience left the young boy more shaken than he had been following his encounter with the old man in the woods years earlier. For several weeks Arthur traveled on the dirt path no farther than where the blueberry bushes—and the burlap bag— were located.

Just like that, stealing hubcaps had become less fear provoking than a walk in the woods.

Chapter 26

Had Arthur stumbled upon a dead body? Since that body had disappeared, the young boy could not be sure.

To take the edge off what had been a stressful few weeks, Arthur treated himself to the movies the following Saturday. He hadn't gone for almost a year and this weekend would be the perfect time to do it. The Port Jefferson Theater was offering a blockbusting double feature of *Invasion of the Body Snatchers* and *The Creature Walks Among Us*. At twelve years of age, Arthur felt he was mature enough to go to the movie house by himself. During the previous summer he'd gone to the movies alone virtually every Saturday and survived. However, he knew better than to reveal that fact to his mother. Instead, he presented his case for cinematic freedom to his mother by noting he was "going to be a seventh grader in a few months", he was "almost a teenager" and he "was pretty big at 5'1"". He finished presenting his case with a supplicating "C'mon Ma, please?"

Marguerite Berndt weighed her options. Was it worth including her husband in this conversation? Or, should she let her son go and keep it a secret between herself and her child? She opted for the latter.

"Okay, Art. You can go this Saturday, but after that we'll have to get your dad's permission to. So this will just be something between you and me, all right?"

"Yup. Good deal! Thanks, Ma!"

That Saturday Arthur left the house shortly after noon. His father had gone to work and wouldn't be home until around six o'clock. His mother impressed upon him the need to get back home before his father did. Arthur promised he would. He would keep his promise, but not without complications.

The young boy rode his bike towards downtown Port Jefferson, going as far as he could before running out of woods to hide it in. That was at the bottom of the hilly section of Brook Road. His mother had given him permission to go to the movies, but his father hadn't. He felt compelled to hide the bike just to make sure he didn't get himself—and his mother—in trouble. After ditching the bicycle, he walked the rest of the way to the theater.

Besides his allowance he had brought several of the foreign coins he'd collected from boxes of Wheaties cereal. The youngster had no qualms about adding "passing counterfeit currency" to his criminal résumé. Armed with so much money, legitimate and illegitimate, he proceeded to load up on candy from the vending machines and found himself a seat. The lights went off and on came the coming attractions. Previews of the next weekend's movie—*The Mole People*—immediately grabbed his attention. No sooner had he planned to visit the movie house the following Saturday then he remembered he'd have to get his father's permission. He convinced himself *The Mole People* probably wasn't that good anyway.

After the coming attractions there was a Woody Woodpecker cartoon, then *The Creature Walks Among Us* began. Thanks to the action on the screen and the candy he was stuffing in his mouth, Arthur had reentered that magical world he'd spent so much time in during the previous summer.

Something hit Arthur in the back of his head. Then, something hit him again. He turned around and saw that Johnny Stefano was sitting two rows behind him and had been trying to get his attention by throwing jelly beans at him. Unsure how to react, Arthur remained frozen in his seat. Johnny tried to get his attention. "Psst!" Hey kid!" Johnny got up from his seat two rows behind Arthur, climbed over the row in front of him, and sat down right behind Arthur. "Hey, it's me, your buddy."

Arthur turned around and said, "I thought I wasn't supposed to talk to you."

"You know kid, I've said it before and I'll say it again. You're pretty smart. I gotta give you credit."

A few teenagers sitting nearby voiced their complaints. "Hey, shut up!"

"Yeah. We're trying to watch the damn movie."

After telling the complainers to "Shut the fuck up!" Johnny leaned forward and whispered to Arthur, "You got your money right?"

"Yup."

"I just wanted to remind you. I'm waiting for more of—". Johnny looked around and said in an even lower voice, "I'm ready to pay you when you're ready to give me you know what. Is there anything waiting for me?"

"Not yet."

"Got anything lined up?"

Arthur answered with a noncommittal, "I think so."

"I can't be checking all the time. I'll look once a week on Sundays. But don't make me keep wasting my time."

Business conducted, Johnny hurdled the row of seats behind Arthur and sat back down next to his brother.

Arthur watched the rest of the first feature and all of the second with his eyes on the screen and his mind on money. At home, Arthur washed dishes and mowed the lawn to get an allowance. Providing hubcaps to Johnny would earn the young boy a far larger "allowance". Arthur thought of Johnny as an additional, intimidating parent, but this intimidation came with a reward.

When the second movie ended and the lights went on inside the theater, Arthur saw that Johnny and Salvatore had already left. Arthur exited the movie house and, on the way home, decided to make a quick stop at Cooper's Stationery.

He leafed through the latest issues in the comic book section. One in particular caught his eye—a 3-D version of *Batman*. Arthur had, on occasion, purchased 3-D comic books but more frequently had stolen them. The twenty-five cent price was prohibitive to a young boy of limited means. He checked his pockets and found only one thin dime. Purchasing the comic book was out of the question. Thus began the familiar battle Arthur so often fought with himself: should he forgo something he wanted due to the riskiness of getting it or should he take the risk and steal it? There was a third option: if he stole four hubcaps, he'd gain the money required to get the comic book. The young boy didn't have the patience to purchase the comic book later when he could take it right now. What if this particular *Batman* issue sold out before he got paid by Johnny? Plus, the thrill of shoplifting was a reward in itself.

With Mr. Cooper up front attending to customers, Arthur took the opportunity to stuff the comic book under his shirt. He then pretended to scan some other comic books before making a quick move to the store's front door.

"Hey, kid! Aren't you forgetting something?"

Arthur ignored the question and opened the door.

"Hey, get back here! "

The youngster knew he'd been spotted. He had to make a split-second decision. If he stayed in the store he'd be forced to fork over the comic book and maybe returning it wouldn't be enough. Maybe he'd be in big trouble. Maybe the owner would call his parents.

Arthur chose the second option—he took off running. Out on the sidewalk he made a quick left down the nearby alley. When he got to the end of it, he made another left turn and, not knowing what to do next, squatted down behind a car.

He heard rapid footsteps—someone was running out from the alley. Arthur peeked from behind the car. It was Mr. Cooper! He was bent over with hands on knees, trying to catch his breath. Severely rotund, he'd given chase and was now paying a physical price. Arthur knew he had to act quickly before Mr. Cooper caught his second wind. While his pursuer continued to wheeze, Arthur crouched down and scurried from behind the car over to a freestanding garage. Alongside it was a path that led out to Bayliss Avenue. Arthur hesitated to take it. He was a vulnerable target and didn't want to walk the streets of Port Jefferson at this particular moment. Instead, he pressed himself against the garage and listened to a conversation between Mr. Cooper and a witness. "Coop, I saw him go on that path there. It'll take him out by the firehouse. If you hurry you can catch him. How far can a young punk like that get?"

"I'll bet anything he's been robbing me blind for a while. I've had my eyes on him. Today, I finally caught him in the act. I know him. He lives up in Suassa Park, couple of blocks from me. A real troublemaker."

"With a name like Berndt whatta ya expect? Something strange about that whole family. Remember that time before the war when Berndt stood up at that meeting and said we shouldn't boycott Germany? He had some balls. Bet he loved Hitler. Fuckin' Krauts."

Arthur snuck a quick look at his adversaries. The witness turned out to be Mr. Dotson, the owner of a new book store that also had a small comic book section. Arthur had recently put Mr. Dotson's store on his mental "must-visit" list. Now, he took it off.

"Today, I finally caught him." With those words Mr. Cooper got into his car and drove back into the alley that led to Main Street. As he left, Mr. Dotson shouted, "I'll keep an eye out for him in case he comes back this way."

Arthur was trapped. He couldn't risk coming out into full view on the sidewalk along Bayliss Avenue. He also couldn't backtrack because Mr. Dotson might spot him. Arthur briefly considered the prospect of ditching the comic book and then appearing in public proclaiming his innocence. That gambit didn't appeal to him, not only because he doubted it would work, but also because he didn't want to risk losing what was now *his* comic book. The youngster stayed put, constantly switching his glance from Bayliss Avenue on his left to what he could see of the area to his right where the two men had been talking. At one point, he saw Mr. Cooper's car go by on Bayliss Avenue. The youngster again crouched down and waited. After a few minutes, he walked to the edge of the garage nearest the back of the alley and scanned the terrain for enemies. Mr. Dotson was nowhere in sight.

A car came out from the alley and into the parking area behind the stores. It was Mr. Cooper. He'd given up the chase. He parked his car, struggled up the stairs and entered the back of his store.

Sensing this was his only chance, Arthur broke into a mad fifty yard dash, totally out in the open as he ran across a batch of barren sand and onto Brook Road. He stopped and looked back at the rear of Cooper's Stationery. The youngster had a clear view and saw no human activity. Not taking anything for granted, he sprinted for another half a mile and then entered the woods where he'd left his bike. He took out the purloined comic book from under his shirt, put on the special 3D glasses and read Batman's latest adventure. When he finished, the young boy decided this was one comic book he didn't want to get caught having in his possession. He completed his journey home, leaving Batman in the woods to face the elements.

While working himself into a sweat over the possibility Mr. Cooper would call his parents, Arthur found the time to mourn what should have been a far less pressing matter, but wasn't to the young thief. In one day, thanks to the meeting between Mr. Cooper and Mr. Dotson, Arthur had lost not one, but two venues in which to commit his sleight of hand.

Arthur spent the next several days in a state of panic. When he was at home, he waited in dread for the phone to ring, fearing the caller would be Mr. Cooper. On the rare occasion the phone did ring, his anxiety shot up to an even higher level until he was sure that it wasn't Mr. Cooper calling. If Arthur went outside, he hesitated reentering the house, fearing he'd find out that Mr. Cooper had called in his absence. Whenever he heard a car engine, the young boy rushed to the window praying he wouldn't see Mr. Cooper showing up in person. Even when things outside were dead silent, the youngster occasionally peeked outside just to convince himself that Mr. Cooper hadn't snuck up on him and was sitting in his car in front of the house.

By midweek and with the threat of Mr. Cooper waning, Arthur shifted his focus to Johnny Stefano. Arthur was eager to get money any way he could, but by the same token, was scared of being caught in the process. His close shave with Mr. Cooper made him more leery of taking risks, at least for the moment. Complicating the situation was Arthur's need to please—and fear of not pleasing—Johnny. If he didn't continue to provide hubcaps, would Johnny let him retire? This was the kind of peer pressure Arthur had dealt with many times before, but had avoided for some time. Now it was back.

***

The following Saturday night, Arthur wet his bed. As was the custom, his father woke him up in the early morning hours of Sunday. He didn't lay a hand on his son, but unleashed a barrage of nonstop insults. "Jesus Christ, twelve years old and still pissing in your bed like a baby."

"What the hell's the matter with you? Are you some kind of sissy?"

"Maybe you should sleep outside at night. How would you like that?"

"You're a disgrace! An embarrassment!"

Arthur proceeded to bathe himself, wash the soiled sheets and make his bed with new sheets. However, he didn't go back to sleep. He didn't want to take the risk of wetting his bed again, so he sat at his desk.

Since he had first learned to scrawl letters, Arthur had been writing notes to himself, at first in print and later in cursive, and stashing them in his desk drawer. He wrote about anything that happened to strike him at that moment. He had held on to all the notes and now had a significant collection that spanned several years of writing: *Rex is the best dog in the world. I have to learn to spell better. I am Ronnie Simpson's best friend. Brenda waved at me on Field Day. Make sure you don't drop stuff when Dad's home. Roy Rogers is the best cowboy ever on TV. I have to pray better so I can stop wetting my bed. Duke Snider is better than Willie Mays. I wish Liz lived at home and Ruth didn't. I want a space station for next Christmas. I will stop wetting my bed when I am 10 years old.*

This early morning, Arthur added to his collection of notes. *I'm going to stop bedwetting now. I will set the alarm clock and get up before my father does and go to the bathroom.*

After writing that message to himself, Arthur counted his stash of money. He was disappointed to find he had only $1.85. The hubcaps scheme quickly flashed into his mind and then just as quickly left it. Then, Arthur played a few IQ Peg games before fatigue overcame him. He lay his head on his desk and went to sleep, feeling more confident he wouldn't wet himself if he remained in his chair.

A few hours later everyone, including a poorly rested Arthur, was up for breakfast. On Sundays the Berndt family, minus Liz, customarily attended church services. Today would be no different. Marguerite and August, the latter there only because of his wife's insistence, sat in the congregation while Ruth and Arthur, the latter also there at his mother's insistence, were in the choir loft behind the minister. In at least one respect, August and Arthur were alike. They both loathed attending church—August because he wasn't a believer, Arthur because he found it boring.

Services began at ten o'clock in the morning. As parishioners filed in, the choir greeted them with a John Wesley Psalm set to music. Following that everyone sat down, but only briefly. As soon as he had led the congregation in prayer, Reverend Mitchell asked everyone to stand and sing a selection from the hymnal.

When not singing, the choir sat quietly and, in Arthur's case, impatiently. The youngster kept looking at the church service program, mentally checking off each part of the table of events as it was completed. When it was the choir's turn to sing, Mrs. Still, the director, led them in a work by Saint-Saëns. Arthur had never learned how to read music and, when singing, essentially guessed at each note he sang. The work by Saint-Saëns did not feature the kind of melody that was easy to predict. The youngster had to take a stab in the dark at virtually every note that confronted him. Faced with such difficult music, he dug deeper into his bag of musical tricks. The young boy had developed the knack of listening closely to his fellow altos and mimicking whatever note they were singing, with an ever so slight time delay. His ruse of last resort was to simply lip-sync.

Every once in a while he earned a disapproving glance from Mrs. Still when his note arrived a bit behind schedule or not at all. Other times, when his guessing was spot on and more timely, she gave him a look of approval. Like his mother, Mrs. Still saw the singing potential in Arthur and had not yet given up on him.

When it was time for the offering, Ruth kept a close eye on her brother when the offering plate was passed around, making sure he gave up his tithe.

For Arthur, the proceedings bogged down when it came time for the sermon. While the pastor used a half hour discussing the intricate connection between John 3:16 in the New Testament and life in 1950s America, Arthur was daydreaming about the Dodger game he'd be watching on television in a few hours.

Once the sermon ended, Arthur knew he was in the home stretch. The final chore was singing a hymn as people exited the church and shook hands with the minister on the way out. After giving a performance that earned a number of smiles and grimaces from the choir director, Arthur was ready to exit the church. He had survived one more Sunday of torture.

Arthur rushed down to the basement of the church where he took off his robe. Feeling out of place surrounded by so many older choir members, Arthur wasted no time hanging up his robe and rushing up the stairs to get out on the street.

Rather than ride in the family car, Arthur preferred walking home from church. Anything to not be in his father's company. Walking also gave him an opportunity to shoplift. Now, with Cooper's Stationery off limits and the youngster still recovering from his recent near-capture, he decided it wasn't time yet to test his shoplifting skills in a new venue. He rode home in the family car and soon became the topic of conversation.

"I told you he needed reform school. If he had gone there, he wouldn't be wetting his bed anymore. They'd have shamed him out of it. Betcha."

"You'd really want your son to go to a reform school?"

"Well, look at how he's turning out. He's twelve years old. If he hasn't stopped wetting his bed by now I'm guessing he'll be doing it his whole goddamn life."

August Berndt turned around and asked his son, "Well, just when the hell do you plan on stopping it?"

"I don't know, Dad. I try."

"Well obviously you're not trying hard enough."

Marguerite had heard enough. "Let's just drop the subject and go home."

Looking in the rearview mirror at his son, August added, "Let me know when you come up with a solution. Twelve years old and still pissing in bed. Pathetic."

For the remainder of the ride, the three passengers in the car remained silent, always the wisest strategy when the man behind the wheel was worked up.

When the Berndts got home, Arthur rushed upstairs to get out of his Sunday clothes and into far more comfortable attire: T-shirt, cargo shorts and sneakers. Ruth began practicing the piano. August went to his bedroom to listen to classical music and Marguerite began preparing Sunday dinner. Liz, not a churchgoer, had ridden her bicycle to West Meadow Beach to go swimming with a friend.

By two o'clock, it was time to eat. At Marguerite's insistence, grace had to be said at Sunday dinner, though it wasn't at meals during the rest of the week. Ruth recited the Lord's Prayer and everybody began to dig into Marguerite's classic pot roast—everyone, that is, but August. He decided he needed something stronger than water with his meal. He went into the kitchen for a beer, but before he got to the refrigerator he saw something through the kitchen window.

"Goddamnit, can't you do anything right?"

Marguerite called from the dining room, "Who are you talking to Gus?"

"Your goddamn son. He didn't hang up the sheets right. They're on the ground and it looks like somebody's dog took a shit on one of them."

August grabbed a beer from the refrigerator and came back into the dining room. After sitting down, he turned to his son and said, "As soon as you're done eating, I want you to clean those sheets again—by hand!"

August Berndt had created the perfect storm. The combination of the insults he hurled at his son on the way home from church had taken their toll. Now, he had issued a directive his son wanted no part of. Arthur did not want to wash his sheets again. He absolutely loathed the idea of then having to hang them up in broad daylight. As he'd grown older, Arthur had become more self-conscious about the fact that neighbors could see what he was doing. Today was a bright sunny day and he would be an easy visual target from the four neighboring properties that had a view of the Berndts' backyard. Arthur had reached an age when such self-revelation had become an unbearable embarrassment.

There was something that ate even more at the young boy: the charade his family played going to church. To Arthur, there was something very wrong about a family that attended church like clockwork on one hand, but had no trouble humiliating one of its own members on the other. Arthur may not have known the meaning of the word hypocrisy, but he knew how it felt to be a victim of it.

Without saying a word, Arthur jumped up from his chair and walked out the front door. August let out a "What the hell?" Ruth stayed silent and Marguerite rushed to the front door. She called out, "Art, where you going?" Arthur ignored his mother's question. He was in a full sprint on Lowell Place heading for his wooded haven. The young boy didn't stop running until he'd gone fifty yards along the dirt path. From there, he walked into the woods towards a trench he'd visited many times before, the same trench where he'd had his encounter with Ernest (the "old man") several years earlier. He hadn't seen Ernest in the woods since that encounter and didn't expect to this day but didn't care if he did. He had something more pressing on his mind. He'd decided he was running away from home.

Reaching the trench, he sat down and tried to collect his thoughts. This was the first time in his life that he fully acknowledged to himself how deeply he resented his father and how alienated he felt from his entire family. He took issue with his father in particular, but felt betrayed by his mother. He considered Ruth, his parents' favorite, a mini-enemy. Liz, the closest he had to an ally, was rarely at home so he couldn't count on her.

He had every intention of running away from home, but it soon dawned on him he had nowhere to go. He had left behind a perfectly good meal and had no idea where his next one would come from. Though he had no idea what to do next, staying away from his house now became a matter of pride. If he went back home, he'd be surrendering and the humiliation he had hoped to run away from would be there to greet him in spades.

The woods had always been his friend, but he knew he couldn't live there. What if he showed up on a neighbor's doorstep? They would call his parents. He needed to get far away from Port Jefferson and Suassa Park and go somewhere where nobody knew him. But, how could he do that? He knew older kids hitchhiked, but he didn't have the courage to do that. He wished he'd taken his bicycle with him. That way he could have traveled much farther away. But, even then, what would his destination be? What if he got caught by the cops and was brought back home? For the moment, he did the only thing he was capable of doing. He sat in the trench and killed time.

Several hours passed. Arthur was feeling hunger pangs. He hadn't eaten anything since early that morning.

"Art! Art!" Liz was calling for him from the dirt path. "Hey Art, come on out!"

The young boy remained seated in the trench. He knew his sister couldn't see him from the path. He heard her calling him, but more faintly. She had proceeded riding on the path towards its end by the railroad tracks. Every "Art!" grew weaker.

Then, his sister's calls became stronger again. She was making the return trip and continued calling for her brother as she passed by him and headed back to Old Post Road. Eventually, her calls stopped. She headed back home.

Around six o'clock hunger pangs began monopolizing the young boy's thoughts. He had left the house on the spur of the moment with absolutely no plan of action or food. The shame of having to walk back through the front door at Twenty-one Lowell Place kept Arthur resolute. Though he was not dealing from a position of strength, and sensed the futility of his effort, he continued to sit...and sit...

By 7:30, the sun was setting and the youngster's need for

food was rising.

Arthur heard a rustling in the woods. Someone or something was coming towards him at a quick pace. Which old man was it? Was it "the old man" that lived in the nearby shack? Or, was it August Berndt, Arthur's old man? The young boy braced himself for either; it turned out to be neither.

Rex! The dog leapt into the trench and jumped on his pal. While he slobbered all over his young master's face, the young boy reciprocated by enthusiastically petting his best pal. Whether Rex had been let out purposely to find him or simply to do his own business, the dog had picked up the youngster's scent and quickly found him.

Now, the situation became even more complicated. Running away from home was tough enough, let alone doing it with his dog as company. He also knew he couldn't get Rex to go back home alone. He'd tried to do that on his journey to the movies and Rex would have none of it.

Arthur got up on his feet, wiped off as best he could the dirt that had accumulated on the back of his shorts and headed back out onto the path with his dog.

The walk home was made with mixed feelings. Arthur had been defeated. His protest against unfair treatment had been a failure. He consoled himself with the knowledge he would soon have something to eat. A runaway kid—like an army—can't march on an empty stomach.

A question crossed Arthur's mind, causing him to slow down his walk: how angry would his father be? Would there be an all-out assault? Should he continue to stay outside or take his chances and go home? It seemed an impossible choice. Ultimately, his stomach made the decision for him. He was starving. Then, another thought popped up in his head. Would part of his punishment for such unruly behavior be getting sent to bed without a meal? That had happened in the past.

He briefly conducted what he thought was a legitimate internal debate, but deep down he'd already made up his mind: he'd return to his house and endure the consequences. Despite any misgivings, his feet took him closer and closer to Twenty-one Lowell Place and finally up to the front door. Taking a huge breath, Arthur opened the front door and entered the house, bracing himself for whatever lay in store for him.

His entrance wasn't grand but, to Arthur's relief, it didn't feature any fireworks either. He could hear the faint sounds of his father's radio upstairs. Downstairs, the rest of the family was watching television.

Rex bolted into the living room as if to say, "Look what I found! I brought him back!" While his sisters remained silent, Marguerite said, "You must be starving. Let me put together something for you."

Nervously, Arthur asked, "Where's dad?"

"He's upstairs. Probably asleep by now. He had quite a lot to drink."

Marguerite heated up leftovers from the Sunday dinner which Arthur proceeded to gobble up.

"Art, I took care of the sheets for you."

"Thanks, Ma."

As soon as he had finished eating, Arthur went to his room and closed the door. He hoped his father would sleep so hard that night he'd be unable to get up to do a bed check in the early morning hours. His wish was granted.

That Sunday, Arthur made a desperate statement that fell on deaf ears.

Chapter 27

Arthur woke up the following morning not soaked by urine, but steeped in resentment. His act of defiance the previous day had gained him nothing other than a feeling of utter humiliation. Though the incident was never discussed again in the Berndt household, it would forever be etched in the young boy's memory.

Arthur immediately ramped up his sense of rebelliousness to new heights. Not capable of escaping jail, he'd remain a resentful prisoner and teach his keepers a lesson by wreaking as much havoc as possible. Fueled by his increased anger, the young boy couldn't wait to get started.

After breakfast, Arthur went out walking through the neighborhood. The idea of starting a fire appealed to him. He had used all of his hidden stash of matches and knew that his mother only had one box in the kitchen. If it went missing, there would be questions. He contemplated stealing matches from the local grocery store, but then something else grabbed his attention.

While wandering through Suassa Park, Arthur couldn't help but notice the variety of cars parked in front of homes. He had always looked at cars as a means of transportation; now he was looking at them as a source of revenue. If he resumed his career stealing hubcaps, not only would he make money and placate Johnny Stefano, he'd be getting away with something right under his parents' noses. This would be a troubled young boy's version of hitting the trifecta. While Arthur didn't know what a trifecta was, he did know what he was going to do next.

The youngster turned around and headed back home. Using the pretext that he was going to shoot pool, Arthur headed for the basement. Once there, he grabbed from his father's collection the same screwdriver he'd used weeks earlier. Stuffing it into his pocket, he didn't bother to go upstairs and announce his exit. Instead, he left by the basement door that opened up to the backyard. He walked to the front of the house, got on his bike and started cruising the neighborhood. Before he got very far, the youngster realized he needed the burlap bag. He retrieved it from the woods and then started his search in earnest.

Being a thief in daylight presented its own set of challenges. Arthur passed up certain cars simply because he didn't like his chances. He traveled all the way to the end of Hawthorne Street where it met California Avenue. He made a left. No longer in Suassa Park proper, he was less familiar with his surroundings. The residents in the area were also less familiar with Arthur, which meant alarm bells wouldn't be set off by his mere presence.

He pedaled along California Avenue headed towards Old Post Road. The youngster was fully prepared to go all the way to Setauket if that's what it took. He was already thinking about stealing hubcaps from more than one car. Just before reaching Old Post Road, an opportunity materialized. On his right hand side, he saw two cars parked in front of a detached garage at 3 California Avenue. This property was similar in set up to the one Arthur had visited several weeks earlier in his first hubcap stealing venture sans Johnny Stefano. Though there were no signs of life coming from the house, with two cars in the driveway the eleven-year-old assumed someone had to be inside. Hell-bent on stealing, Arthur threw caution to the wind.

He rode past the targeted cars and, rather than stash his bicycle in the woods, parked it alongside the road. The young boy sensed he might need to make a quick getaway and wanted his bike ready to roll. After walking back to the property line, Arthur got down on his belly and, burlap bag in hand, crawled from the road up to the side of one of the two vehicles. Without doing further reconnaissance, the youngster brazenly and quickly snapped off all four hubcaps. Only then did he look over to the house. Seeing no one, he removed two hubcaps from the second car. The last two, on the passenger side, would be especially challenging to heist as there was nothing but a low-lying hedge blocking the view between that side of the car and the house. Leaving the bag alongside the driver's door, he crawled over to the passenger side and, remaining on his stomach, removed the final two hubcaps. Keeping close to the ground enabled the youngster to utilize the hedges as a partial obstruction making him far less visible from the house.

Cradling both hubcaps in the crook of one arm, he crawled around the rear of the car and got back to the driver's side. He shoved the two hubcaps into the burlap bag, stood up, and ran as quickly as possible from the driveway out onto California Avenue. The young boy took a quick look at the house and saw nobody coming. He rushed for his bike, threw the burlap bag in the bike's basket, hopped on and began peddling like a mad boy. Reaching Old Post Road, he made a quick left and began heading east towards the dirt path. Every once in a while he glanced behind him. To his great relief, the road was empty.

Nearing the turn onto the dirt road, Arthur happened to glance into his rearview mirror. The boy saw a car far down Old Post Road headed his way. Panicking, he stopped and threw the burlap bag into the woods. He then proceeded to pedal past the dirt road. If the driver was chasing after him and he was confronted, Arthur was prepared to deny everything. He'd said "I didn't do it!" so many times in his life, he could proclaim it with a straight face even when he *had* done it.

Despite having ditched the hubcaps, the closer the car got, the more nervous Arthur got. He tried to convince himself he had nothing to worry about because he wasn't carrying anything that could implicate him—other than the screwdriver which was technically evidence of nothing.

The car pulled up alongside him but, just as Arthur was preparing to refute the driver's accusations, it passed him. The vehicle continued on, heading down the hilly section of Old Post Road that led to Port Jefferson.

Arthur made a U-turn and went back to the spot where he had tossed the burlap bag. He looked both ways on the road. Seeing no cars, he grabbed the burlap bag out of the woods, got back on his bike and made the quick turn onto the dirt path. He pedaled his bike to the drop-off spot and left the bag under the fallen tree.

As he rode back home, Arthur congratulated himself on making a quick fifty cents.

The risky work done, next came the part the youngster disliked the most—waiting. Since Johnny had given Arthur strict orders to stay away from him, the youngster could do nothing but impatiently anticipate his pay off.

When Arthur got home, his mother had lunch ready. "You know Art, you're very hard to keep track of. All this time I thought you were in the basement and then I see you pulling in on your bicycle. Where were you?"

"Nowhere. I was just riding around."

Grilled cheese and Campbell's Tomato Soup, one of Arthur's favorite combos, topped off a productive morning.

***

The fact that the youngster had gone out by himself twice and successfully completed a crime bolstered his confidence. For the rest of July and all of August, Arthur earned $4.75 by providing Johnny Stefano with "hot" hubcaps. During that time, the two did not speak a word to each other. On one occasion, Arthur rode by the Stefano residence and Johnny was outside cutting the grass. Acting like hardened career criminals, they knew better than to acknowledge each other.

The September 7th edition of the Port Jefferson Times reported on a recent spree of hubcap thefts in Port Jefferson (primarily occurring in Suassa Park and a nearby section of East Setauket). John Stewart, the Police Chief of the Brookhaven Town Police Department, commented: "This is a city type of crime. Unfortunately, as more people move into our area from farther west some of them bring along bad habits." Another section of the article outlined how lucrative the business can be. "It doesn't take a lot of skill to remove hubcaps and as long as people are willing to buy them, there will always be a black market. A set of hubcaps can get you anywhere from ten to seventeen dollars. The article ended with ominous words from Chief of Police Stewart: "We will be patrolling the area being targeted by the thief or thieves. We urge residents in that area to remain alert and report to us anything suspicious in nature."

"Anywhere from ten to seventeen dollars." Those numbers jumped out at Arthur. He'd been happy to get his twenty five cents. Now, he couldn't help but think that, while he was the one taking all the risks, he was helping other people get way more money than he was getting. He was even more concerned by the

fact the police were now in the picture.

He'd been instructed not to talk directly with his business partner and since he was also apprehensive about defying the older boy in person, Arthur decided to write a note and leave it in the burlap bag.

Johnny,

I don't want to do this anymore. I don't want to get caught by the police. It's in the papers.

Art

Arthur wanted to complain about his salary, but didn't have the courage. How do you demand back pay from someone who might beat you up?

Chapter 28

On September 9th, 1956, Arthur began the seventh grade. Over the years, Port Jefferson and, even more so, the surrounding area had steadily grown in population. Thus, school enrollment had increased. As a result, for the first time in the school district's history, the seventh grade had to be split into multiple homeroom classes. Unlike kindergarten through sixth grade, each seventh-grader started the day in their respective homeroom and then spent the rest of the day going to different class rooms for each academic subject they were taking. One thing Arthur noticed was that some of the kids being bused in were getting rougher and tougher looking. Especially, in his eyes, the Blacks. To Arthur, they looked bigger and older—and more dangerous—than their white counterparts. There had been only three Blacks in the entire elementary school up to this year. Now there were three in Arthur's classroom homeroom class alone.

Arthur's father had forbidden him from associating with Ronnie Simpson, a one-time classmate and black. Reinforcing his father's viewpoint was the fact that there were still no Blacks living in Suassa Park. The message Arthur received was loud and clear: the races should stick with their own kind.

Despite sensing that things were changing in his school, one custom remained unchanged. At the end of the first day of school, Arthur walked down to the Crystal Fountain and loaded up on candy purchased with stolen money. Some traditions die hard.

When he got home, Arthur changed his clothes and turned on the television. *Laurel & Hardy & Chuck* was on, but couldn't hold Arthur's attention. It had been a week since he left the note for Johnny out in the woods and he decided to take a stroll with his dog up to the dirt path. When Arthur reached his destination he pulled the burlap bag out from under the fallen tree, reached in and felt a piece of paper. When he pulled it out, he realized it was a response from Johnny.

Art,

Don't go chicken on me. You're doing a good job. Why the hell would you want to stop? Just because of some stupid newspaper article?

Your friend,

Johnny.

PS Make sure to throw this note away. Don't let anyone see it.

Johnny Stefano was contesting Arthur's proposal to liquidate their partnership. Arthur had no idea how to respond. If he continued his thievery, he feared getting into big trouble, with the police and at home. If he stopped stealing hubcaps, the youngster was afraid Johnny, his "friend", might beat him up. He might even enlist his older and bigger brother Sal in administering the punishment.

Arthur had again made the wrong kind of friend. He didn't know what to do about Johnny so, for the time being, he did nothing.

Chapter 29

As far as Arthur was concerned, for the moment the best way to deal with Johnny Stefano was to not deal with him at all. When outside in Suassa Park, the young boy kept his distance from Johnny's house. Arthur also altered his walking route to and from school. Though it took him longer to get to his destination, his new route precluded passing the high school, making it less likely he would bump into Johnny.

Because of the increased number of new students, the seventh grade in the Port Jefferson Elementary School was divided into four homeroom classes—7A, 7B, 7C, and Arthur's class, 7D. Arthur found himself amidst a group of exceptionally rowdy students, each member intent on outdoing the rest of the class to gain attention. For the most part, Arthur had always found school to be a respite from the turbulence he dealt with at home and on the street. Now, in his homeroom, he found himself surrounded by chaos. In such a perfect storm of misfits, anything might happen. Fortunately, the homeroom period lasted only twenty minutes at the start of each school day.

Mr. Heinbochel, the homeroom teacher, had little if any control over his students. He was dealing with an adolescent rogues' gallery: Sal Bono, who allegedly carried a knife. Linda Carson, a tough-looking girl who had no trouble getting into fistfights with members of either gender. Richard Clark, who had been Arthur's nemesis starting back in the second grade and had no intentions of giving up that role. The Dillard twins, Hilda and Lucy, who quickly became the class flirts. Ernest Wright, a black student who had reportedly been to a reform school. It quickly became clear his reformation hadn't been complete.

Then there was Marshall Anthony, also black, who had to be fifteen or sixteen years old but, if using size as an indicator, would pass for someone in their early 20s. Marshall had a few distinguishing characteristics. He paraded around school with a variety of ballpoint pens prominently attached and displayed in nerd-like (though nobody would dare point that out to him) fashion from the front pocket of his shirt. Whether he could actually write with any of them was uncertain. He also wore metal taps on his shoes and every school day would announce his arrival by strutting into the homeroom purposely dragging his heels to make as much metallic noise as possible. Mr. Heinbochel would send him back out into the hall with instructions to come back into the classroom quietly. Marshall would exit and reenter, making the same noise with his shoes as he had the first time. Afraid to confront a student that towered over him, Mr. Heinbochel would simply mutter, "That's better."

Taking homeroom attendance was an exercise in futility. For the first few weeks of the school year, Mr. Heinbochel called out names over the din of twenty-five shouting, unruly students. Then, admitting defeat, he resorted to silently eyeballing each student on his list while the class carried on as if he wasn't there.

Aside from his chaotic homeroom class, school remained a refuge for Arthur. Following homeroom, the rest of the school day was far more orderly. Only a handful of students from his homeroom attended each of Arthur's other classes and they were reasonably well behaved in those. Each school day, when the bell rang signaling the end of homeroom, Arthur headed for his first period class feeling he had escaped from a hurricane. No doubt Mr. Heinbochel felt likewise.

***

During the last Saturday in September Arthur found himself alone at home. His father was at work and his mother and sister had traveled to Babylon to go shopping. Arthur was watching television, but was itching to play catch with himself utilizing a rubber handball and the brick chimney in the backyard. His father had warned him not to, as the backyard had just been reseeded.

How could the youngster scratch the itch to play ball without risking his father's ire? A few times he had played catch throwing

169

the handball against the front stoop. The first time his father caught him in the act was the last time he'd done that. His father had been willing to accept some wear and tear in the backyard (only not today due to the reseeding), but never on the front lawn. Today, with his father not at home, the young boy decided to tread on the sacred front yard in the name of baseball.

Arthur went upstairs and got his glove. Then, he went outside to the garage and looked for the handball. He couldn't find it. He considered using the croquet ball, but quickly recognized it was unsuitable for a game of catch. Then, he remembered. Hidden in his bedroom, he had a brand-new baseball he had stolen from Terry's Sporting Goods. Determined to play catch, he had two choices: ride his bicycle downtown and buy or steal another handball or use the baseball he already had. He hesitated at the thought of scuffing up a brand-new baseball, but he also didn't feel like making the trek to Port Jefferson and back. Arthur opted to use his baseball. After all, if he damaged the ball throwing it at the stoop, the youngster knew where to get another one for free.

With Rex as the sole spectator, Arthur began an imaginary baseball game in his front yard. From playing in the backyard against a huge, flat chimney, Arthur had been able to hone his throwing skills so that he could usually guarantee whether the ball would come back to him in the air or on the ground. Now he had to adjust those skills, throwing at a stoop that was seven feet wide but only two feet high, featuring a single step.

Just as he created games of offense with a stick and stones on the railroad tracks, at home he created imaginary defensive games with ball and glove. When the Dodgers were in the field, Arthur made sure all kinds of miraculous catches were made. Playing as a Dodger, the youngster made several classy backhanded grabs and even one over the head with his back to the stoop à la Willie Mays in the 1954 World Series. When the opposing team was in the field, Arthur transformed himself into a butterfingers. The harder he threw the ball the more difficult the catch. Arthur made sure to throw the ball hardest when the opposing team was out in the field.

In the fourth inning of his imaginary game and with the Dodgers at bat, Arthur threw the ball as hard as he had all day. In his effort to maximize ball speed, Arthur sacrificed accuracy. The ball flew above the stoop and went crashing through one of the panes of glass in the storm door. Arthur had been expressly forbidden from playing ball in the front yard and now he would catch holy hell!

The young boy panicked. Then, he segued from a state of panic to one of self-preservation which in turn led to calculation. Fear is the mother of ingenuity. He'd fix the windowpane himself! First, he used the whisk broom to sweep up all the broken glass lying on the stoop. Then, managing not to cut himself, he carefully removed what remained of the broken pane inside its frame, adding those shards to the pile of glass he had already swept together. With the aid of a dustpan, he put all the broken glass into a paper bag. He walked to the garbage pail in the garage and buried the bag underneath other rubbish. He then used his father's tape measure to calculate the size of the replacement pane he needed to purchase.

After putting Rex back inside the house, Arthur grabbed all the money he had stored in his desk, got on his bicycle and headed for Port Jefferson. After arriving there, he went into the local hardware store. This was a place of business Arthur had never set foot in, so he wasn't greeted with suspicion. Mr. Barker, the owner, started the conversation. "What can I help you with, son?"

"Well, I need a piece of glass and something to put it in with. It's for the front door of my house."

"What's the size?"

"Eight inches long on all four sides."

"All right. A square. I can help you with that. Have a little accident?"

Though used to instinctively lying in response to such a question, Arthur didn't feel the need to do so in this case. After all, he was in the process of hopefully rectifying a problem before it would ever show up on his father's radar. No need for self-protection.

"I was playing ball in front of my house and it went through the door."

"Well, I guess that's the last time you're going to do that, right?"

"I guess so."

"Wait here a minute." Mr. Barker went into the back room. A few minutes later, he came out holding a brand-new piece of glass.

"Okay, young man. Is that it?"

"I don't know, sir. Is there anything else I need?"

"You'll need some putty. And some glazier points. You have those items?"

"Nope."

The store owner looked at Arthur skeptically. "Are you sure you can handle this job?"

"Yup. My father is gonna help me. It'll count as a project for Boy Scouts."

"Atta boy! Good for you! That's what I call learning from a mistake."

Mr. Barker put together the additional items and rang up the total, Arthur paid him and left the store armed with the keys to his salvation.

Time was now of the essence. His father would be home in a couple of hours, probably before his mom and sister would be. Arthur pedaled his bike furiously back home. He immediately got down to the task at hand, but didn't get far. He couldn't quite get the knack of inserting the new glazier points (and didn't know he had to remove the old ones), so he tried to simply putty the window into place. Not familiar with the use of putty knives, he tried to apply the putty with his fingers. He was making a mess and time was running out.

Where to turn? He couldn't go to the Sinclairs because of the ongoing feud between his father and Mrs. Sinclair. Besides, August Berndt had convinced his son that Mrs. Sinclair was crazy. He couldn't go to the Barneys because Mr. Barney, like Arthur's father, was an angry drunk. Arthur opted for his neighbors to the back—the Silkworths. Since time was crucial, instead of taking paved streets the youngster walked through his father's reseeded backyard into the Silkworths' backyard.

Like the hardware store owner, the Silkworths had never been negatively impacted by Arthur's behavior. However, thanks to their birds-eye view of the Berndts' backyard, Arthur was sure the Silkworths knew he did laundry in the wee hours of the morning. Whatever else they might know about the young boy, this was not a time to let embarrassment stop him in his tracks. Swallowing his pride, the youngster walked up to the front door and knocked.

Seconds later, the door opened and Mr. Silkworth asked, "Arthur, how can I help you?"

"Do you know how to put in window panes?"

"I think so. Why do you ask? What happened?"

"I had a little accident."

"Let me finish dinner and I'll be over. Nobody at home to help you?"

"Nope. Just me and Rex."

"Okay. I'll see you in a few minutes." Arthur wanted to cry out *I can't wait a few minutes. I'll get caught and my father will beat me up!* but those were not the kind of thoughts he could share with anyone. He would just have to anxiously wait on the front stoop at home, hoping Mr. Silkworth would show up before anyone in his own family did.

True to his word, a few minutes later Mr. Silkworth arrived, carrying a tool kit complete with putty knife. "Well, I see you bought everything you need. And you did a good cleanup job too."

Not used to getting compliments, Arthur was also not used to saying thank you. He didn't.

Mr. Silkworth got to work. As he expertly inserted the new pane of glass, he told Arthur to watch closely and described the procedure as if he was giving a tutorial to an apprentice. Arthur had trouble paying attention because his mind was solely focused on getting the job done and getting this Good Samaritan off the premises before his father got home. As desperate as the young boy was to hasten the process, he could not reveal to his neighbor why.

After Mr. Silkworth put the finishing touches on his repair job, he turned to Arthur and said, "That new putty doesn't quite match with the rest of the door. Do you have any white paint?"

"I think so. I can do that myself though." Hoping to get his neighbor off the property, Arthur fumbled in his pocket and pulled out six dollars. That was all he had to his name after his purchase at the hardware store.

"Here, sir. Is this okay?"

Mr. Silkworth laughed. "Hey, neighbors don't charge neighbors." In a hushed, understanding voice Mr. Silkworth confided, "I know you have a tough time getting along with your father. Glad to be of help here."

Arthur felt a brief flush of embarrassment. Just how much did this neighbor know? No time to dwell on that question. The last thing he wanted was for his father to pull up with anyone on the property. He remembered when his father had threatened Mr. Juska, another neighbor, with a shovel. After saying "This should do the trick," Mr. Silkworth collected his things, picked up his toolbox and headed behind the Berndt residence back to his house. Unlike Arthur, he walked on the edges of the Berndts' backyard, respecting August's lawn work.

Arthur scrutinized the front storm door. Other than the freshness of the new putty, it was as if nothing had happened.

Just then he heard a car turning off of Old Post Road onto Lowell Place. Arthur rushed inside where Rex happily greeted him. He peeked out the window and saw his mother and sister returning from shopping. The young boy turned on the television, but his viewing was distracted. He would not be able to rest until the repair job had passed the test. The fact that he had not been able to paint the fresh putty might prove to be his downfall.

Armed with packages, Marguerite and Ruth entered the house without incident. Apparently neither had noticed anything odd about the storm door.

An hour later, August Berndt was dropped off at home by a coworker. Arthur held his breath as he watched his father walk up the driveway. Instead of turning onto the flagstone walkway to come inside through the front door, August went around the side of the garage and entered the house via the basement. The youngster was swamped with an ambivalent mixture of short-term relief and long-term angst. His father hadn't seen the front door from close-up so Arthur could rest easy—at least for now. He still didn't know if he was in the clear and wouldn't until he was sure his father had eyeballed the storm door and noticed nothing.

In his sleep that night, Arthur hatched a plan. The following day was a Sunday. When his mother called for him to come downstairs for breakfast he declined and stayed in bed.

His mother went upstairs to check on him.

In a raspy voice, he said, "I don't feel good, Ma."

"What's wrong?"

"My throat hurts bad."

Marguerite went upstairs and touched her son's forehead with the palm of her hand. "Well, you're not warm."

"All I know is, my throat hurts real bad."

"You insist on running around without a jacket even when

174

the weather's starting to get cooler. It would be nice if you listened to me a little more often."

Arthur didn't answer. He acted as if it was too painful to talk. He was feigning a sore throat and giving a stellar performance.

Marguerite asked, "Do you want me to bring you some toast and eggs? Hot cereal?"

Though he was hungry, Arthur had to stick to the script. "No, Ma. It would hurt my throat too much eating that stuff."

"Well, we're going to church. I want you to stay in bed. Can I count on that?"

The youngster answered "Yup!" and added a couple of forced coughs.

"I'll have Ruth let Mrs. Still know why you couldn't make it today."

Arthur listened from his bed as the rest of the family got ready for the Sunday service. A half hour later August, Marguerite and Ruth left the house and headed out to the car. Marguerite had given her son one last reminder, "Stay in bed!"

Arthur heard the car start up and pull out of the driveway. He rushed to Ruth's room and from a window saw the car turn right onto Hawthorne Street, in the direction of Port Jefferson. No one had noticed the repair job on the front storm door.

Arthur had work to do and he had created the opportunity to do it. The young boy climbed out of bed and went downstairs. He rushed to the basement and grabbed a can of white paint and a couple of paintbrushes. He ran back upstairs and went outside onto the front stoop. He tried to pry the top off of the can of paint but it was stuck. He reentered the house to retrieve a screwdriver from the basement but instead took a butter knife out of the kitchen drawer and used that to get the lid off the can, damaging the knife in the process. Then, after stirring the paint with a paintbrush, he prepared to apply it to the new putty. He quickly realized the brush was too wide and if he used it he'd do a sloppy job that would not escape detection. He went upstairs to his room and got a very small paintbrush that he used on occasion when assembling plastic models. Back down and onto the front stoop he went. Still in his pajamas, he sat down and began methodically painting the putty on all four sides of the new window pane. Using such a small brush made the job especially tedious. Arthur used one hand to support the other hand that was holding the brush, enabling him to maintain a steady accurate stroke as he applied the white paint. When the job was finished, the youngster didn't have the luxury of admiring his handiwork. To save time, instead of cleaning the two brushes he had used, he buried them in the garbage pail along with the mangled butter knife. He forgot about the shards of glass he'd put in the pail the day before and cut his finger on one. Sucking the blood from his wounded finger, he carried the paint can back to the basement. He then took damp paper towels and, as best he could, cleaned up the older putty on the storm door so that his new paint job would be that much less noticeable.

Checking the clock, he saw that it would be at least another half hour before the rest of the family got home. Ignoring his mother's admonition to stay in bed, he made himself a bowl of cereal and turned on the television. After finishing his Wheaties, he washed and dried both the bowl and the spoon and put them away, giving the impression he'd never left his bed. Arthur went out front one more time to assess his paint job. If one looked closely, they might notice that the putty around the new pane had been freshly painted. Fortunately, the pane he had broken was near the bottom of the door and not at eye level.

Arthur went up to his bedroom and got in bed. Fifteen minutes later he heard the family car pull into the driveway. The youngster braced himself. He heard footsteps going up the walkway. First the storm door opened and then the main door. When Arthur's father, mother and sister were all inside the front door was closed. The young boy waited for a few more anxious seconds, fearing that his—and Mr. Silkworth's—handiwork had been discovered.

Marguerite said, "I'm going upstairs to check on Arthur." Arthur heard two sets of footsteps. His father was following his mother upstairs.

Conditioned by years of bedwetting, whenever Arthur was in bed and heard his father's footsteps anywhere in the house, it generated fear in the youngster. But today he was bone dry. Today's fear was brought about by a still wet paint job on a door. In Arthur's world, fear had seemingly limitless and often unlikely occasions to rear its head.

As his mother headed for his bedroom Arthur heard his father say, "I can't wait to get out of this monkey suit." Wearing a tie and jacket was just another reason August Berndt loathed church services.

Arthur sensed he was in the clear. When his mom came into the room he continued to complain of a raspy voice just to be on the safe side. After taking his temperature, Marguerite said, "You don't have a fever. That's a good thing."

"So is it okay if I get up?"

"Yes. You're just not going to go outside today."

Not being able to get outside the house—especially when his father was home—would normally be a disappointment to the youngster. But today it was a small price he was willing to pay for the thrill of getting away with something right before his father's eyes.

Arthur didn't have too many people in his life that he could count on. He would forever include Mr. Silkworth in the small group of people he could.

Chapter 30

After escaping certain death at the hands of his father for breaking a window pane, Arthur was further rewarded with several weeks of relative tranquility. Apart from the usual punishment the youngster suffered on those occasions he wet his bed, Arthur and his father had no run-ins. Except for his homeroom period, school also was uneventful and continued to be the safest place in the world for the young boy.

On the last Tuesday of October, the temporarily calm seas began to again stir up. Arthur was walking home from school. The youngster was reading a comic book he'd stolen from Anderson's Market. Since Cooper's Stationery no longer welcomed Arthur's "patronage," he'd taken an alternate route home so that he could stop by Anderson's and profit from his lower profile in that establishment. From there he began walking up Old Post Road which took him past the high school. Engrossed in the latest edition of *Plastic Man*, he was startled by a voice he instantly recognized. It was Johnny Stefano's. With his head stuck out of the passenger window of a car in the student parking lot, Johnny called to the youngster. "Hey, Artie. What the hell ya doing?"

"Nothing. I'm going home."

In a half-friendly, half-commanding voice, Johnny yelled, "Get the hell over here." Sitting alongside Johnny in the driver's seat was his brother Sal, a high school senior.

Johnny was the last person Arthur wanted to talk to, but if he ignored the older boy he knew he wouldn't get far on foot if the two older boys decided to pursue him, with or without their vehicle. Reluctantly, Arthur crossed the street and walked over to the auto in which Johnny and his brother were sitting.

Johnny reached back and opened the rear door. "Hey, hop in!"

Arthur declined the invitation and a conversation ensued during which the back door remained open and Arthur kept out of Johnny's reach.

"Hey, I checked the bag, I checked the bag a couple of times. Nuthin in it. What's up?"

"Nothing. I don't want to get in trouble."

"You're not going to get in trouble. Have you so far?"

"No, but..."

"You like money, right?"

"Yup."

"So let's make some!"

"I don't wanna get in trouble with the police."

"No shit, Sherlock. Who does? I haven't seen any cops in Suassa Park. Have you?"

"Nope. But it said in the newspaper—"

"These local yokels are all talk. They can't cover the whole territory."

Arthur worked up the courage to question the older boy. "I read in the newspapers that these hubcaps... well, people pay a lot of money for them."

"Yeah... So?"

"Well I'm only getting twenty-five cents." Arthur took a deep breath and asked, "Who's getting all the rest of the money?"

Acting as if exasperated, Johnny answered in a condescending tone. "Well, here's how business works. There is you, there's me, then there's the guy that actually sells the hubcaps. Everybody gets a piece of the pie. That's how it works."

"Well, I'm just saying. Twenty-five cents is okay but maybe I—"

"Do you have any idea what kind of risk I take? You're hiding when you do your work. I'm right out there in the open. I've got to worry about snitches a lot more than you do."

Sal interrupted. "Hey, Johnny. The kid's doing a good job. Why dontcha give him a bonus?"

"Like what?"

"I don't know. Fifty cents a cap?"

"Christ Sal! You're pretty generous with my money."

179

"Whadda ya mean 'yours'?"

Johnny answered his brother with a testy, "Alright! Alright! Ours."

Sal made a final point. "Look, he's the only kid you got. We couldn't find anybody else."

"You're right about that. Bunch of punks living out here in the sticks."

Turning to Arthur, Johnny said, "So how about it? How about if I give you fifty cents a hubcap."

"That's for each one?"

"That's what I'm talking about."

"So if I steal the four caps hubcaps I'll get two dollars?

"You're real good at math, kid."

Even with the pay raise, Arthur was hesitant. "I gotta think about it—"

"Time's up!"

Arthur's sole wish was to get away from the two boys and get home. To placate them, he mumbled a lukewarm "Okay" and began walking away from the car.

He got back out onto Old Post Road and resumed heading towards his house.

Sal started up his car, drove out of the student parking lot and swung the car onto Old Post Road heading in the same direction as Arthur was. Before passing by the youngster, Sal pulled his car alongside and Johnny said, "So when should I check the bag again?"

"I don't know. I have to be ready."

"I'll tell you what. I'll give you two weeks to get ready. Today's Tuesday. Two weeks from today, I'll be checking the bag. Don't make me waste my time. Remember, there's a lot more money in it for you now."

Arthur answered with an unenthusiastic, "Okay, Johnny."

The older boys drove off. Arthur stuffed the comic book in his back pocket. He had lost his interest in reading.

When he got home, Arthur took Rex for a walk on the dirt path. He avoided going near the burlap bag.

***

For the next several days Arthur debated what to do. He was fearful of resuming his hubcap stealing career, but at the same time afraid of what Johnny would do to him if he didn't. Added

180

to that mix was the temptation of making more money than he had ever made before. Lots of money and avoiding getting beat up by Johnny was a carrot that came with its own stick—the possibility of getting into trouble with the law and, even worse, his father.

Fate—in the form of Father Time and Mother Nature—stepped in to assist Arthur with his criminal calculation. The seasonal changing of the clocks would play a huge part in Arthur's decision-making process.

On October 28, 1956, clocks were set back an hour, ending Daylight Saving Time. That day, the sun set at 4:57 P.M. Entering the month of November, it would set sooner with every passing day.

Inspired by the earlier sunset each new day brought, Arthur hatched a plan. There was a Dodge-Plymouth dealership on Main Street in downtown Port Jefferson. It had a large group of new and used cars for sale, all sitting on an outside lot. The only security was a chain-link fence that was four feet high. Once over the fence, Arthur would be surrounded by scores of hubcaps ripe for picking. Monday to Friday the dealership closed at 6:00 P.M. Those were school days and there was no way Arthur could be out of his house after six o'clock. Saturdays the dealership closed at three o'clock when it was still light out.

Sundays the dealership was closed all day. That worked for Arthur. If he pulled off the heist in the late afternoon on a Sabbath, he'd be operating under the cover of darkness. In his mind's eye, he envisioned taking a lesser risk than he'd taken when stealing hubcaps from cars on homeowners' properties. To boot, he would make more money in one operation than he had in all his previous efforts combined.

The only challenge he saw was accounting for his whereabouts with his parents. That would take some creativity on the youngster's part. Temporarily stymied, he put his plan on hold.

Tuesday, November 13th. That was the deadline Johnny Stefano had given Arthur to produce some hubcaps. Arthur spent the day on edge, first in school and later at home where he watched television with disinterest.

Johnny, his part-friend, part-intimidator, lived just 100 yards away on Hawthorne Street. For the first time in his life, Arthur felt safer in his house than outside it. He was fairly certain Johnny wouldn't show up at Twenty-one Lowell Place, demanding Arthur explain his failure to live up to his part of the bargain. But Arthur knew *he* couldn't stay inside his house forever either. Eventually he and Johnny would meet. Add Sal Stefano, even older and bigger than his brother, to the mix and Arthur feared for his life. As fearsome as his father's beatings were, up to now he'd always survived them. These two older boys were from a rougher part of the world his father called "the jungle". They spoke English with a sinister-sounding city accent. Their father was in jail; Arthur wondered if he was there because he had killed someone. Had Johnny? Sal? August Berndt was the devil Arthur knew all too well. There was something even more frightening about dealing with devils the youngster had only recently met.

Two days later, Arthur was walking on the dirt path leading to the railroad tracks. Curiosity got the best of him. He didn't expect to find anything in the burlap bag, but he was compelled to check it anyway. To his surprise—and alarm—the young boy found a cryptic unsigned note. There was little doubt who had written it:

Cut the fucking crap. Get to work, chickenshit. I'm giving you one more week.

Let's make some money. Two bucks for every four you-know-whats.

Arthur had been on the fence about resuming his hub cap stealing. Johnny's threatening message ended the youngster's indecision. If Johnny was the stick, Christmas was the carrot. With the holiday season approaching, Arthur hoped to be the same generous gift giver he'd been the previous year. Stealing hubcaps would not only ensure his physical safety by mollifying Johnny, it would also enable him to again shower gifts on his family at Christmas time—perhaps without feeling compelled to steal his sister's money.

November 25th. A Sunday for everyone else, but D-Day for Arthur. After church and dinner, the youngster headed for the woods with Rex. There, he spent time trying to figure out how he could leave the house later that day without raising suspicions. He was already outside with his dog. Why not just stay outside, steal the hubcaps and come home in a few hours claiming he'd been searching for Rex after the dog had wandered off? That wouldn't work because he knew his dog would insist on following him to the car dealership. Plus, it was still too light out to conduct business. He thought of going home and volunteering to go downtown to buy something that his mother needed. If she didn't need anything, that plan would immediately fall flat in its face. Finally, he decided on a course of action. The young boy headed back home.

When he got inside his house, Arthur went to his mother who was in the kitchen.

"Ma, can I go over to David's house?"

"David Blake?"

"Yeah. I saw him in front of his house. His parents remodeled the basement and he's got a ping-pong table and everything down there. He's even got an official sized pool table. He asked me if I wanted to come over and play."

"Well, I'm glad. I think it would be great if you and David could get along again. But it's kind of late. You have school tomorrow."

"Come on Ma. It's not that late."

His mother glanced at the clock. "It's quarter after four. I thought it was later than that, but I guess that's 'cause it gets dark earlier now. All right. You can go but make sure you're back here at six—six thirty at the absolute latest. Don't get lost along the way."

"Okay, Ma."

Arthur went outside into the garage and got his bicycle. He grabbed two burlap bags. He wanted to take even more of them so that he could steal as many hubcaps as possible but was afraid his father might notice if too many bags were missing. Instead, he rode his bike back onto the dirt path and retrieved the burlap bag hidden there. Three full bags of hubcaps would net him a tidy sum.

Arthur pedaled his bike down Brook Road and then walked it over a sandy patch of land and onto the paved parking area behind the stores on the west side of Main Street.

With every store closed except for the delicatessen and a restaurant, the town was Sunday-quiet. Arthur leaned his bike against the rear wall of the Bohack supermarket, grabbed both burlap bags and proceeded to walk along an alley that led past the car dealership's outside car lot before ultimately ending at Main Street.

The young boy reached the parking lot filled with new and used automobiles. The car lot itself was not illuminated. The only light was coming from a nearby streetlamp. The youngster's confidence was growing. After throwing the burlap bags over the fence, Arthur quickly scaled the short chain-link fence and hopped onto the lot. He picked up the bags and went to the area of the lot farthest from the Main Street sidewalk.

Arthur got to work. He quickly separated a 1952 Studebaker from its hubcaps. Next, he moved over to 1955 Buick and did likewise. After he had filled his burlap bag chock-full of hubcaps he went back to the fence. He gently lowered his bag of goodies on the other side of the fence, careful to minimize the noise his metallic stash might make. He scaled the fence, picked up the bag and carried it over his shoulder to the rear of Bohacks. There, he placed it out of sight under a nearby staircase, just a few feet from his bicycle. He then scurried back to the car lot and filled up a second burlap bag. After hiding that one under the staircase he went back to the car lot and got to work filling up the third bag.

While removing a hubcap, the youngster heard voices and quickly ducked behind the car he was "working on", sneaking a peek out onto Main Street. A couple was walking hand-in-hand by the car lot, chatting amiably. They crossed the street and headed into the Elk Hotel and Restaurant. Silence returned, aside from the occasional passing car on Main Street.

By 5:30 P.M., the youngster had filled up the third burlap bag. He lowered it to the other side of the fence and then climbed over the fence himself. Just as he landed on the alleyway he heard someone shout, "Hey! You! What the hell ya doin'?!"

Arthur panicked. Leaving a bag full of hubcaps behind him, the young boy scrambled down the alley and over to where his bicycle sat. He dared not go back and retrieve the bag he'd left at the scene of the crime, but he grabbed the two bags from under the staircase and tried to shove them in his bicycle's basket. Both wouldn't fit so the young boy threw one bag back under the staircase and headed off with the other.

Fearing that he was being chased by someone on foot, Arthur couldn't risk pushing his bicycle through the sand to get back onto Brook Road. Instead he pedaled his bike through the alley next to Cooper's Stationery and continued his escape on the sidewalk, steering the bike with one hand while using the other hand to secure the bag of hubcaps in the bike's basket. He turned onto Bayliss Avenue and pedaled with all his might up that street's sharp incline. Then, he made a right onto Barnum Avenue. A hundred yards later he turned left onto Brook Road and headed home. When he got to the steep upgrade near Suassa Park, he dismounted his bike and began pushing it uphill. He lamented the loss of one bag of hubcaps, but calculated that with the hubcaps he had in his possession he'd made at least ten dollars.

If he hurried he'd be able to drop off the bag in the woods for Johnny to pick up and then get back home by six fifteen.

Behind him, Arthur heard the sound of an approaching vehicle. He debated whether or not to duck into the woods with his bike, but before he could make a decision the car pulled up alongside him. A police car!

"Hey son. Where you headed? Whatcha got in that bag? Looks like quite a load."

Arthur answered the first question. "I'm going home." He had no interest in answering the officer's second question.

"Just stay where you are, son." The officer exited his vehicle and approached Arthur, who was straddling his bicycle. "You mind telling me what you have in that bag?"

Arthur was suffering an emotional freefall. This wasn't like getting beaten by his father. That physical disciplining, as painful as it was, had a time limit to it and usually occurred in private. Right now, he was facing a bad situation that he sensed wasn't going to be resolved any time soon. And this one was in the public eye.

Seeing no way to lie successfully, the young boy answered with a terse, "They're hubcaps."

"Really. Mind telling me where you got them?"

Now Arthur got creative. "I found them on the ground behind Bohack's."

"I see. It's six o'clock at night on a Sunday. What are you twelve, thirteen?"

"Eleven."

"So what are you doing behind Bohack's? It's closed and just about everything else is, too."

"I was just riding my bicycle."

"I don't think that's what you were doing. And I think it would be better if you just told me the truth right now before things got worse."

Arthur gave a stab at going on offense. "Isn't it okay to pick up stuff you find on the street?"

"Yeah it is—if it's not stolen."

"I didn't steal anything."

"Well, there's a witness that says you did."

Crying had rarely worked as a means of self-protection when Arthur was younger. Now Arthur had reached a point in his life when tears no longer seemed an age-appropriate defensive strategy at all.

He opted to remain in denial. "I didn't take anything. I found these on the street."

"What would you say if we took these hubcaps and found that they happen to fit on cars that are missing hubcaps at the Dodge-Plymouth dealer?"

"I don't know."

"I bet you don't know. That would be pretty hard to explain, wouldn't it?"

"I guess so."

"Your name, son?"

Not wanting to give any more information than necessary, the young boy answered with a flat "Arthur."

"Okay Arthur. What's your last name?"

"Berndt."

"And where do you live?"

"Suassa Park."

"Oh, Suassa Park. Very interesting. They had a bunch of hubcap thefts up and around that area not that long ago. Did you have anything to do with those?"

"Nope."

"The officer headed back to his car to respond to a call. Arthur listened intently.

"This is Officer Peavy." That last name sounded familiar to the young boy but he couldn't quite place it. "Yeah, I'm talking to the perpetrator right now. Turned out to be a young kid. Name of Arthur Berndt."

Arthur heard the dispatcher say, "Oh, now there's a familiar name. (Chuckling) Don't let him out of your sight. He's got a bit of a history."

Purposely speaking loud enough so that he was sure Arthur could hear him, Officer Peavy said, "So you have the statement of that eyewitness. He saw it all, right?" Arthur paid scant attention to the rest of the conversation. He'd heard too much already.

Hanging up the car phone, Officer Peavy exited his vehicle and headed over to Arthur. The youngster switched from denying his guilt to attempting to keep his parents in the dark. He was already going to get in trouble for getting home late, but that was a price he would gladly pay if his parents never found out about this crime.

"Officer, I'm not saying I took anything, but if I say I did can I go home?"

"I don't think it's that easy. At your age there's gotta be some consequences. Plus, I understand you've got a bit of the history with us."

Arthur's desperation began to show. He was now physically trembling, not from the chilly night air but from fear. "I just don't want to get into trouble. Can I just give these back?"

"What about the other bag of hubcaps?"

"I left them back at—" Too late to shut himself up. Arthur had let the cat—and the hubcaps—out of the bag.

"All right. I'll take that as an admission of your guilt. I guess I can say you didn't resist arrest. Let me talk to the Sarge." The officer got in the car, closed the window and conducted a conversation on his phone.

After it was over, he came back to Arthur, who hadn't moved an inch.

"Well, I have good news. We tracked down the owner of the dealership. Apparently, he's willing to forget the matter as long as all the hubcaps are in good condition. There's still the matter of all those thefts around your neighborhood. Right now, the thing we definitely have to do is let your parents know. Just to make sure you don't do something like this again. Overall, I'd say you're one lucky kid."

Lucky kid? The officer didn't understand. Arthur would rather take his chances with the legal system than with his father. As far as Arthur was concerned, his luck had totally run out.

He pleaded with Officer Peavy. "Do we have to tell my parents? Isn't there anything—if the owner gets all his hubcaps back, isn't that okay?"

"Believe me, if all the hubcaps weren't retrieved, he would

187

press charges. Like I said, you should consider yourself lucky."

The police officer grabbed the bag full of hubcaps from Arthur's basket and put them in the trunk of his patrol car. Then he told Arthur, "I'm going to follow you home. I'll be right behind you. We'll let your folks know what happened and that'll be that for now. Do you want to tell me anything about those other hubcap thefts?"

"Nope. It wasn't me."

"I'm having a hard time believing you. Maybe we'll have to chat down at the station. Whadda ya think?"

Arthur remained silent. He didn't need to be read his rights. He knew anything he said could be held against him.

"You remind me of my brother when he was your age. Got into all kinds of mischief. You know what happened to him?"

"No."

"He started breaking into businesses. Finally got caught and did some jail time."

Arthur suddenly remembered where he'd heard the name Peavy before. The teenager he'd known as Four Eyes—that was his last name! Arthur was being grilled for a new crime by the brother of one of his cohorts in an old crime.

"Right now it's time to get you home. "

The policeman returned to his car. As instructed, Arthur resumed pushing his bike up Brook Road with the police officer right behind him. When the young boy got to the intersection of Hawthorne Street, he hopped on his bicycle and began pedaling. When he got to the first vacant lot, Arthur jumped off his bike and tore into the woods. As he rushed farther into the woods, he heard the squad car door slam shut. Officer Peavy was giving chase on foot!

Running in the woods made too much noise so Arthur squatted down and stayed put in an attempt to hide from his pursuer. The officer scanned his surroundings with a flashlight while calling out, "Arthur! Don't make things worse than they have to be. I don't want to have to add any charges. Show your face!"

Arthur was now lying flat on the ground, belly down, trying to control his heavy breathing, fearful it would give him away.

He heard the officer's footsteps. At first they were headed away from him, then back in his direction. Suddenly, the glare of the officer's flashlight was directly on him.

"Get up on your feet!" The officer grabbed Arthur roughly by the arm and pulled him back to the squad car.

"You act like a criminal, you'll get treated like a criminal." Officer Peavy pushed Arthur into the back seat of the car. It was the first car Arthur had ever been in that had no inside door handles for rear passengers.

"Now, where do you live?"

"I can't tell you."

"Well, I can take you home or I can take you to the police station. Which would you prefer?"

"Well, if I go to the police station can I walk home from there?"

"No! You don't get it! I'm trying to give you a break by taking you home."

Arthur didn't get it, but resentfully blurted out, "Twenty-one Lowell Place."

"Now we're getting somewhere."

Officer Peavy pulled his vehicle in front of the Berndt residence and parked it there. He let Arthur out of the back seat and the two walked up to the front stoop. Marguerite, having already heard the car, had turned on the outside light. She opened the front door and when she saw that her son was accompanied by a police officer, became faint. August Berndt caught her before she fell to the floor and assisted her onto the sofa, where she began sobbing.

"Mr. Berndt?"

"Yeah. Go ahead and tell me. What has he done now?"

"I have some good news to go along with the bad news. Your son got caught stealing hubcaps, but Mr. Chambers, you know, the owner of the Dodge-Plymouth on Main Street, isn't going to press charges."

August shot his son an angry stare and didn't bother to censor his words. "What the fuck were you doing? What the hell is wrong with you?" Arthur had no answer for either of his father's questions.

"Mr. Berndt, I completely understand your anger. I'm hopeful there won't be any formal charges pressed in this matter. But the dispatcher was telling me Arthur has a bit of a history with the legal system so I felt the best thing was to make sure that you folks found out about this."

From the sofa and in between sobs, Marguerite said, "Thank

189

you, officer."

His eyes blazing with anger, August simply gave the officer a nod of the head. "Years ago I wanted him in a reform school, but that never happened. This just proves to me I was right."

"Well, hopefully this'll be the lesson he needed and he'll grow out of this kind of stuff."

"Yeah, well we've been waiting for him to grow out of this kind of stuff since he was born."

Fearing that at any moment the policeman would bring up the subject of the large number of unsolved hubcap thefts in the neighborhood, Arthur felt a welcome measure of relief hearing his captor's next words.

"Again, I'm Officer Peavy. If you have any further questions about this incident don't hesitate to give me a call. As of now, I'm hopeful the matter's closed and I'm leaving him in your hands."

Though he was being released from police custody, Arthur had no time to savor Officer Peavy's departure. The policeman was handing the young boy over to a fuming father.

As the patrol car drove off into the cool autumn night, things began heating up inside the Berndt residence. Ruth, who had been listening from upstairs at the foot of the staircase, went back into her room seeking shelter from the impending storm.

Marguerite remained on the sofa, disappointment and stress shaping the drawn expression on her face. Arthur and August Berndt stood just a few feet apart. Familiar with the drill, the young boy expected a tongue-lashing followed by a belt lashing.

"So, who put you up to this? Hanging out with Stanton again?"

"No."

"So who the hell was it? You certainly weren't going to sell those goddamn hubcaps by yourself."

Determined to keep Johnny Stefano out of the picture, Arthur lied. "I read about it in the newspaper."

Marguerite blurted out, "Oh my God! That article in the Times a couple of weeks ago."

With a mixture of sarcasm and skepticism, August asked his son, "So, because you read an article in the newspaper you go out and break the law?"

Arthur couldn't fully explain his actions—even to himself. He offered what he thought was his best defense. "I thought I'd get money to buy everyone Christmas presents."

Answering his own question, August correctly concluded, "So, instead of stealing from your sister you stole from somebody else."

Arthur had no response. He knew better than to counter his father when the latter had already made his mind up.

August Berndt was not acting in character. Normally, by this time he'd have been administering a beating. Instead, he'd only been engaging in a verbal assault. Surely now August would literally take matters into his hands. But instead of telling his wife to leave the living room and then administering a beating on his son, August himself exited. Arthur assumed his father was getting some kind of weapon. The memory of being chased by his father brandishing a fireplace poker suddenly came to Arthur's mind. It quickly vanished when August came back to the living room with an open can of beer. He sat in his recliner, poured the beer into an already used glass and resumed the drinking that had been interrupted by Officer Peavy's visit.

Arthur wanted more than anything to go upstairs to his room but wasn't sure how his father would react if he attempted to. An odd silence pervaded the room. Marguerite, who remained seated on the sofa, began cross stitching. As he continued drinking, August began perusing the newspaper. That left Arthur still standing by himself, frozen in place and not knowing what to say or do.

Marguerite broke the ice. "Art, you've got school tomorrow. Why don't you go upstairs and go to bed?"

Out of the corner of his eye, the young boy saw his father was engrossed in whatever he was reading in the newspaper. Sensing it was best to say nothing, he followed his mother's instructions and headed up the staircase and then into his bedroom. From there he listened intently, hoping to hear whatever his parents said downstairs. His fate was on the line.

Marguerite spoke first. "Gus, I'm so relieved by the way you handled the situation. "

"Well, make no mistake. I'm pissed off at him." August took a swig of beer. "But I have to admit...drinking beer does take the edge off."

"It puts me to sleep. Speaking of which, I'm exhausted."

"I'm going to stay up a while and try to figure out what to do with my goddamn son. If he keeps this up you know someday the cops won't be bringing him home, they'll be taking him to jail."

191

"I know, I know. Don't think I don't worry about it. I keep thinking he'll grow out of it. He seems to do so much better in school than out of it."

"You know his grades aren't as good as they should be."

"I was talking more about his behavior. It seems like he's a different person in school."

"Thank God for Ruth, that's all I can say. I guess when it comes to kids you have to take the good with the bad."

Marguerite got up, went over to her husband and surprised him with a kiss on the cheek. "Tonight you made me proud to be your wife. You shouldn't let your son get you down. I'm still trying to get him interested in some kind of activity that would keep him busy."

"You know, enough about him. I'm going to watch the rest of *The Ed Sullivan Show*."

With that, August got up and turned on the television while Marguerite went upstairs to bed.

Later that night, August Berndt barged into his son's bedroom and discovered he'd wet the bed. The beating Arthur had eluded earlier in the evening finally found its mark.

Chapter 31

The following morning Arthur was back in school. He sat at his homeroom desk, so deep in thought he was oblivious to the chaos going on around him.

The young boy had to make a decision: he knew the police didn't have all the hubcaps he'd taken. A third of the stolen goods were in the burlap bag he had tossed under the staircase behind the butcher shop. If he turned those over to the police, he'd most likely be in the clear legally. But then, he'd have to deal with the Stefano brothers. It was a tough decision and one that the fear of his father helped him make. If he gave the bag to Johnny Stefano he'd make money, but he'd have to continue dealing with the legal system and that would also mean he'd have to continue dealing with his father's anger. The previous night, his father hadn't hit him after he'd come home escorted by a policeman. Had August Berndt changed his ways? Arthur doubted it. He attributed his father's temporary lenient behavior to beer consumption, which often put the elder Berndt into a short-lived sweet spot mentally. The physical punishment Arthur had received later that night for wetting the bed was much more in keeping with his father's M.O.

If he turned over the remaining bag of hubcaps to the authorities, he'd most likely avoid any further legal consequences, which would also keep him out of his father's clutches—at least with regard to this matter. However, he'd not only make no money but he'd have to explain himself to Johnny Stefano.

Ultimately, the fear of physical pain took precedence over fear of the legal system or financial loss. Which to risk: a certain beating from his father or a possible pummeling from a sketchy neighbor.

Arthur made up his mind. When the bell rang, like all the other students in his class Arthur got up and headed out of the homeroom. Unlike all the other students, instead of going to his first period class Arthur headed out the exit door and headed straight for the Suffolk County Police Department station on East Main Street.

Before he got there, he decided to make a detour. He had to make sure *all* the stolen goods were returned to the authorities before the owner of the Dodge-Plymouth dealership made the youngster's life even more miserably complicated than it already was. From Main Street he walked into the same alley he'd visited the night before. Reaching the end of it, he walked over to the staircase under which he'd left the bag of hubcaps. When he got there, he couldn't find it. He combed through the little bit of brush under the stairs, but there was no doubt—the bag of hubcaps was gone! The young boy panicked. Now he was facing the worst possible scenario: legal problems and possibly two beatings, with no financial gain to ease the pain.

Arthur ran back to school. He hurried to his locker to get his math textbook for his second period class. He'd have to come up with an excuse to explain his absence during the first period when he showed up for that class tomorrow. Right now, that was the least of his problems.

For the rest of the school day, all Arthur could do was to mentally push back at the walls that were closing in on him.

While walking home from school, the pressure got the best of him. He had to sit down on a rock to catch his breath. His forehead and armpits were drenched with sweat. His heart was pumping furiously. When the tension subsided to a more manageable level, he resumed his journey towards his house. His thoughts condensed into a single question: whom would he have to deal with first—the law (and then his father!) or the Stefano brothers?

Arthur was the first person in his family to get home that day. He arrived at 3:15 P.M. The young boy decided he'd wander in the woods with his dog. As he was letting Rex out the front door, the telephone rang. Arthur went to the dining room, and picked up the phone. The youngster answered with a cautious "Hello."

194

"This is Officer Peavy. Is that you, Arthur?"

"Yes sir."

"I'm very disappointed. I was hoping you were telling me the truth."

"I did, sir."

"Well, you certainly didn't tell me about the bag of hubcaps under the staircase, did you?"

"Oh, well I forgot about them. I was scared when you stopped me. I remembered them today and I went to get them to bring them in to you."

"Yeah, I'm sure that's what you were doing. The butcher found them this morning and turned them into us. Technically, we've got all the hubcaps and they are in good shape. But I don't like the fact that you were holding out on me. You know, I was talking to my brother, the guy you know as Four Eyes..."

Arthur's face turned crimson. This officer and his brother had talked about him! Arthur worked hard to keep his life a secret, desperate to avoid being the topic of anyone's conversation.

"...he said I should give you a break. I don't know..."

Arthur had been so engrossed in the conversation he hadn't heard his mother pull into the driveway. She entered the house and found her son talking on the phone.

"Who are you talking to?"

"Oh, it's just somebody."

On the other end of the line Officer Peavy asked, "Is that your mother?"

"Yeah."

"Put her on the line. I have to let her know what happened."

Arthur did as told and handed the phone to his mother. He lingered nearby, out of curiosity and fear.

"Mrs. Berndt. This is Officer Peavy."

"Hello. How can I help you?"

"I just wanted to relay some information to you. We did get all the hubcaps. They're in good condition and the owner is not going to press charges."

"Oh, thank God."

"I should let you know that your son wasn't totally honest. Some of the hubcaps were turned in by Jack Williamson, the owner of the butcher shop. They were found in back of his store. Your son says he forgot about them, but I doubt it. I just think you have to keep a real close eye on him. He's heading into delinquent territory."

"Oh, we are very concerned."

After an awkward silence the officer continued. "Mrs. Berndt, can I ask you this? Does your son have any interests, you know hobbies, sports?"

"Well, he tends to stay by himself and that's something we've been working on. I was hoping at one time to get him into Cub Scouts but he's too old for that and he doesn't show any interest in joining Boy Scouts."

"What about the P.A.L.?"

"What's that?"

"It's an organization sponsored by the police that gets kids involved in playing ball games, you know, like baseball, basketball and so on. It'd keep your son busy."

"That sounds very interesting. Arthur loves baseball on TV and is constantly playing games of catch in our yard. He loves gym class at school. That might be something that would be very good for him."

"Do you have a pen and paper handy?"

"Yes."

"Let me give you a phone number. PO3–5555. That's PO3-5555. They'll help you get the ball rolling. You know, I've seen some kid kids that I just knew were going to be lost causes. I don't know if Arthur is there yet, but he's working on it. The older he gets, the greater the consequences for lawbreaking. I could make an issue out of him not being 100% honest with me last night. By the way, I didn't tell you this yesterday but he *did* run away from me. So there's a few charges that could be made. He gets a break this time, but that's it as far as I'm concerned."

"Thank you, sir. I completely understand. And I'll call that number you gave me."

"Okay ma'am. Nice talking with you. Hopefully the next time—if there is the next time—we'll be talking about how well Arthur is doing."

"I hope the same."

After hanging up the phone, Marguerite turned to her son and said, "You are fortunate, very fortunate that this officer is such a nice man. Apparently, you weren't totally forthcoming with him. Because of him, it looks like you're not going to be in any legal trouble as a result of your nonsense. Just what were you

196

going to do with those hubcaps, may I ask?"

"Well, I guess I was going to sell them to get money for Christmas."

"There's that 'ill-gotten goods' thing again. We talked about that. You have to learn there is a correct way to earn money. I'm just curious. Who would you sell them to?"

His mother was doing too much probing so he answered with a simple "I don't know. Somebody. I guess I didn't figure that part out."

"Well, now you won't have to. There was a lot of friction between you and your sister over what happened last Christmas. I admire your wish to be a gift giver. However, everything has its limits. You buy what you can with your allowance you've saved and any money you've gotten from raking the neighbors' leaves. Nobody in this family expects you to spend any more than you have."

"Are you going to tell dad? You know, about the other bag of hubcaps?"

"Well, part of me says I should, but why throw fuel on the fire? Arthur, do you realize how difficult you make things for me and your father?"

"Yeah, I guess so."

"You know, Officer Peavy made a very good point. You're getting to an age where bad behavior leads to more serious consequences. You understand that, right?"

"Yeah, I do Ma."

"He mentioned something called the P.A.L. I think he called it the Police Athletic League or something like that. It might be just the thing for you. I'm going to look into it."

"Ma, can I go out with Rex?"

"I suppose so. Get back here around 5:30."

Eager to be free, Arthur shot out the front door where he found Rex waiting for him on the stoop. The two then headed up Lowell Place, their destination the woods.

While walking on the dirt path, Arthur assessed his current situation. He was in the clear with the law and with his father, if his mother kept her conversation with Officer Peavy to herself. Unfortunately, he wouldn't see the big payday he had hoped for. Of much greater concern was how he would handle Johnny Stefano or, more to the point, how Johnny Stefano would handle him.

197

Chapter 32

Typically, after Arthur had gotten in trouble for something he did outside the house, the Berndt family was on edge more than it customarily was. That was the case following the young boy's hubcap venture. For several days, everyone else in the family made an extra effort to not do or say anything that might touch off the head of the family. What was normally a house of few words rendered itself virtually mute. As he did so often, August Berndt brought the silence to an end by cracking a joke. His unexpected and uncommon stab at levity signaled that the coast was relatively clear—for the time being.

This particular cease-fire in the Berndt household was especially timely, coming as it did at the beginning of the Christmas season, the one time of the year Arthur and his family lived in quasi-normalcy.

Arthur lost out on the money he'd hoped to gain from his final theft of hubcaps. Due to the fact Ruth kept her money in a far more secure piggy bank, stealing money from his sister was not an option. For this year's Christmas shopping, he would have to content himself with spending only money he earned legitimately.

As for Arthur Berndt and Johnny Stefano, their paths had not physically crossed since that meeting outside the high school back in October. Since he had received that threatening note from Johnny, Arthur had not dared to check the burlap bag alongside the dirt path to see if there were any follow-up messages from his one-time partner. What he didn't know wouldn't hurt him—or would it?

For the next few weeks Arthur dedicated himself to purchasing the few gifts he could for family members and to enjoying the annual Christmas spirit that helped lighten the load of living at Twenty-one Lowell Place.

School also was uneventful in the month of December, except for Arthur's homeroom. One day two students got into a fight that required three teachers to break up. A few days later, Hilda and Lucy came to school wearing matching low-cut sweaters and were sent home. Two days before Christmas vacation began, Mr. Heinbochel let out a "Damn!" as he sat down at his desk. Such language was out of character for the teacher. He got up, groped at the seat of his trousers and pulled out a tack. "Who's responsible for this?" Though all twenty-seven students knew Marshall Anthony was the culprit, no one responded to the teacher's question. Mr. Heinbochel threatened to give those same twenty-seven students detention if he didn't get an answer, but backed off. He realized that having to sit with his unruly homeroom class any longer than the one period he was required to would have inflicted more punishment on him than the tack had.

When school ended early on Friday, December 21st, Christmas vacation began. Time off from school was always a mixed blessing for Arthur, even during the Christmas season. Like any child, he enjoyed the reprieve from school work, but, unlike most of his peers, he was not enthusiastic about spending more time at home.

While leaving the school at twelve noon, Arthur chucked into a trash bin the box of candy "Santa Claus" (a.k.a. Mr. Jackson, the new janitor) had given him, just as he had to each student in school that day. That candy was simply not up to Arthur standards and, with that in mind, he headed to the Crystal Fountain to purchase some higher caliber sweets. He came out of that establishment twenty-five cents poorer in money, but twenty-five cents richer in sugar, artificial flavors and artificial colors. He decided to start ingesting Candy Buttons as he continued his walk home. The youngster became so engrossed in making sure his mouth didn't miss a single button he missed his turn onto Bayliss Avenue. Instead, he absent-mindedly proceeded along Main Street, oblivious to the world around him.

"Hey, punk! What are you doing, punk?!"

The unfriendly greeting instantly got Arthur's attention. He saw Sal Stefano leaning out the driver-side window of his car. Arthur instinctively sought shelter by entering the closest store, Woodfield's, a men's apparel shop. He walked in and immediately felt like a fish out of water. This was a store that offered clothing for adult men. Since it was just days before Christmas, the store was quite busy. Arthur pretended to be looking over possible purchases.

"Can I help you with something?" The store clerk had come over to assist the youngster. "You here buying something for your dad?"

"Not exactly. I'd have to come back with more money. Is it okay if I see what you have?"

"Certainly. Just give a holler if you have any questions."

Arthur had already seen that the prices were way out of his shopping range, but he was stalling for time so he pretended to be seriously looking over the merchandise. He saw that there was a rear exit to the store and decided that leaving the store via the rear exit was safer than coming back out onto Main Street. As he headed for the rear exit door, the same store clerk asked, "Did you see anything you like?"

"Yeah, lots of stuff. I'll be back."

"Great. Just ask for Jack. That's me. We close at nine today."

"Okay."

Arthur left the store and came out into a rear parking lot used by customers visiting several stores that sat along the west side of Main Street. To his relief, the young boy didn't see Sal's 1947 Plymouth. But he was still faced with the task of getting from downtown Port Jefferson to Twenty-one Lowell Place without incident. He decided to avoid streets at all costs. This meant laboriously making his way through vacant lots and surreptitiously trespassing through backyards. Reaching Barnum Avenue, he gave a quick look in each direction and then made a mad dash across the thoroughfare. Reaching the other side of the street, he continued his undercover walk home.

When Arthur reached the lower of the two high school athletic fields, he climbed over a fence and began walking across the football field. When there were no sports activities going on, both fields were blocked to vehicular traffic. Feeling he was in a safety zone, the youngster scaled a hill and came out onto the upper field. He continued his journey and ultimately reached the intersection of Brook Road and Emerson Place. He was so close to home yet so far. If he went up Brook Road he might be spotted by the Stefano brothers and he also might have to deal with Tar, a dog so nasty he was probably itching for a rematch since Arthur had escaped his jaws of death the previous year. If he headed onto Emerson Place he'd also be putting himself out in the open. However, he'd only have to walk on Emerson Place for about fifty yards before he could duck into the woods and walk the rest of the way home hidden by foliage, to the extent it existed in late December. Arthur opted for the latter strategy.

He climbed over a fence and came out onto Brook Road. He took a quick look up and down the street. The coast was clear, so he ran across Brook Road and onto Emerson Place. After passing two houses on his left he ducked into the woods. He briefly stopped to catch his breath and then resumed walking at a normal pace, filled with the comforting optimism that he was home free. It proved to be short-lived.

Arthur heard a car behind him on Emerson Place come to a screeching halt. Car doors opened and quickly slammed shut. Then he heard the sound of feet rushing up behind him. Someone shouted, "Get 'im!" It was Johnny Stefano!

Arthur started running for his life. He was being pursued in the same woods in which, years earlier, he'd been chased and collared by an angry motorist whose rear window he'd shattered with a rock. Now, he was in danger of being trapped in those woods by two thuggish teenagers that threatened to mete out a much darker punishment. As desperate as he'd ever been in his life, Arthur pleaded with God to let him make it home. Arthur's house of horrors had suddenly become his only safe haven.

From behind him Johnny shouted, "Get the fucker!"

Was there any chance Arthur could make it to his house unscathed? Maybe, but, in a sudden change of heart, he decided he didn't want to find out. What if his father was home? To Arthur, it was critical that his father and Johnny Stefano never crossed paths. Johnny Stefano would be an embarrassment to the young boy in front of his father; August Berndt would be an even greater embarrassment to the young boy in front of Johnny Stefano.

Arthur slowed his pace, allowing Sal to tackle him by his ankles. The older boy got back on his feet but Arthur turned around and remained on the ground, in a submissive position.

Johnny caught up with the two other boys and asked in an unfriendly tone, "Where the hell were you running too, hotshot?"

"I don't know. I was going home."

"Aren't we friends anymore? Don't you want to talk to us?"

"It's not that. I just don't want to steal hubcaps anymore."

"That's not what you promised me. Remember?"

"I did. I tried, but I got caught. "

"Yeah, right."

"I swear."

"You shouldn't swear. You'll go to hell." The two older boys chuckled.

"I really did. It was at the Dodge-Plymouth downtown."

"You mean Chambers?"

"Yeah. That's the place."

"What a fucking asshole you are. That's one of the places we sell to!"

Johnny looked at his brother. "Can you imagine if we had showed up at his place trying to sell him some of his own hubcaps? This little punk really almost screwed things up big time."

Johnny turned back to Arthur who remained on the ground. "You know, you're as stupid as you look. I changed my mind. I don't want to do business with you. You can't be trusted. You don't have the street smarts. And you know what, I never liked the way you tried to shake me down for more money."

"Johnny, I did my best. But now the police follow me everywhere." That last statement was a lie, but Arthur figured he'd say anything he could to make himself appear too hot to do business with. He hoped Johnny would be as eager to end their relationship as he was.

"You know little kid, you're a stupid jerk. There's just one thing..." Johnny gave a knowing look to his brother. "When anyone ends an association with the Stefano brothers, there's a price to pay."

Rather than say anything, Arthur thought it better to wait for a bill he was in no hurry to receive. He didn't have to wait long.

Johnny gave Arthur a swift kick in the ribs. "Get up on your feet, squirt!" The young boy grimaced in pain. He took another kick and then struggled back to his feet. Sal assaulted him with a series of rapid-fire punches in the stomach and then an overhand right to the solar plexus. Arthur temporarily lost his breath and became nauseated. Johnny took over and, after slapping Arthur several times in the face, kneed him in the groin. The youngster experienced a pain unlike any other he had experienced up to that point in his life.

Johnny stepped back and let his older brother take over. Sal let go with a right cross that landed directly on the bridge of Arthur's nose. Crack! Blood began to trickle out of one nostril. Arthur fell back to the ground. Sal fell on top of him and raised his fist, ready to deliver a knockout punch. Before he could, Johnny grabbed his brother's arm. "Hey, man. I think that's enough. We don't want to kill the kid. Or do we?"

The older brother asked, "I dunno. Whadda ya think?"

Fearing for his life was nothing new for Arthur but that didn't make it any easier to deal with. The youngster lay pinned to the ground under Sal's 225 pounds while his fate was being decided.

Johnny smirked. "Hey, I'm too young to get the electric chair. This asshole ain't worth it."

Sal responded, "Yeah, I guess you're right. Damn, I was just getting warmed up."

Sal got off Arthur, allowing the young boy to sit up. Johnny squatted down and got eyeball-to-eyeball with Arthur. "Okay little boy. You can go home to mommy now. If you tell mommy and daddy we did this, you won't be so lucky the next time I see you. Got it?"

"Yes."

The two older boys turned around and walked back out onto Emerson Place where they'd left their car. Arthur woozily got to his feet and stood alone in the woods, licking his wounds. Though his ribs and chest still hurt him, it was his nose that would give him away when he got home. It was broken.

Arthur stumbled through the woods until he came out at the intersection of Hawthorne and Lowell Place. The young boy was the first to get home that day. His fear that his father and Johnny might have met had been unfounded. He realized he should have kept running. A lesson learned, but too late.

The youngster immediately rushed upstairs to examine the damages to his face in the bathroom mirror. He saw a swollen nose, a partially closed left eyelid and blood that had trickled out of one nostril.

Arthur's major concern was not the pain, but how he would

explain his condition to his parents. He had to come up with an alibi that didn't involve the Stefano brothers. His first thought was that he had walked into a door that opened on him. But that would mean there were witnesses and he wouldn't be able to produce any. He finally decided on a story: he had been so absorbed reading a comic book he just bought that he walked into a telephone pole on Main Street. The youngster strained his imagination to come up with an alternative explanation for his physical condition, but nothing better came to mind, so he decided to stick with this one.

Arthur heard the front door downstairs open up. Ruth had come home from school. This would be his alibi's first test.

Arthur walked out of the bathroom and came downstairs. Ruth took one look at him and said, "What happened to you?"

"I was walking on the sidewalk and accidentally walked into a telephone pole."

"You've got to be kidding. No, I guess you're not. You should go to the hospital."

"Nah. It's not that bad."

"Betcha mom takes you to the doctor or something."

"I'll be okay in a few days."

"You're nuts." A car pulled into the driveway. "Well, here comes mom now."

Arthur steeled his nerves. Getting his fabricated story past his mother was far more challenging and critical than getting it past his sister.

The minute Marguerite Berndt entered the house and saw her son she exclaimed, "Oh my God! What happened?"

Arthur repeated his script. "I bought a new comic book and I was busy reading it and walked into a telephone pole."

"Well, I'm calling Dr. Mills right now. He's got to take a look at that. You might have a broken nose."

"It's no big deal." Physically, the young boy was still in discomfort. Emotionally, he was relieved to see that his mother was not questioning his story.

Marguerite made a phone call to Dr. Mills. After explaining her son's emergency situation, the doctor decided he would see Arthur that afternoon.

At three o'clock Marguerite and Arthur arrived at Dr. Mills' office on Prospect Street. Arthur was the last patient of the day and was ushered in after a brief wait.

The normally reserved physician took one look at his young patient and exclaimed, "Wow. Who got mad at you!?"

Just a common expression uttered by the doctor, but as far as Arthur was concerned the question came too close to the truth. The youngster answered defiantly, "No one!"

"O.K. I believe you, son. So what happened?"

"I was walking along Main Street reading a comic book and I walked into a telephone pole."

Dr. Mills was able to stifle what would have been an unprofessional chuckle and replaced it with an "Ouch!" "Well, they say you should look before you leap. Perhaps you should look before you read." The doctor's attempt at humor fell flat on its face.

Dr. Mills examined Arthur's swollen and partially closed left eye. Then, he washed away dried blood under the left nostril. After his examination he suspected that Arthur might have broken his nose. In reality, someone else had, but that was Arthur's secret.

Dr. Mills turned to Marguerite and said, "I'm going to take some X-rays. Just to rule in or rule out a fracture."

X-rays showed a nondisplaced fracture. This required no medical treatment, simply time to heal.

"So Arthur, do you hurt anywhere else?"

"Nope." The slightest movement on Arthur's part and his right rib cage exploded with pain. The young boy didn't want to let anyone know about that part of his injuries because he feared it would make his account of what happened less credible.

The doctor directed his next remark jokingly to Arthur. "I have to say Arthur you're the first patient I've ever had that broke his nose while reading." Arthur didn't find the statement any funnier than the doctor's earlier stab at humor, but far more importantly to him, that made two adults who were buying his alibi.

The visit over, mother and son headed out of the doctor's office and back home.

Later in the day August Berndt walked in the door, took one look at his son and said, "What the hell happened to you?"

"I walked into a telephone pole."

"Come on. Only drunks walk into telephone poles. What really happened?"

"I was reading and lost track of where I was going."

"You look like you spent ten rounds in the ring with Rocky Marciano. I guess you realize now it's dangerous to walk and read at the same time. I've heard it all. Now, I've heard everything!"

To Arthur's relief, his father dropped the subject. To his dismay, his mother took up the gauntlet. "I took him to Dr. Mills. He has a broken nose, but it doesn't have to be set. " Turning to her son, she added, "I'm still having trouble picturing this actually happening. Whereabouts were you?"

"I was walking on the sidewalk on Main Street getting near Bayliss Avenue." Arthur had no idea where the nearest telephone pole was in that area. All he could do was hope there was one, just in case his parents checked the scene of the "accident". Arthur spent much of his life covering his tracks.

Marguerite reminded her son that the doctor said it would take several weeks for the nose to heal and that meant, for safety's sake, the young boy's outdoors activities would be severely limited. In essence, he was quarantined at home until school began the following January.

Chapter 33

For Arthur, Christmastime in 1957 was quite different from the previous year's. He abstained from stealing from his sister Ruth and, as a result, he spent far less lavishly on family members than he had the year before; he also endured a recovery from painful injuries throughout the holiday season. That meant having to spend much more time trapped inside his house. All in all, a Christmas not worth remembering.

Had Arthur's ribs been fractured or bruised by the Stefano brothers? No one, including Arthur, would ever know because the youngster gutted it out until the pain finally subsided weeks after his pummeling. During the recovery period, pain frequently and unexpectedly shot through his rib area. Arthur did his best to stifle any verbal or facial expressions of pain in front of family members. To make his cover-up easier, Arthur spent vast amounts of time in his room, where he could hurt and grimace in privacy.

There was one temporary benefit to the rib pain: at night when Arthur was sleeping, his slightest turn would provoke shooting pain that would jolt him out of his sleep. Awakened, he would take the opportunity to go to the bathroom. As a result, the youngster set a lifetime record for consecutive days without wetting the bed. That string of victories would end on January 8th.

By the time the holidays were over and Arthur had returned to school, his nose was back to its normal size and his eyelid was no longer swollen. When asked by fellow students, Arthur attributed the remaining skin discoloration to getting hit in the eye with a football. He looked presentable enough not to warrant any further probing questions. For that he was immensely grateful because he could all too easily imagine the ridicule he would have suffered if he'd been forced to utilize his made-up telephone pole story. As for revealing the real cause of his injuries, that was a dark tale the young boy would never tell.

#

As one set of physical ailments healed, another health issue was making itself more noticeable. Arthur's deteriorating vision had begun to impact his studies, most noticeably in English class. Every school day the English teacher, Mr. Bangs, wrote vocabulary words on the board for his students to copy down. As homework, they were to look up and write down each word's definition. These assignments were handed in and graded. Arthur was having difficulty seeing the board but, being self-conscious about that, he didn't ask to be moved closer to the front of the room. Instead, with squinting eyes, he attempted to decipher Mr. Bangs' writing. Sometimes his efforts were successful and sometimes they weren't. Consequently, the work he was turning in was getting sloppier, as his stabs at some words were incorrect, while others he gave up trying to decipher and simply didn't bother to write down. In less than a week he had homework grades of 68, 61 and 64. Mr. Bangs had seen enough. One day, the teacher called Arthur up to his desk at the end of class for a brief chat.

"Arthur, how do you explain the drop-off in your work? It looks like someone else is doing your work for you, but I know that's not the case. You've always been one of my best students. How do you explain it?"

"I don't know. Maybe the words are getting harder."

"You're misspelling words that are right in front of you on the board. Some you're not even writing down at all. Are you having any difficulty seeing the board? I could move you closer."

"No," Arthur answered defensively.

"Well then, pay better attention. If this keeps up, I'm going to have to talk with your parents."

Even that threat was insufficient to get Arthur to spill the beans about his worsening vision. He simply answered with an "I'll try to do better, Mr. Bangs."

Chapter 34

February 13, 1957. A Wednesday. The day Arthur became a teenager. That morning before he left for school, he received two birthday gifts—a model kit of an Atlas ICBM missile and a book about the history of the Brooklyn Dodgers.

At school, Mr. Heinbochel announced to the homeroom that it was Arthur's birthday. The class let out one huge roar that mixed cheers with good-natured razzing. A couple of students started chanting "Speech! Speech!" That was the last thing Arthur wanted to do. He wouldn't have to because he was saved by the first period bell.

When school ended, Arthur headed straight home. He didn't bother to stop at the Crystal Fountain because he knew his sweet tooth was going to be satisfied after dinner with a chocolate devil's food cake and ice cream.

Once he got home, the youngster turned on the television. He was enjoying *The Three Stooges*, but when his father pulled the car into the driveway, Arthur went upstairs to begin working on his model kit. Arthur's first instinct was always to put distance between himself and his father if possible.

While the young boy was assembling a guided missle, the rest of the family had returned home and they were all busy downstairs: his sister was playing the piano, his mother was preparing dinner and his father was drinking.

At six o'clock Marguerite shouted, "Time for dinner!" and the four Berndts sat down at the dinner table. By this time, August Berndt, who was drinking bottled beer in sets of two, had already consumed eight.

Marguerite started the conversation. "Well Art, what did you think of your birthday presents?"

"They're great. Especially the Dodger book."

His father chimed in. "Yeah, I picked it out myself. It's got a great photo of Snider climbing a wall to catch the ball."

"Yeah, Dad. I saw that one. It's really neat!"

August switched gears. "Now you're a teenager, it's time to get a little bit more serious. You know, next year you can get working papers and get a job. By the way, you'd better stop screwing up with the law. They treat teenagers differently. Another thing, don't you think it's time you stop wetting your bed, for God sakes?"

"I'm trying, Dad."

"Well, I'd have to say that you're not trying good enough. Did it again today, didn't you?"

Arthur's face turned a bright red. Even though his father was disclosing something already known by the entire family, the youngster preferred to imagine it was his well-kept, private secret. Before Arthur could answer, his mother chimed in. "Gus, you think we can talk about something else at the dinner table? This is Arthur's birthday."

"I know it is. I just want to make sure he knows he's getting older."

"Well he *is* getting older. And I don't think you're disciplining him with the bedwetting has really helped much—"

"You have any better ideas?"

"Well, I've always wanted to talk to a doctor again or some kind of expert and you always pooh-poohed it."

"Damn right. What the hell do they know? You want to let the whole world know we have a bed-wetter for a son?"

"I wouldn't care if I knew they could help him."

August got up and stumbled out into the kitchen where he retrieved two more bottles of beer, popped the tops off them, and came back into the dining room. He sat down clumsily on his chair and proceeded to pour one of the beers into his empty glass.

Turning to his son, August asked, "So whadda ya say? Is this the year you stop pissing on yourself?"

"I'm going to try."

Marguerite chimed in. "Gus, I think that's enough. Let's everybody enjoy the roast beef, so that we can get to the dessert."

Ruth had been ignoring the conversation and was just about finished with her dinner. "Can't wait for the devil's food cake. Next month when I have my birthday, we'll have something even better, Mom. Pineapple upside down. Yum!"

August Berndt poured the second bottle of beer into his glass. He mumbled something, but his slurred speech was unintelligible.

Ruth turned to her mother and, in a hushed voice, said, "I hate when he gets that way."

Not hearing his daughter, August Berndt started a conversation of his own. "You always stick up for him."

Assuming his words were directed at her, Marguerite asked, "Stick up for whom?"

"Arthur, your son."

"If you mean 'support,' that I do."

Garbling his words, August said, "You don't care what he does outside the house, or inside the house, for that matter."

Marguerite was quick to respond. "Gus, is that you talking or the beer?"

"Oh, so now you're being a wise ass?"

Arthur and Ruth shot each other a quick look. Their mother was being more assertive than usual and that made the two siblings equal parts happy and concerned. They were pleased to see their mother show this rare display of courage against the family tyrant. However, they both knew their father was into the ugly phase of his drinking bout and they weren't sure why their mother was testing her luck.

August Berndt sucked the last drops of beer from his glass. He started to get out of his chair but then fell back into it. Marguerite offered to get him some more beers. August answered with an insincere "Why thank you very much young lady!"

Marguerite went into the kitchen and took two bottles from the refrigerator. She found one of the many church keys in a drawer and opened both bottles. She then proceeded to empty the bottles, one in each hand, into the kitchen sink. August spotted her from his seat at the dinner table, awkwardly got to his feet, and navigated himself into the kitchen. "What the hell are you doing?"

"August, I think you've had more than enough."

"The hell I have."

211

He rummaged in the refrigerator and then realized there was only one bottle of beer left.

In a fit of rage, he grabbed the bottle and threw it at his wife. Before she could get her hands up the bottle hit her on the head. She staggered back and leaned against the kitchen counter, trying not to fall to the floor. Arthur ran in from the dining room and grabbed his mother around the waist, helping to keep her from collapsing. Without apologizing or showing any concern for his wife's well-being, August picked the beer bottle up off the floor. He opened it with gusto and half of it foamed out. He cursed at what was left in the bottle and took it upstairs to the bedroom. He then blasted the classical music station as loud as he could. Ruth cleaned up the spilled beer while Marguerite wrapped some ice in a dish towel and placed it on the lump forming on her forehead.

Ruth said, "You know Mom, you should get a divorce."

Marguerite answered, "That's not how you handle problems like this. Besides, that's not what Catholics do."

"Well, we're not Catholics. Just because you try to make dad happy by pretending we are, the fact is we aren't."

"When you marry, you take an oath for better or worse. I don't take that oath lightly."

Arthur was only vaguely aware of what a divorce entailed, but if it meant putting greater distance between him and his father he was all for it. After hearing his mother's words, the youngster concluded that a divorce was not going to happen so why get his hopes up? Thirteen-year-olds were not in a strong position to advocate for their own well-being.

Mother, son and daughter cleared the dinner table. In a rare display of teamwork, Ruth washed the dishes and Arthur dried them. Marguerite walked Arthur's birthday cake, complete with thirteen candles into the living room. There they each helped themselves to a slice of cake and watched *Disneyland* on television. It was silently understood there was no point in inviting the head of the household to the festivities.

The birthday party over, Ruth and Arthur headed for their bedrooms. Marguerite slept downstairs in the living room. August Berndt slept in the upstairs bedroom with blaring classical music until the station signed off at 2 A.M.

The following day, it was as if nothing had happened the previous evening. August was the first to go to work. Then Arthur and Ruth set out for school. Finally at 7:45, Marguerite, sporting a golf ball sized lump on her forehead, left the house and headed for her job at the high school cafeteria. When explaining to her coworkers how she got the injury, her husband was not part of the story. Like son, like mother.

Chapter 35

Had Marguerite's confrontation with her husband been a watershed moment for her? If so, that wasn't immediately apparent. August Berndt continued his drinking, Marguerite tolerated it and their children lived with the consequences.

On the first school day in March, Mr. Heinbochel handed out report cards, each contained in a protective envelope, to his homeroom students.

Since winning the medal as the best student academically in the 4th grade, Arthur had made a silent vow to never win the medal again. But he also knew he had to maintain better than average grades to avoid his parents' disapproval in general and his father's ire in particular. Thus, he was always curious to see his latest grades, hoping he again successfully straddled the fence between the highest academic achievement on one side and academic mediocrity on the other.

Arthur pulled the report card out of its envelope. When he opened the card up, he saw something on it he'd never seen before—written in bright crimson red ink was a 60 in English. Following his conversation with Mr. Bangs weeks earlier, the youngster had followed up with homework grades of 61 and 58 and gotten a 59 on a spelling/definition of word test based on words students had to copy from the blackboard. Though Mr. Bangs was an English teacher, he also knew how to do the math and Arthur's average for the marking period had been a failing grade—the first red mark Arthur had ever gotten in his scholastic career.

Arthur's report card put a damper on the rest of the school

day. He spent it desperately searching for some way to hide this failure from his parents. His search proved futile. After school, he reluctantly headed home. On the way, Arthur was so distraught he passed by the Crystal Fountain without giving it a second thought. When he reached Twenty-one Lowell place, nobody was there except Rex, happily barking from the inside of the house. Arthur didn't know what to do with the report card so, for lack of a better option, he slipped it into the milk box alongside three fresh quarts of milk that had been delivered earlier. Then, he let Rex out and, as he so often did under duress, headed for the woods. He walked by the burlap bag that had been used to conduct business with Johnny Stefano. He didn't check to see if there were any notes inside it. The young boy was in the middle of an academic crisis; the last thing he needed was added drama. Besides, he convinced himself that the beating he'd taken at the hands of the Stefanos weeks earlier had served as an exit interview from his job as a hubcap stealer.

Arthur sat down on a tree stump and, while watching Rex entertain himself, reflected on his situation. For several years he had refused his mother's suggestion to read downstairs in the living room during the early evening. He had done so primarily to avoid being in the same room with his father. Instead, he'd read his comic books upstairs in his dimly lit bedroom. Over time, he'd noticed that his vision was worsening. Nevertheless, he had stubbornly and spitefully made the choice to keep allowing his eyes to deteriorate rather than read in the living room in the presence of his father. At the deepest of levels, he was both angered and upset at what he had done to himself. Arthur sensed the bitter irony—years of punishment at the hands of his father had led the young boy to isolate even at home and that isolation had cost him his good eyesight. Self-consciousness over his poor vision compelled the youngster to keep the problem a secret. As a result, he now was faced with a red mark on his report card that demanded an explanation to his parents—the very people who had forced him to damage his eyesight in the first place!

It was starting to get dark. He considered running away from home, but quickly remembered the time he tried that the previous summer. He didn't want to suffer another such embarrassment.

Reluctantly, Arthur headed back to Twenty-one Lowell Place. Along the way, he thought a familiar thought: how lucky Rex was to be a dog. When he arrived at his destination, he knew that his mother and sister would most likely be home. The absence of the family car meant his father wasn't. Before entering the house, he checked for the report card in the milk box. Both it and the quarts of milk had been removed. There was no turning back. Arthur took a deep breath and entered the house. He saw his mother seated at the dining room table going through the day's mail. His report card, out of its envelope, was in plain sight.

"Arthur, what is this all about?"

Unable to think of something better to say, the youngster replied, "What is 'what' all about?"

"You know what I'm talking about. Why a 60 in English? That's one of your best subjects."

Though he had long ago mastered the art of crafting an alibi, this time Arthur saw no alternative but to tell the truth. "I can't see the board good anymore, Ma."

"What do you mean? Are you too far away from it?"

Arthur didn't know for sure. He'd refused his teacher's offer to let him sit closer to the blackboard. Rejecting a teacher's proposal might meet with his parents' disapproval. When in doubt, Arthur felt more comfortable lying.

"No. I sit up close and still can't see the board real well."

"Why in the world didn't you say something? Why did you let it get to this?"

"I don't know Ma. I thought I might get in trouble."

"You know I wear glasses all the time and your dad wears them for reading. I kept telling you to read downstairs with better lighting, remember?"

"Yeah, I know."

"So we have to take you to an optometrist."

"Do I have to get an operation?"

Marguerite laughed. "I certainly hope not. You'll probably have to start wearing glasses though."

A half-hour later August Berndt came home. Marguerite told him about their son's vision problem. Then she showed her husband his son's report card. In a rare display of even temperament, practicality and fear instilling, August Berndt said, "If glasses are the problem, we'll know when the next report card comes around, won't we?"

A trip to the optometrist provided conclusive evidence—Arthur had become nearsighted. He was prescribed glasses which he took with him wherever he went—primarily hidden in his pants pocket, not on his nose. Perhaps because of the fact that he was now a teenager, Arthur was more self-conscious about wearing glasses than about not being able to see. Virtually the only time he wore his glasses was in Mr. Bangs' class and then only when there was board work to be done. On those occasions, he'd surreptitiously remove his glasses from his pocket, slip them on and then, telling himself no one in the room was watching him, proceed to copy down all of the vocabulary words as quickly as possible so that he could again stuff his glasses somewhere out of sight.

Chapter 36

Thanks to the judicious use of his glasses, Arthur resurrected his academic performance. In Mr. Bangs' class, he leapt from a 62 to a 91 in the space of one marking period. Occasionally he found it best to use his lenses in some of his other classes, further raising his overall academic average. At the end of the school year Among all the students in the seventh grade, he ranked third overall academically. His improved schoolwork got him out of his parents' crosshairs, but was not quite stellar enough to garner him the medal. That suited Arthur fine.

***

Mr. Heinbochel had long ago stopped trying to interact with his raucous homeroom students so the day he asked for their attention, the room got quiet out of curiosity. "I want to let you know...the faculty had a meeting yesterday after school and there was unanimous agreement that 7D is the worst behaved homeroom in the school."

The students let out a roar of self-approval. Such a dubious distinction was a badge of honor for this band of misfits. Unlike his fellow students, Arthur didn't feel the urge to celebrate. He was relatively well-behaved, not only in his homeroom, but throughout the school day—and with good reason. Unlike the other students, he had to account to August Berndt for his behavior.

Throughout the school year, Arthur constantly worried that members of his homeroom class would at some point force the homeroom teacher's hand by misbehaving drastically enough to earn the entire class after-school detention. If his parents were notified, would he be able to convince them he was a victim of circumstance, that this was a case of undeserved guilt by association? Much more likely, Arthur would have to account for himself and blaming his classmates would never pass as an excuse with his father. Would he be able to get Mr. Heinbochel to exclude him from the group detention? Not likely. That would enrage every other student. Could he convince Mr. Heinbochel to explain to his parents that their son was a well- behaved boy that unfortunately had to pay the price for his fellow students' misdeeds? Again, not likely unless he revealed what might happen to him at home. That would require disclosing the twisted nature of the relationship he had with his father— something Arthur would never do. There were still over two months of school to go. Over two months for the 7D classroom to push its teacher over the edge. That never happened. Arthur fretted over nothing. Mr. Heinbochel dragged himself to the finish line in June without ever keeping his homeroom class after school.

As it turned out, the biggest threat in school to Arthur's well-being at home came not from his homeroom classmates, but from his social studies teacher, Sidney Wickersham.

Mr. Wickersham and his wife Stephanie were both teaching for the first time that year at the Port Jefferson Elementary School. Mr. Wickersham quickly established himself as the quirkiest and meanest teacher in the school. He routinely hurled petty insults at students for their classwork, mannerisms and appearance. Mispronounce a word you were subjected to ridicule. Due to his calling another student "four eyes," Arthur avoided wearing glasses in his class altogether. Mr. Wickersham chided another student for her drawl saying, "That might play well in Mississippi, but we're here in New York." He told a black student, "You better smarten up in class. You're never going to be a pro athlete. I've seen you play softball. No one would mistake you for Hank Aaron."

Mr. Wickersham could also get physical. In a fit of rage, one day he grabbed a student by the neck, briefly lifting him off the floor with one hand. Arthur silently—and gratefully—noted that was something his father had never done to him.

His combination of brutality and unpredictability earned Mr. Wickersham the reputation as the most hated—and feared—

teacher in the school. Perhaps more than his fellow students, Arthur had expertise in dealing with this teacher's type of personality. Arthur kept as low a profile as possible in Mr. Wickersham's class. He would always volunteer to give an answer he was sure of, thereby lessening the chance of being called on to respond to a more baffling question. He was quick to volunteer to read in class, confident he would not miss a word, thereby enabling him to avoid Mr. Wickersham's scrutiny.

***

One day in early April, Arthur woke up to two positives: he hadn't wet the bed and it had snowed overnight. There was a coating of thick, damp snow on the ground. Had school been canceled?

When he got downstairs, his mother was already listening to the local radio station for any possible school closings.

"Art, I think you're out of luck. I've been listening and only the Catholic school is closed."

"Darn. Well, you always make us eat fish on Friday. Why can't I be a Catholic today?"

"Don't be a smart aleck. Port Jeff is probably going to be open today. I'll keep the radio on, but eat your breakfast and then get ready to go to school."

Two hours later Arthur was sitting in his homeroom class, resigned to getting a full day's dose of scholarly enlightenment.

When the bell rang, Arthur headed directly across the hall to his first class. Social studies with Mr. Wickersham. He was accompanied by his fellow homeroom classmate and chronic nemesis Richard Clark. The two took the short walk into the classroom. Richard headed to a seat in the back of the classroom while Arthur stayed up front, gazing out a window at the wet snow that covered everything but the street. Mr. Wickersham came over to Arthur, opened the window, grabbed some snow from the ledge and made a snowball. With his forefinger on his mouth, he signaled for Arthur to remain silent. To Arthur's disbelief, the teacher hurled the snowball at Richard, while simultaneously shouting, "Look out!"

"Ow! Ouch! Shoot!" The snowball had made a direct hit and Richard was holding his eye, jumping up and down in pain. "Dammit."

With blinding speed, Mr. Wickersham closed the window,

220

dried his hands on his pants and quickly sat down at his desk. Then he asked, "What happened?"

"I got hit with a snowball. Man, it hurts!"

Other students were now filing into the scene of the crime. Mr. Wickersham turned to Arthur, who was still standing by the window. "You better hope he's not hurt too badly. I'm going to give you detention. This might even call for a suspension."

"What? I didn't do anything."

"You were the only one in the room stupid enough to do something like that."

Richard was sent to the nurse's office, still holding a hand over his eye. Once he left the room and Arthur resentfully took his seat, the other students settled down and the class began.

Arthur was boiling with anger. In his world, the only thing worse than getting blamed for something he did do, was getting blamed for something he *didn't* do. Arthur drank his anger with a chaser of fear. If his parents found out about the teacher's allegations, he had little doubt whom they would believe and who would pay the price. Arthur tried to prop up his spirits. *Mr. Wickersham was only kidding; he wouldn't pin the blame on an innocent student. After all, he's a teacher; he wouldn't lie.*

Arthur spent the forty minute period in an anxious fog. He didn't volunteer to participate and Mr. Wickersham didn't ask him to.

When the bell rang, the teacher called Arthur up to his desk. Arthur felt confident the teacher would make things right.

"We'll see how Richard is. If he's not too bad, maybe I'll let this whole thing slide."

Arthur wanted to scream out his innocence, but that would mean declaring his teacher guilty. The young boy said nothing and left for his second period class.

Later in the day, Arthur and Richard crossed paths in the hall. Richard's eye was heavily bandaged.

"When I get better, I'm gonna beat the shit out of you."

"I didn't do anything. The teacher threw it."

"Yeah. Sure. There's something wrong with you."

That last comment stung. Arthur labored under that same belief himself and didn't appreciate anyone confirming his suspicions.

Chapter 37

During homeroom class the following day, students ribbed Richard for his swollen eye.

"Did mommy hit you?"

"Hey, next time watch where you're going! Ha! Ha!"

"Ew! You look creepy."

Richard let everyone in the classroom know what had happened and how he was going to exact revenge. "As soon as I get better, Artie boy and me are going to have a little meeting after school."

When the bell rang, Richard purposely pushed Arthur's books off his desk as he passed by. Mr. Heinbochel didn't see it happen or perhaps he did and simply chose to do nothing about it.

After collecting his books from the floor, Arthur headed across the hall. Following the previous day's incident, Arthur had decided he would never again enter Mr. Wickersham's room until a number of other students already had. The young boy no longer trusted this teacher and, in order to never again be set up, he wanted to be certain there would be witnesses.

Once the social studies class began, Arthur sat through a lecture on the Revolutionary War, a lecture he hardly heard. He spent the entire period fretting over what awaited him when class finished—detention or suspension. Throughout the lecture he preoccupied himself with exploring different ways to minimize his potential punishment. If he was given a note to take home, he'd simply destroy it. If the note was mailed, he'd intercept that note and dispose of it. If the note had to be signed, he'd forge his parent's signature. If the school called home, he'd have to come up with another line of defense—one that didn't immediately come to mind.

The bell rang. Arthur got up from his seat and followed the other students to the door. Out of the corner of his eye, he saw Mr. Wickersham had gotten up from his desk and was rolling a movie projector to the back of the classroom. Nothing happened. No suspension. No detention. Not even a comment from the teacher about the previous day's events. Greatly relieved, Arthur exited the room and headed to his second period class.

Arthur couldn't totally relax yet. Maybe Mr. Wickersham would bring up the matter over the next few days. Maybe the teacher had already sent a letter to his parents.

Arthur waited for a shoe to drop that never did. During the rest of the week there were no comments from Mr. Wickersham in class and no letter arrived at home from the school.

By the following Monday, Arthur was convinced he had successfully run the gauntlet—at least as far as the threat of formal disciplining went. He couldn't rest on his laurels very long. That same day, Richard made it clear *he* hadn't let the issue go. During homeroom period, Richard walked over to Arthur's desk and said, "I'll see you in the playground behind the school tomorrow after school. That's if you're not a chicken."

"Hey, I didn't do anything."

"So, you're chicken."

"No, I'm not. I'm just saying —"

"See you behind the school. Don't chicken out!"

Arthur and Richard had never gotten along. Back in the second grade, they had a brief skirmish on the school bus while heading for the circus. Since then, they kept their distance from each other by mutual consent. Now things had gotten up close and personal.

Both boys had grown considerably in the past five years. Richard was larger than Arthur in the second grade and he remained larger now by some two inches in height and almost fifteen pounds in weight. Should the two fight, Arthur didn't like his chances. He knew he wouldn't be getting the kind of beating he often endured at the hands of his father nor would it be like the one he'd taken from the Stefanos just months earlier. This fight *could* damage his pride more than the others had. If Arthur didn't show up for the scuffle or, if he did and Richard won, either fact would be broadcast all over the school. Arthur would have to endure the scorn of more than 300 of his peers. Though he had already suffered a long string of humiliations in his short life, the feeling of being humiliated never got any easier—and this one would be in the public domain.

The following morning Arthur headed off on foot to school with a lump of fear in his throat that he couldn't swallow. He thought of claiming he was sick so he'd be sent home early from school, but then pictured the taunts of "chicken" he'd have to endure the following day. The young boy walked on, as if headed to his own funeral. Richard, the would-be funeral director, shot Arthur several menacing looks during homeroom period.

Throughout that morning and afternoon, Arthur felt like a prisoner who had run out of appeals and was counting the hours to his execution. Normally, the youngster looked forward to hearing the dismissal bell and making a subsequent trip to the Crystal Fountain. Today was a school day the youngster wished would never end. At three o'clock, it did.

Arthur left his eighth period classroom. He headed out the exit on the north side of the school building. He walked down the sidewalk alongside Spring Street passing the playground in back of the school. He scanned it, looking for Richard. He was relieved not to see his mortal foe. Arthur waited, but not for very long. After a less than a minute, he told himself he'd waited long enough and his opponent had failed to show up. Arthur continued down Spring Street and then along Main Street. Arthur was in a celebratory mood. What better place to celebrate than at the Crystal Fountain!

Chapter 38

The next day in homeroom Arthur pushed his luck. He walked over to Richard's desk and asked, "Where were you? I waited a long time."

"Yeah? Well, I didn't see you either."

"I was by the monkey bars. I waited so long I got in trouble for getting home late."

"You're lying. I would have seen you. I knew you wouldn't show up. Anyway punk, I don't have to beat you up. My parents already called the school. You're in big trouble."

No sooner had Arthur dodged one bullet, then another shot was fired at him. Richard was no longer his problem, the system was.

An announcement came over the intercom: "Mr. Blake, will you please monitor Mr. Wickersham's first period class in room 107. Mr. Wickersham, please come to the office. Also, student Arthur Berndt, come to the principal's office immediately."

As homeroom students filed out of Mr. Heinbochel's room, Arthur was serenaded by discouraging words:

"You're gonna get it!"

"Arthur's in trouble now!"

"I wouldn't want to be you for nothing."

The previous school year he'd received a paddling from the principal, Mr. Tolleson. Quick and painless. He would gladly settle for that again.

As Arthur entered the principal's office, he hoped and prayed neither of his parents would be there. They weren't, but somebody else's parents were—Richard's! Mr. Toal's secretary ushered Arthur into the principal's office where Mr. and Mrs. Clark were already seated. Three adults and a youngster waited in an uncomfortable silence for Mr. Wickersham. He arrived shortly and the conference began.

"Mr. Wickersham and you, too, Arthur, I called you in to discuss a problem that the Clarks have brought to my attention. They tell me that you, Arthur, apparently hit their son with a snowball, not outside, but inside the building! Is that true?"

"No. I didn't."

"Well I have it from the nurse that Richard came to her office on April 8th—two Mondays ago. He had a swollen red eye and claimed you had thrown a snowball at him."

"Well, I don't care. I didn't do it."

The principal turned to Mr. Wickersham. "Can you straighten this out?"

Mr. Wickersham said, "Well, I guess I made the mistake of leaving a window open. It snowed earlier in the day but it was getting warm. So before I could do anything Arthur made a snowball from snow on the ledge and threw it at Richard. I didn't actually see it happen, but they were the only two students in the room at the time, so I think everyone can pretty much figure out who did what."

Arthur was shocked that a teacher could lie so blatantly and calmly. In the young boy's eyes, this was pure betrayal from a member of a profession that, up until now, he always had complete faith in—school teachers.

Mr. Tolleson turned to Arthur and said, "Son, what do you have to say for yourself?"

"Nothing. All I can say is I didn't do it."

"Well, certainly you're not saying that Mr. Wickersham did it, right?"

Arthur wasn't sure how to respond. If he didn't defend himself, he was going to be convicted by the adults in the room. If he accused a teacher, he was just as certain he wouldn't be believed *and* he'd have to deal with that teacher for the rest of the school year. Unable to decide what to say, he said nothing.

Mr. Tolleson commented, "Your silence speaks volumes, son." Then the principal turned to Mr. Wickersham and asked," Why didn't you bring this to my attention immediately?"

"I certainly intended to. I wanted to see just how serious Richard's injury was before recommending detention or suspension."

"Poor judgment on your part. Very poor. Here we are ten days later and the first I find out about this is from Richard's parents. I prefer to take the bull by the horns. I'm sure Arthur was happy you didn't report it right away." Mr. Tolleson turned to the Clarks and said, "I assure you, this isn't how we normally handle these things. I apologize."

Mrs. Clark responded. "Well, we didn't get a call from anybody, not even the nurse. That day when my son came home I was shocked. We kept asking our son if anything was done about it and we kept waiting to hear from the school but nothing..."

"Again, I apologize to both of you for what happened and the way it was handled. I'm just glad that Richard didn't lose an eye."

Mr. and Mrs. Clark answered in unison. "So are we!"

"Now I have to decide on a punishment for this. I was leaning towards in-school detention for a week but I'm bothered by the fact that Arthur refuses to tell me the truth."

"But I *am* telling the truth! This isn't fair."

"A lesson in life. You have to pay for the consequences of your actions, whether you admit to them or not. Lying won't work, young man. What I want you to do right now is apologize to the Clarks."

Arthur balked. An anger welled up inside him. He shot Mr. Wickersham an expression of disappointment and bitterness followed by a look of hopefulness that the teacher would right this wrong. He wouldn't.

Looking at the floor, Arthur muttered, "What am I supposed to say? I'm sorry for something I didn't do? Okay. I'm sorry."

The principal responded to Arthur's lukewarm apology. "I guess that's about the best we're going to get from this youngster. Again, I apologize for the lack of communication and again I'm very relieved that your son didn't suffer more serious injury. I'm going to determine Arthur's punishment and I will let you folks know what I come up with."

Mr. Clark nodded his head. "Fair enough."

Everyone got up to leave, but Mr. Tolleson grabbed Arthur by the shoulder. "You and I have to talk a bit." Arthur instinctively flinched when the principal restrained him but quickly sensed he wasn't about to be hit.

After the other adults had left the room, Mr. Tolleson sat down behind his desk and directed Arthur to take a seat in the chair across from him.

"Arthur, in all your years in the school I only remember you coming to my office one time. I know for a fact that you are a very good student. I've heard you've had a little bit of trouble up there in your neighborhood. I just don't want you to start acting up in school. I won't tolerate it. Do you understand?"

"Yes sir." Arthur resigned himself to the fact that justice was not going to be done in this case. No one was going to believe a student—especially one claiming that a teacher had thrown a snowball inside the school. Since absolution was no longer a possibility, the young boy's focus shifted to worrying about the punishment he was going to get.

"You know, Richard could've lost his eye and then we'd have big problems. Let me ask you Arthur, what do you think is fair in this case?"

"I don't know." Arthur weighed his options and decided he'd rather take his chances with in-school detention.

"If I'm not mistaken, both your folks work, right?"

"Yup."

The principal thought aloud. "So if I expelled you from school you'd be home alone?"

"Yes."

"Sort of left to your own devices?"

"What do you mean, Mr. Tolleson?"

"Well, as they say, when the cat's away the mice will play. I'm going to give you five days of detention after school. It will start next Monday. I'm going to send a note to your parents letting them know the details of what happened. Does that sound fair?"

It didn't sound fair to Arthur, but the youngster knew there was nothing he could do about the situation. "I guess so."

"Okay. Your second period class begins in a few minutes. You can go now. Detention starts immediately after the end of the school day. 3 P.M. on the button. You're to report to room 110. And make sure you get there on time. That's Monday through Friday next week, got it?"

"Yes, Mr. Tolleson."

Arthur left the principal's office grateful for not having been expelled from school but with a new concern: the school was going to send a letter to his parents.

Arthur spent the rest of the school day calculating his chances of escaping his father's wrath. Detention lasted until

3:45 P.M. After it ended, if he ran all the way he might make it home before his mother and father did, but most likely not before his sister arrived. He'd have to come up with an explanation for his late arrival so that Ruth wouldn't blab to their parents. A more pressing problem was the letter being sent home. He had to make sure no one in his family ever saw it. Today was a Wednesday. Arthur hoped and prayed the letter would arrive on Thursday or Friday. On those days, he could retrieve it the minute he got home from school. Saturday would be more complicated as other family members might be home. If it arrived the following week he'd be sitting in the detention room and his sister would most likely find the letter. He had no doubt she would relish the opportunity of turning it over to their parents.

***

Thursday came and went. No letter. Friday came and went. Still no letter. To Arthur's great relief, on Saturday his father worked overtime. Another unexpected bonus: Ruth was participating in her high school choral group's practice in the town of Islip, in preparation for an upcoming music festival featuring high schools throughout Suffolk County. She'd be gone most of the day.

Saturday's mail usually arrived between 12 and 1 P.M. Arthur took up residence in the living room watching television from a distance. He set up shop on a chair near the front window of the living room so that he could more easily monitor mail delivery. The TV was at the opposite end of the room. When his mother questioned why he was sitting so far away from the television set, Arthur answered, "With my new glasses I can see the TV from anywhere now." At noontime, Arthur went on high alert. He spent five minutes looking out the window for every one minute he spent looking at *Sky King* on television. His mother had gone upstairs and was sewing in her bedroom. Thus Arthur didn't need to explain his overt surveillance.

Shortly after the noon whistle sounded, Joe, the mailman, reached the Berndt property. He began rummaging through his bag, selected a few pieces of mail and placed his bag on the ground. Years ago he'd learned to leave the bag behind him as it provoked Rex. Arthur dashed out of the house with Rex close behind and met the mailman just as he began walking up the

229

driveway.

"Thanks for saving me a few extra steps son. You must have something really important coming to you."

"Yup. I do."

Arthur grabbed the mail and Joe did an about face to continue on his appointed rounds. While walking back to the house Arthur went through the day's mail. He stuffed an envelope with his school's address on it under his shirt and went into the house. He placed the rest of the mail on the dining room table. From upstairs Marguerite called, "Arthur, are you ready for lunch?" Though he was famished, he had to see the contents of the letter from school before he did anything else.

"Nah. I think I have a stomach ache."

"You *think* you have a stomach ache? You're not sure?"

"I know I have a stomach ache."

"Well we've got some Pepto-Bismol. Try that."

"I think I'll go outside a little bit."

"Stomach ache and all?"

"Yeah. I'll come back and take the Pepto stuff if it still hurts."

Arthur headed out the door with his dog as company. Though the letter was in no danger of falling out, Arthur pressed his hand against his shirt just to be on the safe side. He walked briskly up Lowell Place, turned right on Old Post Road and immediately scooted onto the dirt path. He sat on the first fallen tree he came to and pulled the form letter out from under his shirt.

To the parents or guardian of Arthur Berndt:

This student will be serving five days of after-school detention from April 22 through April 26. Detention period lasts 45 minutes from 3:00 p.m. to 3:45 p.m. The school does not provide transportation home following detention. If you have any questions regarding the administering of this punishment by the Port Jefferson Elementary School please feel free to contact me.

Please sign this letter where indicated and return same at your earliest convenience. If you have any questions I can be reached at HR 3–5555.

Respectfully,

Lawrence Tolleson

Principal

The letter had to be signed! Arthur hadn't figured on that. He put the letter back in the envelope and headed back home. Now he lost his appetite for real, his hunger pangs dulled by stress. He couldn't tell his mother the real reason for not being hungry, so he continued with the stomach ache alibi, even taking some Pepto-Bismol to reinforce his story's validity.

Arthur went to his room and, after closing the door, took out a pen and paper. He attempted to write his mother's name. Then, he made a stab at writing his father's. Both efforts were in vain. He wasn't trying to mimic their signatures; he was simply attempting to write their names as if he were an adult. He tried a few more times, but had no confidence in the results.

He had to find an older person to sign this critical correspondence. He couldn't count on Ruth. Liz might bail him out, but she was living in Hempstead and there was no time to do this by mail.

He couldn't go to a neighbor—that was out of the question. It would take a unique adult to willingly aid and abet a teenager trying to get away with something

Maybe there was a neighbor. The old man! Ernest! Would he help Arthur? Did Arthur dare ask him for help? They had met in the woods once several years earlier and that meeting had been rocky. Everyone said Ernest was crazy. Arthur wasn't sure. Ernest could be scary, but so could Arthur's father. Right now, the drunken loner living up the street qualified as Arthur's only lifeline in his current crisis.

He knew the old man visited the trench where they had initially met because, on occasion, the youngster would find an empty liquor bottle there. Yet, as often as he'd visited the woods since their initial encounter, Arthur had never again bumped into Ernest.

There was no time to wait for a chance meeting. Arthur would have to summon up the courage to set foot on Ernest's property. After telling his mother he was going out bike riding, he left the house again, this time without Rex. He wasn't sure if Ernest was dog-friendly.

Arthur rode up Lowell Place and out onto Old Post Road. Ernest's shack was the very first building on the south side of the road. Arthur pedaled a few more yards and then veered onto the dirt path. He jumped off his bicycle, lay it down, and covered it with brush. This operation required complete secrecy.

On foot, Arthur made his way back to Ernest's shack. The young boy steeled himself for the job at hand.

Not much had changed over the years at Ernest's residence. Perhaps the out-of-control foliage had become a bit more out-of-control. Perhaps there were a few more grocery bags full of empties. Perhaps a few more window panes were broken. All in all, Ernest inhabited the only residential property in Suassa Park that was losing value. Stepping onto the old man's property was like entering a no man's land. The thought occurred to the young boy: *Will I come out of this alive?* He quickly reminded himself he'd survived their first encounter and Ernest was the only person he could turn to save his life. Hopefully, he wouldn't end it.

Arthur walked from a weed infested driveway onto a weed infested walkway that led to the front door. He stepped onto a rickety porch that could barely support the thirteen-year-old.

When Ernest was having one of his fits, his screams echoed throughout the neighborhood. When Ernest wasn't ranting and raving, it was hard to tell if anybody was inside his house. The shack had no doorbell or knocker so, summoning up all his courage, Arthur rapped on the door with his knuckles. No reply. Arthur thought his first attempt might have been too halfhearted, so he again knocked, this time with more gusto. No reply. Though the young boy had been extremely nervous at the thought of dealing with Ernest, now that he had come this far he did not want to turn back. He desperately needed a piece of paper signed. He knocked on the door a third time. From inside the house came a faint moan. Then a "Goddammit!" That was followed by "Who the hell is it?"

Every bone in his body told Arthur to take off running. The young boy ignored his own warning. For the sake of a signature, he put his life on the line.

"It's me, Arthur. I'm the kid you met in the woods. Remember?"

"I don't remember shit. Get the hell off my property!"

Ernest's cold reception forced Arthur to second-guess his mission. A thought flashed through Arthur's mind: *what if he has a gun?* After all, this was a man that had killed a kid younger than Arthur. That had been during war time, but if he did it once, could he do it again? The young boy realized that he had walked into this dangerous situation in hopes of getting himself out of another precarious situation—one he didn't deserve to be in but was, thanks to Mr. Wickersham. Arthur was determined not to let his parents get wind of the trumped-up charges against him. The youngster's resolve gave him the courage to proceed with the uncomfortable task at hand.

The front door opened just a crack and with the one eye he still had, Ernest peered out at his visitor. "Who the hell are you kid? I'm not taking visitors today." Ernest laughed at his own joke.

"Mr. Ernest, I—"

"If you're going to call me mister then it's Dawes. Mister Dawes."

"Yes, Mr. Dawes. I really need your help."

Ernest let out a laugh. "That's a good one. You need my help? What the hell for?"

"Well, it's kind of complicated. It's because no one believes me and I'm telling the truth."

"What the hell could be so bad for a kid your age?"

Ernest opened the door a bit further. There he stood in the same outfit he'd been wearing out in the woods when Arthur met him three years earlier. None of his attire appeared as if it had been washed since then. Arthur wondered to himself if Ernest ever washed the patch that covered his empty eye socket.

A foul odor emanated from within the shack, unlike any Arthur had ever smelled before in his life. He hoped he'd be able to complete his mission on the porch. No such luck.

"Oh, what the hell. Come on in and tell me your sad tale. Shit, it might do me some good to have a guest."

233

Though entering the smelly hovel of a madman was the last thing Arthur wanted to do, it was also the first thing. His hopes of getting the school document signed took on new life.

After entering Ernest's "home," Arthur heard his host close the door behind him.

All the window shades were drawn and only a single table lamp illuminated the 20' x 25' combination living room/bedroom/kitchen in which Ernest spent the majority of each day of his life. There was a single threadbare throw rug that covered two thirds of the wood floor. The exposed part of the floor had not seen polish in years, if ever. Furniture consisted of a now-barely-upholstered chair, with an even older table lamp, and a cot. For appliances, Ernest had a stove that looked too dangerous to use and a twenty-year-old icebox. There was a hot plate on which sat a pot of beans that had been cooked weeks ago and left uneaten.

The floor was littered with empty liquor bottles and the occasional empty carton of milk. Newspapers dating back as far back as 1948 were piled haphazardly against one wall. Arthur couldn't hide his fascination with the dingy spectacle that surrounded him.

"Yeah, it's a real palace right? This is what happens when you fight for your country." Ernest rubbed his chin and then said, "I remember you now kid. I remember telling you to stay out of the Army." He gestured at the layout of his shanty and said, "See what I'm talking about?"

The old man went into the bathroom and came out with a stool. He placed it next to his chair.

"Here you go, young fella. Make yourself comfortable."

The old man plopped into his chair while Arthur sat on the stool, resting the heels of his sneakers on the stool's rail.

"So, what's going on?"

"Arthur pulled out the envelope from under his shirt.

"Oh, what you got there? Some kind of secret document?"

Yes, as far as Arthur was concerned. He definitely didn't want his parents to lay eyes on it.

"Mr. Dawes, I got blamed for something in school that I didn't do. I have to go to detention for it. I just don't want my parents to find out because my dad will get real mad. And since I didn't do it—"

"That's what they always say. 'I didn't do it.' If I had a dollar for every—"

"Yeah, but this time I really didn't do it. I swear."

"And what's 'it'?"

"A kid in my class got hit with a snowball. The teacher threw it and blamed it on me."

Ernest guffawed and then asked skeptically, "So the teacher threw the snowball and not you?"

"I swear to God. Cross my heart and hope to die. I swear it."

"You better not be lying to me."

"I'm not Ern—I mean Mr. Dawes. I promise."

"Hey, you're a German kid right?"

"Well, my parents are...they're German."

"Me... me helping a German? I don't know."

Arthur remembered how much Ernest disliked Germans due to his war experience. The young boy had to act quickly.

"I'll help clean up some stuff for you if you help me."

The old man glowered at his youthful guest. "You saying my place is a mess?"

"I'm not saying that. I just mean—"

"Well, it is. Don't be a lily-liver. You know a pigsty when you see one. I know I do."

After a brief pause, Ernest looked Arthur in the eye and asked, "Now what the hell is it exactly you want me to do?"

"I need... I would like you to sign this piece of paper so I can take it back to school. That's all."

"And I'm the only person in the world that can do it?"

"I think so."

"Hey, I'm an important guy." The old man got up from his chair and began strutting around, stumbling on some of the empties lying on the floor.

Arthur remembered that during their first meeting there came a point when Ernest had started ranting and raving and then another when he had frozen stiff. Arthur knew he had to get the piece of paper signed before Ernest became incapacitated.

He took the letter out from the envelope and showed Ernest where a signature was required. Arthur had forgotten to bring a pen with him and it took a lengthy search to find one lying on the floor near a mouse trap. "Yeah, I had a few of them vermin some years ago, but haven't seen one in quite a while."

With Ernest's permission, Arthur grabbed an old *Daily Mirror* from one of the many piles of newspapers and on the

235

front page printed out his father's name. He handed it to Ernest. "If you could please just write that name on this letter where it says to sign."

"I can't see for shit. Hey, before I do anything else I have to get something."

Ernest walked over to a wall cabinet, opened it up and pulled out a half-finished bottle of vodka. After examining several dirty glasses in the sink, he decided to drink straight from the bottle. He took a couple of hearty swigs and then came back to his chair.

"There. Now I can function. Remember, like I told you last time, never touch this shit. It's killing me."

"Yes sir."

"'Yes sir.' I like the way you answered. 'Yes sir'. Good discipline. You must come from a good family. Wait, how can I say that? You're German. Oh, what the hell. That war's over. These days we got to worry about the goddamn commies. Besides, you seem like a well-behaved youngster."

"Well behaved." Surprising and pleasant music to Arthur's ears, even if it was coming from a madman.

After another swig of vodka, Ernest asked, "Okay, where were we?"

"You were going to sign the paper, but you said you couldn't read well."

"Yeah that's right. I got some glasses around here somewhere, but I'll be damned if I know where."

"So Mr. Dawes, why don't I read the name to you and you can write it down."

Grabbing the pen from Arthur and laying the letter on the lamp table the old man said, "Fire away!"

"A–U– G–U–S–T."

"Hey, slow down. I'm not some damn stenographer."

Arthur spelled out his father's first name more slowly.

"Oh, like the month?"

"Yup."

"Okay. I got it. Yeah. And now the last name."

"B-E-R-N-D-T."

"Damn! That's a Kraut name alright."

Ernest handed the signed letter to Arthur. Arthur looked it over and for a split second thought Ernest's handwriting might not convince the school principal. Too late now.

Ernest began drinking feverishly, as if he were behind a self-imposed schedule and had to make up for lost time. Arthur tucked the letter back in the envelope and slid it under his shirt. Now, just as had happened the first time they met, he was unsure exactly how to take his leave without upsetting his guest. He didn't want to risk angering Ernest like he had done years earlier when he'd abruptly ended their first meeting.

"Thank you very much, Mr. Dawes. "

"Hey, wanna stick around? Not too often I get company."

"I have to take this letter home so I don't lose it."

"Bullshit. You won't lose it here. I did you a favor. Now I'm asking you to do me a favor. It's a tit-for-tat, got it?"

"But, Mr. Dawes —"

Ernest lunged at Arthur, and tried to pull his shirt out from under his pants so he could get at the envelope. Arthur shoved Ernest and the older man reeled backwards, losing his balance and falling to the floor. As Ernest struggled to get to his feet, Arthur bolted from the shack and ran out onto Old Post Road. He didn't head back to his house, fearing the old man would follow him there. Instead he continued along Old Post Road and turned onto Whittier Place, the first intersection. He looked back and saw Ernest standing at the edge of his property, shaking a fist. "We'll meet up again, you fuckin' scumbag Kraut."

Though Arthur sensed Ernest had given up the chase, the young boy took no chances. He ran to the end of Whittier and then turned onto Hawthorne Place. From there he made his way back home.

There his mother was still sewing. Arthur immediately went upstairs to his bedroom and placed the envelope in his drawer. From her bedroom, Marguerite called, "How's the stomachache?"

"It's okay now. It went away."

(Laughing) "I'll have to remember that the next time I get a stomach ache. Just take a walk."

"What's for lunch, Ma?"

"Wow! Your stomach ache really did go away!"

After a late lunch Marguerite went back to her sewing and Arthur went back to his scheming.

While his mother was upstairs stitching, Arthur was downstairs in the living room, rummaging through the drawers and pigeonholes of a writing desk. He helped himself to a stamp and a return address label. The youngster took both up to his room and affixed them to the envelope. As he did so, Arthur got an uncomfortable feeling. During his brief scuffle with Ernest, the envelope had been crinkled. Fearing a battered envelope would sound alarm bells at school, the young boy went back downstairs and grabbed a fresh envelope from the same writer's desk. After returning to his bedroom, he took the letter out of the damaged envelope and saw that it had a few creases. He attempted to smooth them out but to no avail. He would have to work with what he had. Trying to get the school to send a second letter for signing would be a complicated task and trying to get Ernest to sign another letter would be an impossible one.

Arthur prepared the letter for mailing. On second thought, he decided not to affix a return address label. Why take any chance of the letter coming back to Twenty-one Lowell Place and possibly falling into the wrong hands?

It was too late in the day for a trip downtown to mail the letter. The young boy would have to stop by the post office first thing Monday morning on the way to school. Later that same day he'd begin his weeklong after school detention. Would the forged signature on the letter pass the muster? Could he make it to his house from detention for an entire school week without raising suspicions at home? This would be a nerve-wracking week.

There was another source of stress—Ernest. What if he knew where Arthur lived? What if he didn't, but was determined to find out? Until today, Arthur had never once imagined Ernest showing up on the doorstep at Twenty-one Lowell Place. Now, it seemed all too possible. Even if he didn't find out where Arthur lived, what if the two met up in the woods? Arthur was fairly certain he could outrun the old man, but if he ever fell into his clutches there would be hell to pay. Then there was a possibility that, on one of Ernest's rare walks into town, he might spot the youngster there.

The Stefano brothers, Peter Stanton and his crew, Ronnie Simpson, Richard Clark, Warren Howell—all these and more were on Arthur's to-be-avoided list. Arthur did not want to add this highly fearsome neighbor to that list. Arthur had to take the initiative and somehow placate his volatile neighbor. He figured he'd do that the following day, but then he remembered—his bicycle! He'd left it in the woods by the dirt path. His father would be home soon and if he went into the garage he would see the bicycle was missing. Which was riskier? Going by the old man's house to retrieve his bike or acting as though someone had stolen it from the garage? Had his mother seen him leave earlier with the bike and then later seen him come home without it? Maybe, maybe not. If not, and his parents assumed the bike had been stolen, how long would Arthur have to wait to get a new one? Though Arthur typically walked to school, he planned to ride his bike to school the upcoming week so he could get home from detention as quickly as possible. Arthur had to get his bike right now!

"Ma, I'm going over to the Blaskowitzes' to see if the big kids are playing ball. Maybe they'll let me play."

"I hope they do. I think sports would be a good outlet for you. But don't be too late. Dinner will be around 5:30."

"Okay."

Again leaving Rex home, Arthur walked up to the end of Lowell Place. When he got there, he peeked across the street at Ernest's shack. There were no signs of life, but that was proof of nothing; Even when Ernest was at home, his residence had all the earmarks of an abandoned building. Arthur hustled along Old Post Road, onto the dirt path and up to the spot where he had left his bike. He brushed aside the foliage he'd covered the bicycle with and stood it upright. He hesitated to hop on and start pedaling. He couldn't leave his business with Ernest unfinished. He would apologize to Ernest and let the chips fall where they might. If Ernest was belligerent, Arthur would simply take off running as he had earlier in the day. If Ernest accepted his apology the youngster would go back to having only one angry old man to deal with—his father. Just in case things didn't go well in the second meeting, Arthur made sure he'd at least come back home with his bicycle. He pushed it to the end of the dirt path and left it standing. Should he have to make a quick escape from Ernest's shack his bike would be there ready to use.

For the second time that day, Arthur walked up to the front door of Ernest's hovel. He knocked on the door only to find it had been left unlocked and very slightly ajar. The young boy's knocking opened the door a bit farther, just enough for Arthur to see the old man's body lying on the floor. Was Arthur seeing a dead body for the second time in his life? He called out, "Ernest! Ernest! It's Arthur. I came back to apologize." The body lying on the floor didn't respond.

Arthur opened the door to let more light into the room. He

could see Ernest's chest rising and lowering. He wasn't dead, he had passed out from drinking. In one hand, he clutched a bottle of vodka from which some of its contents had emptied onto the carpet. The rest of its contents had been emptied into Ernest's stomach.

Arthur wasn't sure exactly what to do next. When his father passed out from drinking at home he was usually left in place to sleep it off. Arthur was disappointed that he was not going to be able to mend fences with the man who had done him a big favor. He was afraid to touch Ernest, so he simply kept calling his name in hopes he would wake up. The creature didn't stir. Admitting defeat, Arthur reluctantly headed for the front door.

"Oh... God dammit... I feel like shit."

Arthur turned around and saw Ernest still lying flat on his back, but holding his head with one hand.

"See why I told you never to touch this stuff?"

"Yes, sir."

"There is that 'yes sir' again. I kinda like it and I kinda don't. Respectful, but reminds me of the damn military."

"Ernest. Mr. Dawes. I came back to apologize. "

"Apologize? For what?"

"Well, you did me a favor. You really helped me by signing that paper. So I didn't mean to push you."

"What the hell you talking about? What paper?"

Arthur wasn't sure if Ernest was playing dumb with him or had forgotten the events of earlier in the day. He did know that sometimes when his father sobered up he apparently had no recollection of what he'd said or done during the previous day's drunken stupor. Could that be happening with Ernest? Arthur decided to do everything he could to leave on a positive note.

"Do you remember when I offered to help you clean some stuff up in the house?

"Oh, so I can win the Good Housekeeping seal of approval?" Ernest laughed at his own joke.

"Well, I don't know what else I could do for you."

"Well I do. Get me up off this goddamn floor."

Arthur walked over to Ernest, squatted down and grabbed him under the armpits. As Arthur stood up, Ernest put one hand on his recliner. Their combined effort got Ernest back on his feet, but he immediately collapsed into his recliner, causing it to squeak and groan from years of use and abuse.

"Thanks, Sonny. The next thing you can do is get me a bottle out of the cabinet right over there. There's only one full one left, the one with the cap on it." Arthur did as told.

"Do you want a glass with that?"

"No, just bring me the bottle and make it snappy."

Arthur knew better than to delay an adult's order. He brought the bottle over to Ernest who immediately spun off the cap and took a couple of hearty swigs. "When you get like me, it hurts more not to drink than it does to drink. At least that's what I tell myself."

Ernest briefly studied the bottle he was holding and then asked, "Hey kid. You know why I live like this?"

"No."

"Because the war fucked me up. That's why. Didn't I tell you about that kid I shot?"

"Yeah."

"Never got over it. I came back home. Couldn't live with my own goddamn parents. They were afraid of me. The VA tried to fix me, but I guess I'm not fixable." He lifted his bottle triumphantly. "Here's my cure. Trouble is—the cure is killing me. I know it, but I just don't want to think—" The old man stopped himself in midstream. He scrutinized the young boy in his presence. "You have any idea what I'm talking about?"

Arthur thought it best to answer affirmatively. Then, he admitted something he'd never admitted to anyone else. "I guess I do. I get scared sometimes."

"Hah! What the hell do you get scared about? You're how old?"

"Thirteen."

"You got the whole rest of your life in front of you. So what's there to be afraid of?"

Arthur could never divulge the major source of his fears—his father—and the details of their relationship. He gave a less revealing, yet still truthful answer. "If I get bad grades in school, I'll get in trouble."

"If that's... the... worst..."

The old man's voice trailed off. He remained seated in his recliner, but more like a statue. He looked straight ahead, his eyes frozen in place. Arthur had seen this side of Ernest a few years earlier when they first met. Back then, the catatonic state had lasted only a few minutes. Arthur decided this was an opportunity for him to take off. He wasn't sure if he was leaving on good terms, but he'd had enough of his unpredictable neighbor for one day. He carefully screwed the cap back on the vodka bottle without ever removing it from Ernest's tight grasp.

He left the shack closing the front door behind him. From there, he quickly made his way to his bicycle. He pedaled back home, put the bike in the garage and went inside.

Ten minutes later his father arrived home from work. His son told him he'd been allowed to play softball on the Blaskowitzes' field. He hit a double and then scored the winning run. His father gave him an unconvincing "Way to go!" and headed for the kitchen and his first beer.

Chapter 39

Monday morning arrived. Arthur told his mother he was going to ride his bike to school because "it was neater than walking." He didn't bother to add that it was also faster and thus better for getting home from detention without raising anyone's suspicions. Thanks to some furious pedaling Arthur arrived in front of the post office early in the morning at ten minutes before eight o'clock. He had to be in his homeroom by 8:15. The post office opened at 8:00. Arthur parked his bicycle and stood by the post office's front doors, eager to be the first customer. At exactly 8 o'clock Mr. Floyd opened up the post office for business. Standing in front of him was a thirteen-year-old clutching a letter ready for mailing.

"Hey, shouldn't you be in school?"

"Yup. And I'll be there as soon as I mail this letter."

"Okay. Give me the letter."

Arthur did as requested and then asked, "Are you sure this will go out today?"

"Sure as shootin'. Now get on up to school."

As the young boy got back on his bike Mr. Floyd looked at the envelope. "Hey, you could've saved the postage. It's going to your school. Why didn't you just deliver yourself?"

"It's a letter signed by my father. He forgot to mail it. I figure it's more official with that stamp thing the post office does."

"I guess so. I'll see this goes out first thing. Top priority, son."

That was the second time in his life Arthur had been addressed as "son" by Mr. Floyd. Son. A word Arthur had never heard once from his father, at least not as a term of endearment.

Arthur got on his bike and took off for school. When he got there, all the slots in the bicycle rack were filled so Arthur propped his bike alongside a fence. From there, he ran into the school, up to the second floor and, not a moment too soon, scooted into the classroom behind Marshall Anthony who, at Mr. Heinbochel's request, was entering the classroom for the second time that morning.

Arthur spent the entire school day swimming in anxiety. Most of his thoughts centered on the challenge he faced trying to serve detention for five days without his family being any the wiser. In between those thoughts, he found the time to convince himself that Ernest's signature would not be spotted for what it was—a forgery.

Once again, Arthur found himself in the odd position of wanting a school day to go on eternally. Every time a class period ended he was that much closer to his moment of reckoning. Arthur had already faced many moments of reckoning in his life, but that didn't make today's task any easier.

At three o'clock the dismissal bell rang. While his fellow students happily rushed out of the school building into sweet freedom, Arthur dutifully trudged himself to room 110. Sal, a homeroom classmate, was already there. He'd gotten caught throwing an eraser at another student. The two sat down at desks. Gradually, the remainder of academic delinquents entered the room. Peter Fox, a consistent troublemaker, was there for cursing at a teacher. Jimmy Keating was being punished for starting a fight in study hall. Anthony Bordone's infraction immediately got Arthur's attention. Anthony had gotten detention for forging a parent's signature on his report card. Now Arthur knew that if he got caught falsifying his father's signature at the very least he would be getting additional detention he'd have to cover up. Far worse, the principal might decide it was time to talk directly to Arthur's parents. If that happened, undoubtedly the snowball incident would come up in the conversation. The anxiety Arthur had been experiencing all day ratcheted up a few more notches.

In walked Mr. Seitz, a math teacher and one to be feared. It was doubtful even he knew how mean he looked. Mr. Seitz immediately rearranged the seating so that the students were as far from each other as possible. The teacher then took attendance. Arthur felt he didn't belong in the detention room because he was there on trumped up charges, yet there was something "cool" about being a part of this edgier crowd of students.

Arthur continually looked at the clock on the wall as time marched on towards 3:45. He was prepared to set a cycling speed record the minute the detention ended. Meantime, his fellow detainees were doing whatever they could to provoke Mr. Seitz. Peter had an obnoxiously loud and phony coughing fit. Sal kept purposely shoving a book off his desk, letting it fall to the floor. Out of the corner of his eye, Mr. Seitz spotted Anthony throwing a crumpled up piece of paper at Arthur. "I guess you folks want to stay here until 4 o'clock?" Arthur certainly didn't. He couldn't afford to. Fortunately for him, none of the other students wanted to either. Things calmed down and at 3:45 the students were set free.

Arthur ran outside, jumped on his bicycle and started pedaling furiously. There would be no Crystal Fountain today. When he got to the hilly part of Brook Road, he hopped off his bike and pushed it uphill as fast as he could. To get home as quickly as possible, he'd have to take his chances with Tar. Fortunately for Arthur, his owners kept their volatile dog inside this day. When Arthur got home, he found only Ruth there, practicing the flute in the living room. Though she didn't ask for one, Arthur offered an alibi for his whereabouts. In a burst of creativity, he came up with an excuse he could use for the rest of the week. "They're letting us play softball after every school day."

Ruth answered with a tepid "That's good." It *was* for Arthur. He repeated the same line to his parents at dinner and he was "home free" for the rest of the week. His luck didn't run out in school either. Days and then weeks went by and no one from the principal's office called the Berndt residence to express concerns over the letter signed by Ernest.

An old man living up the street had spared Arthur from the wrath of the old man he lived with.

Chapter 40

Arthur burst through the front door at Twenty-one Lowell Place. He was home from another day in school. His mother had a surprise for him. "Arthur, you've got a letter."

"Yeah, Ma? Who sent it?"

"I don't know. There's no return address on the envelope. The postmark says it's from Coram. Maybe it's from a friend in school?"

Arthur wasn't sure he had any friends in school let alone one that would write him a letter. In fact, he couldn't think of anyone who would write him a letter. Though his curiosity was piqued, the young boy acted nonchalant. He started playing with Rex, who was happily celebrating his master's arrival home.

"Don't you want to open it?"

"I will. First, I want to take Rex for a walk."

"Fair enough."

Arthur changed his clothes and headed into the great outdoors with his dog for a brief walk.

When he got back home, his mother and sister were in the living room. Ruth was practicing the piano and Marguerite was knitting. Occasionally, Marguerite offered an encouraging word as Ruth attempted to master a difficult piece by Liszt. In Arthur's eyes, the family favorite was getting her typical royal treatment.

On the way to the kitchen, Arthur spotted the mysterious letter lying on the dining room table. The young boy grabbed the envelope and headed up to his bedroom. He didn't know if the letter contained good news or bad and he wanted to open it in private in case the contents spelled trouble.

Arthur tore open the envelope and took out the letter. He read its short, semi-sweet contents:

Arthur,

Hello. We used to be in the same class together. You used to like me and I liked you. I had to start going to another school this year.

I hope you're having fun. Maybe I will write again.

Very sincerely,

?

Arthur excitedly re-read the short, unsigned missive. He examined the writing. He wasn't sure if it was that of a girl or a boy, but guessed it was a girl's. There was something about the fact that the letter came from Coram, but the young boy couldn't put his finger on it.

Arthur detected a not unpleasant odor. He held the letter to his nose. It was scented. He put the letter back in its envelope and secreted both under some clothes in a desk drawer. Then, he went downstairs and entered the living room. His mother asked, "Well, did you look at that letter?"

"Yeah. It was stupid. The person didn't even sign it."

"Really?! What did it say?"

"It was stupid stuff."

"What kind of a 'stupid stuff'?"

"Well, they said they used to go to Port Jefferson Elementary School and now they don't. What am I supposed to do about that?"

"Anything else?"

"Not really."

"What a strange letter. Coram. You know anyone in Coram?"

"Well, probably some kids in my classes."

"Would you mind if I looked at it?"

"Oh, I already tore it up and threw it away."

"Oh well, maybe you'll get another letter with a name signed

247

to it."

"Maybe."

Ruth had been listening while remaining perched on the piano bench. Teasingly, she offered, "Maybe Arthur has a secret admirer."

Marguerite responded, "Hmm... I hadn't thought about that." Turning to Arthur she said, "You're getting to that age."

A red-faced Arthur asked, "Ma, what's for dinner?"

Following supper, Arthur went back up to his room and took out the letter. Though he had acted blasé about the letter in front of his mother and sister, the youngster wracked his brain trying to figure out who had sent a letter. Then it hit him. Carolyn Marino! That's who sent the letter! He had been right about her all along! Though he desperately wanted to be sure this was her handiwork, he couldn't be. There was no signature and no address he could respond to. All he could do was wait anxiously for a follow-up letter that wouldn't be anonymous. None would ever arrive.

Epilogue

Arthur has crossed the threshold into adolescence. The way he has spent his life up to now doesn't bode well for the youngster's teen years.

Still not daring to openly confront his father, Arthur continues to channel his pent-up anger into antisocial behavior on the street. That self-defeating pattern of behavior shows no signs of ending.

Whenever he does something wrong and gets away with it, Arthur savors the feeling of having avoided detection—both by the legal system and his own father. Getting away or getting caught—in both cases his acting out is a mostly subconscious knee-jerk response to his resentment towards his treatment at home.

Every once in a while—especially if he gets caught—the thought briefly flashes across his mind Why do I keep doing the next wrong thing? Is it because I hate my father? Is there something wrong with me? Such uncomfortable thinking quickly evaporates.

If his father were to declare cease-fire, would Arthur call a halt to his delinquent behavior? That question isn't likely to be answered any time soon because this battle between father and son appears destined to rage on with no end in sight.

Author Bio

Walter Stoffel is a freelance writer and publisher who specializes in human interest memoir and fiction. His newest book, *Arthur: The Struggle Continues*, is the sequel to *Arthur: The Beginning*. Both books are works of historical fiction that describe a young boy's struggle to survive his childhood. His debut dog rescue memoir *Lance: A Spirit Unbroken* has achieved five-star book review status on three continents.

The author has a rich work history that includes teaching GED and providing substance abuse counseling at correctional facilities. He also has experience as a certified mental health screener. For many years, he lived and worked in various South American countries. Most unique occupation: chipping excess concrete off the undersides of bridges in Virginia. All his coworkers were wearing prison stripes.

Mr. Stoffel is a member of the Greater Lehigh Valley Writers Group, Pennwriters and Barbara's Writing Group, a critiquing association.

When not writing, he loves to read, travel, work out, and watch bad movies.

The author has a B.A. in psychology, is a credentialed alcoholism and drug counselor and also a certified mental health screener. He lives in Canadensis, PA with his wife Clara and their dog Heidi (the Hooligan!).

Personal accomplishment: after having hip replacement surgery, Walter entered a marathon and finished it—dead last.

Interview with Walter Stoffel

How about a quick overview of Arthur: The Struggle Continues?

It picks up where *Arthur: The Beginning* left off. This second book covers him from age eleven to thirteen. At home, he remains in the crosshairs of his father. On the street, he continues to commit antisocial acts. There are some surprises—for one, Arthur has another encounter with the "old man" that lives up the street. Readers will no doubt remember the tension that existed during their first meeting in *Arthur: The Beginning*.

So the story remains edgy?

I'd like to think so.

First an abused dog (*Lance: A Spirit Unbroken*) and now Arthur, an abused boy. Do I detect a pattern?

Well, the goal of an author—at least this author—is to catch the reader's attention. If you can also capture a bit of their heart and soul that's an even greater accomplishment. If you can do all that writing about an important issue like abuse so much the better. If a reader comes away from your book with a heightened awareness of what's going on in this world, you've hit the jackpot! I can only hope I'm able to do that.

What motivates you to write about Arthur?

Arthur is very near and dear to my heart. He is a fictional character that I'd like to think speaks for all the children growing up in dark households.

How is the Covid era affecting you?

Last year I had multiple personal appearances scheduled that had to be canceled along with presentations I'd planned to give in schools. The in-person book readings also went by the wayside. But, putting things in perspective, no one close to me has succumbed to the virus. Also, during the quarantine I ramped up my writing efforts. So there is a silver lining.

What can we expect from you in the future?

Currently I'm writing a third book in the Arthur series, a work of children's literature about a boy and a dog, and a book that recounts my experiences as a drug and alcohol counselor in a correctional facility. That last work is proof positive that truth is *indeed* stranger than fiction.

Three manuscripts? And you say you are procrastinator?

Well, for most of my life I was. Just goes to show that even the most unlikely changes in a person's life can occur—and they can be positive!

Suggested Reading Guide and Discussion Questions

1-What do you like best about this book?

2-What do you like least about this book?

3-What other books does this one remind you of?

4-Which characters in the book do you like best?

5-Which characters do you like least?

6-Share a favorite quote from the book. Why does this quote stand out?

8-Would you read another book by this author? Why?

9-What feelings does this book evoke in you?

10-If you got the chance to ask the author of this book one question, what would it be?

11-Which character in the book would you most like to meet?

12-What do you think of the book's title? What other title might you choose?

13-What do you think the author's purpose was in writing this book? What ideas is he trying to get across?

14-How original and unique is this book?

15-If you could hear the same story from another person's point of view, which would you choose?

16-Which scene has stuck with you the most?

17-What do you think of the author's writing style?

18-Did certain parts of the book make you feel uncomfortable? If so, why?

19-If there is a sequel to this book, what do you think will happen to the main characters?

20-What do you think were the advantages and disadvantages of living during the 1950s?

Printed in Great Britain
by Amazon